Depart in Peace

Depart In Peace

Copyright © Ian Douglas Wilson 2021 All Rights Reserved

The rights of Ian Douglas Wilson to be identified as the author of this work have been asserted in accordance with the Copyright, Designs and Patents Act 1988

All rights reserved. No part may be reproduced, adapted, stored in a retrieval system or transmitted by any means, electronic, mechanical, photocopying, or otherwise without the prior written permission of the author or publisher.

BookPrintingUK
Remus House
Coltsfoot Drive
Woodston
Peterborough
PE2 9BF

www.bookprintinguk.com

A CIP catalogue record for this book is available from the British Library.

The views expressed in this work are solely those of the author and do not necessarily reflect the views of the publisher, and the publisher hereby disclaims any responsibility for them.

DEPART IN PEACE

IAN DOUGLAS WILSON

BookPrintingUK
Peterborough
2021

*To my beloved wife, Beatrice Mary.
Angel Sweet Pet Dove Darling!*

Contents

Foreword 1

BOOK ONE

Domestic Reflections And Reminiscences

Getting To Know You 5
That Shepley Trip 11
A Lasting And Creative Friendship 17
Recruitment And Potential 21
To Tell Or Not To Tell: What Is The Question? 28
Why Is Laura? What Is She – To Me? 34
The Order Of The Bath And Other Honours 39
The Afternoon Of A Phone 42

BOOK TWO

The Flooded River Horst Moves To Centre Stage

A Tide In The Affairs Of A Man Taken By The Flood 58
Laura Is Not Home For Her Tea 65
Safe As Houses 72
Waiting 78
A Real Adventure 81
Still Not Found 84
Refuge 89
Help Is At Hand 97
A Tale Told By A Page 106
Hike And Ye Shall Find 116
Charlie Tells All 123

Rescue And Recovery 128
A Very Close Friend 135
A Deeper Look 141
Meet The Porters At The Rectory 145
Gossip At The Golden Unicorn 151
A Special Request For Jacob 160
Meet The MacDonalds' 167
Reg Talks To The Drews 175
Proposal, Property And Problems 179
Charlie, Chase And Follow 195
Recovery! Recovery! Recovery! 205
Talking And Telling Tales 208

BOOK THREE
The End Of The Beginning And The Beginning Of The End

Tell It On A Sunday 222
Shadows On The Road Ahead 228
Early One Morning – And Afternoon 231
The Evening And The Morning Were The Cursed Day 239
A Time To Pee And A Time To Cry 244
Where There's A Will, There's A Thrill 251
Where There's Will, There's A Won't 260
It's Not Over Yet 270
The Funeral 276

Acknowledgements 298

FOREWORD

I started writing this novel after my wife Mary died in 2013. I had written several 'scenes' on related themes in the past, with the idea of turning them into a play; which experience emboldened me to think that I could write something more substantial, and so this book emerged.

It interests me that gossip and chat, can often bind people together, but also has the capacity to destroy as well as to build up.

I am also concerned with the gradual disappearance of the Yorkshire dialect, so I have depicted characters who speak in this dialect; such folk can still be heard in some of the more remote villages of the Yorkshire dales to this day.

Writing this book has answered a creative urge, which in the past was answered by my acting and directing in the theatre.

BOOK ONE

DOMESTIC REFLECTIONS AND REMINISCENCES

CHAPTER 1

GETTING TO KNOW YOU

Ernest Silver had begun every day of his retirement with a reassuring routine, but today was to be the beginning of a cruel and violent end to that pleasant life: destructive both morally and physically.

Ernest drew back the bedroom curtains. It was raining. What else could he expect? After all, it was mid-October.

Every morning Ernest routinely gave his appearance a serious examination in the Cheval mirror. What he saw daily told him that he was, against unfounded hope and studious determination, showing unmistakable signs of his getting older. The physical exercises he had performed religiously every morning meant that, for his age, he was comparatively lithe and sound in mind and limb; he could still touch his toes and perform strange contortions that would cripple a man half his age. After a gargle, his vocal exercises kept his musical voice youthful and supple.

In the afternoons he would still go for long walks without pain and reassuringly without the aid of a walking stick: however, there was unmistakable evidence that his waistline had expanded somewhat, though it would be wrong to call his midriff a paunch.

Daily applications of unctions, patents, ointments, and balms to his face had not sufficiently delayed the aging processes; where there had been creases, there were now hills and valleys. His once attractive laughter lines were now deeply engraved folds.

His hair, in youth golden and curly, had almost disappeared many years ago; he had grown used to that, and what remained round the edges had become snowy white. Ernest had known as a boy that he was fated to become bald. He had observed that fair-haired, middle-aged men often lost their hair in early manhood. Why should he expect better?

He had grown accustomed to his bald pate, but he was finding it hard to observe other, more insidious evidences of growing older. Was he vain? Not really, but he was perhaps rather too proud that suits, jackets, and trousers, bought when he was much younger, still fitted him without too much pressure on the buttons.

On this stormy day, after he had performed his exercises, brushed his teeth, showered, counted out and washed down his pills – controlling blood pressure, heart disease and cholesterol – Ernest dressed for comfort. He went downstairs, tapped the barometer, which confirmed that this was indeed a wet and stormy day, and turned on Radio 4 for a dose of John Humphreys – more for company than for argument or information.

Whilst half-listening to Humphreys' merciless exposure of weaknesses in whichever politician was brave or unwise enough to undergo his verbal scarifications, Ernest poured out a bowl of cereal with the essential half a banana, sliced not mashed, and began to eat in the pursuit of health. Reading the damp Telegraph (wet after being shoved through his letter box in the downpour) he ignored the radio, though the weather summary did penetrate.

"It will be soggy everywhere today and, if you have to go out in it, you'll know about it!"

Ernest had long made a point of staying at home, warm and comfortable, whenever the weather turned sour. On this day, however, he had overlooked that it was Thursday, and Thursday was 'Bins-day'. He hadn't remembered in time so, cereal unfinished, he rushed round the house to tidy up and collect the wastepaper baskets. He was upstairs when the doorbell rang.

"Dammit," he said to himself. "I thought I'd unlocked the door; that'll be Maureen."

Door unlocked, he greeted a drenched and dripping Maureen.

"By Go', it's a rare wet 'un this mornin'; teemin' it down."

"Come in, Maureen. Hang your raincoat near the Aga – it'll soon dry."

"Thanks, I will. It's a real wet 'un an' no mistake. I'm wetshod an' all, so I'll tek mi shoes off an' mount 'em by t' cooker. I've browt mi slippers in mi bag just in case."

"Before you do, I haven't done the dustbins this morning. I'm sorry. I woke late. I set the alarm as usual for seven so I could get up and have all that sort of thing completed before you arrive, but I must have slept through it."

"There's no need to tidy up afore I come. I know where everythin' goes. If it's not in t'right place I'll put it there, so nivver you bother. 'Ow are you this morning? It's a chilly mornin'. We don't want you gettin' a chill like last year, do we? Ee, you was proper poorly."

"I'm not planning to go out today. 'Stay home and stay safe', that's the motto for today."

"Stay at 'ome and stay warm, that an' all. It's not as bad like a year since what were turrible."

Ernest had been very foolish last year. He had decided to risk a brisk walk to the Co-op to get a few items to tide himself over the weekend. There was no urgent need to do so, but he popped up there anyway and purchased a couple of bags of groceries. Bringing them home he slipped as he entered the garden, fell against the gate post and knocked himself out.

How long he had laid there, Maureen didn't know. She had gone round a bit later than usual because her daughter Laura had a bad cough. The seven-year-old girl wasn't well enough for school, so Maureen had given her cough medicine and tucked her up in bed with a book before she went to clean for Ernest, as per usual.

And there she'd found him, unconscious by the garden gate. At first she'd thought he was dead, he was so pale and grey. She managed to get him inside and rang the doctor, who had him taken by ambulance to the Iverdale General Hospital. He'd been very ill with pneumonia, but thanks to antibiotics Ernest had quickly pulled round.

"It were new-monics I think they said it were. Any roads on, when you cem round after a few days they sent you 'ome."

"I am still eternally grateful for all you did for me. Looking after me and bringing homemade soups and tasty dishes to bring me back to the hale and hearty. I wouldn't be living now if it hadn't been for you finding me in the first place and feeding me up after I came home."

"You said ta enough at the time and that number of times since. There's no need to 'arp on and on about it."

"Anyhow, there's no danger of my repeating that foolishness on a filthy day like this. If I haven't got it today, the Co-op and I can wait until tomorrow. I have more sense than to try to repeat that experience; one year older and a thousand years wiser."

"That's enough of that. Now what's to do today? I'll do t' outside bins later at after the rain's debated a bit. T' bin men don't come 'til at after dinnertime so there's no rush. Right, owt special this mornin' or 'ow?"

"I had thought you could do the outside windows but it's pointless in this weather. So, I'll tell you what: we could do the brasses together after you've done upstairs. Give us a chance for a chat. Is that alright with you, Maureen?"

"Okey dokey. What about downstairs? Shall I do a swift vac and puff up cushions. Will that do? Then we'll get on wi't' brasses."

And she disappeared upstairs in a puff of smoke.

Later that morning with Maureen doing the bedrooms, Ernest had read *The Telegraph* cover to cover and, but for a couple of clues, had finished the cryptic crossword. He had scanned the hatched, matched, and dispatched columns without finding anyone of interest who had either emerged from the egg or dropped off the perch: in fact nothing to laugh at all! He had covered the kitchen table with old newspapers, assembled the ornaments to be polished and made a start.

Maureen bounced down and said, "I've done upstairs. You need more lavvy paper in the bathroom – I think you've plenty downstairs. Shall I get some for you at Co-op? I can't promise today and you've enough to last, but I'll get some when I can. An' while I'm at it, your bread bin's nigh on empty and there's only a bit of butter left in t' fridge. Ee, you need a bit of lookin' after, you do."

"I think I do pretty well for my age, Maureen. It's very kind of you. You could get those items you've mentioned and anything else you think I might fancy. I'll give you £20 to be going on with when you go, and we can settle up when I come round to your house next Tuesday. Is that fair enough?"

"Nay, I'll bring it all 'ere tomorrer and you can settle up then. Keep yer brass in yer pocket 'til you 'ave to spend it; you can pay me when I've got t'stuff. You can't last out ovver t' weekend wi'out I bring it tomorrer. Now, I see you've made start wi't brasses, but we can finish 'em together like. 'Av yer plenty of Brasso for today?"

"Yes, just, I think; you might add Brasso to your shopping list, though. Your coffee's ready for you to pour hot water on when you've done the hoovering."

Maureen took no time and in a flash was busy with the elbow grease. As they were putting the polish on, she said, "This weather in't lettin' up. T' river'll be ovver runnin' if it goes on. I 'ope it lets up afore I go, an' I can do t' bins in t' dry afore bin men come."

"It's nice just to sit here and chat over the brasses. You're often in such a hurry to get things done – both here and at home – there isn't time to talk. In your kitchen you're always cooking or washing up, or ironing or watching the television. We've known each other for quite a while now, but we haven't done a lot of chatting, have we?"

"Oh aye! I were just thinkin' t' other day about that time you gev me an' little Billy a lift into town. Do you remember? I'd just missed t' bus. We've supped many a cuppa tea sin' that day, 'aven't we just?

"Yes, indeed we have."

"It were a while ago. It were just afore our Billy died."

CHAPTER 2

THAT SHEPLEY TRIP

This is how I remembered the trip into Shepley all those years ago. I had lived in Holsterdale about a year. The actual date I couldn't recall but the details I could recite verbatim. Mine was that sort of memory.

That day, the day that Maureen was talking about, after an early lunch I had set out for Shepley: not a vital journey and one I could perfectly well have put off to another day. It must have been a day in late February. As I was driving, I saw a young woman pushing a pram and running towards the bus stop. By the time she reached it, the bus had already drawn out into the road and was gone, leaving her stranded.

I thought, *I'll stop and give her a lift if she wants,* and I pulled up beside her.

"Can I give you a lift? I'm going into Shepley if that's any help?"

"Oh, ta. Yes please." She was out of puff.

I jumped out of the car and said, "Here, you hop in and carry your baby in your arms; I'll just put the pram in the boot."

In seconds it was done. She sat in the back and made her little one comfortable on the seat beside her.

"Ta, ever so. This is a real 'elp. Most days I would tek the car wi' Billy but today it's bein' serviced and I just 'ad to go into Shepley. Next bus is an hour off."

"I've seen you before, haven't I ... in church?"

"Yes, maybe you 'ave. Is it you 'as just joined the choir? We don't go as oft as we used to, it being 'ard wi' the kiddy. I used to be in t' choir mesel' but since 'e cem along it's a full-time job looking after 'im," she replied, somewhat jocularly.

"You young parents just don't know what you're letting yourselves in for until it happens – bang." I laughed as I addressed the rear-view mirror. "How old is the baby? Billy, did you say his name was? No don't tell me; let me guess. I'd say about eight, or maybe nine months. Am I right?"

I was pretty confident I was right. I hadn't judged pretty baby competitions for nothing; being a minor celebrity in a small Scottish town had had its dubious rewards!

"Actually, Billy is nearly two and a half. "

"Is he really? Don't tell me anything more unless you want to. I'm so sorry. I really am very sorry."

The rest of the journey passed in silence – embarrassed or preoccupied – until I asked, "Is there anywhere I can drop you? Anywhere at all? Just say the word."

"Anywhere near the market'd be best, but you can't stop on the Main Street. Central car park will be fine. It's not far to t' shops from there. Ta for the offer."

"If you're sure? I'll risk a ticket on the Main Street if it really is best for you."

"Central car park's okay, ta."

As I parked the car I offered, "Look I'm in no hurry to get back. What time do you plan to go home? I'll tell you what: you say a time and we'll meet here at the car. Let's see, we're in lane three near the top. Meet me here at about … say four and I'll take you and young Billy home. Blue Ford in case you haven't noticed."

"I couldn't put you to all that trouble."

"No trouble. Or as they say these days, no worries! Silly thing to say, that, as if we all went about worrying all the time. What's the use of worrying? It never was worthwhile. There's no rush for me to get home."

"No, I couldn't."

"Why not? Look, is four o'clock fair? Does that give you enough time? You can't rush with the pram anyhow. Can you manage for four?"

"I think so, if I get a shift on.

"Are you sure?"

"Well, mebbe a bit after four. It depends on the chemist: queues for the pharmacy an' that."

"I'll wait for you. But don't go by bus and leave me stranded 'til midnight!" I joked.

So saying, we departed in different directions, promising to keep our rendezvous. Actually, I had very little to do in Shepley: a browse in Waterfalls, a long established and old fashioned bookshop, on the off chance that a title would jump out of the shelves at me; buy a new pair of gloves to make up for the glove I had lost last weekend; bits and pieces and that was all.

I passed the morning sitting in the Pink Teacup taking a pot of Earl Grey, when a lady I had never met approached me and said, "You are Mr Silver, I believe."

"I certainly am. What can I do for you?"

"Let me introduce myself. I'm Lucy Hepworth. We live at the Grange just outside Holsterdale. The MacDonalds tell me you are something of a pianist."

"That's very kind of them. Won't you sit down and join me for a cup."

"Thank you." She sat opposite.

I ordered another pot of tea. "Anything to eat, a cupcake perhaps?"

"No, thank you. What I want to talk to you about is my daughter, Felicity. We think she is quite good when she tinkers about on the piano."

"What is it you want me to do?"

"Just come to the Grange and listen. See what you think about her potential."

"Does she sing?"

"All the time; I find it hard to stop her."

"I'm not a qualified piano teacher, Mrs Hepworth. But her singing will tell me what musicality she possesses. How old is she?"

"Seven and a half. Then you will come? Delightful. Would tomorrow afternoon be convenient?"

"Yes, that should be fine. Whatever time suits you. I am free all afternoon, I think."

"Excellent. Come at four for a cup of tea so we can get to know each other, then you'll meet Felicity and hear her sing and play the piano when she comes home from school at five o'clock."

Mrs Hepworth thanked me and left me in The Pink Teacup.

At ten-to-four I settled up, picked up my few bags and walked slowly up to the car. I was expecting to have to wait until this young mother arrived, but she was already there. The screech of Billy wailing in the pram reverberated through the car park, wall to wall. Folks in the next county must surely have heard him. The young mother had taken the opportunity, on the promise of a lift home, of buying more items than she had originally intended; she was burdened with heavy and bulging plastic bags, her shoulders sagging under the weight: not exactly grunting and sweating, but clearly glad to get into the car.

Travel arrangements were as before: we sat in the car, both of us full of unnecessary apologies. The return journey was passed in what in conversational terms might be called total silence, if silence meant we didn't or couldn't talk over the incessant loud wailing. Billy was seriously uncomfortable. I had to get home quick.

As I drove into Holsterdale, the young mother's voice penetrated through the wall of sound. "Next left into Water

Street and number 47 – the one wi' the black door and the golden privet 'edge."

"You get yourself and young Billy sorted and I'll help to carry in the shopping," I offered as I pulled up.

As she went in she called out, "Put the shoppin' on t' table. I'll 'ave to change 'im upstairs."

She disappeared to do so. It took several trips to bring in the pram and all the shopping. I looked round as I lingered by the door to say goodbye. The room was neatly furnished with evidence of inexpensive Scandinavian taste: a few books on shelves; telly in one corner; old fashioned black iron fireplace – no fire, just a vase of dropping tulips in the grate – and a well-used, comfortable looking sofa and easy chairs.

Shortly the young mother reappeared downstairs without the bairn.

"'E's settled down. It must 'ave been 'is mucky nappy what's upset 'im. There in't enough places in the town to 'elp with such like. Would you like a cup o' tea?"

"Thanks; I'd better be off."

"Come on. You've been a massive 'elp. In any case, what's the 'urry? You do live by yourself, I expect, don't you? Or 'ave you a dog or a goldfish or somethin' to let out?"

"None of the above and no, I don't even have a goldfish. Yes, you're right, there is no hurry – a cup of tea would be very acceptable."

"I'll put t' kettle on and get out the teapot. Ordinary tea. Nothing fancy, sorry. Look, when it boils you mash the tea – two bags – you mash it 'an I'll just go up to check he's lying down proper."

And again she dashed upstairs. I did as told. When she returned she insisted, "Sit yoursell down – you're not the rent collector."

As I sat down I said, "I think it's time we introduced ourselves. I'm Ernest Silver and who may I ask are you, dear lady?"

"Maureen 'Irst," she replied as she went to the fridge. "Milk?"

"Just a splash. No sugar, thank you."

I sat at the table with Maureen opposite.

"Excuse me askin'. You've only just landed in 'Olsterdale. 'Ow long is it?"

"Actually I've been here for over a year, but I've kept a low profile whilst I settled in. I have joined the church choir as you seemed to have noticed. The choir is a good place to see who comes and goes, and it is a nice way to meet people. Now I come to think about it, I recollect seeing you in church when you've now and then brought Billy to the altar for a blessing."

"That's right, though it's a while since we last went, what wi' Billy bein' as 'e is an' that."

"I understand. Is he really poorly? No, don't tell me if—"

"They say 'e won't last the year out. I try to keep 'im comfortable. I don't want 'im to die in 'ospital an' that's all I can do. I give 'im 'is medicine, o' course, but they don't seemingly make much difference."

"The doctor must call, surely."

"Aye, but he can't do much. There's nowt much can be done. Best keep 'im at 'ome, 'e says."

"Look, I'm sorry to intrude. I must leave you to get on with things. Thank you for the tea – it was just right."

"No worries. See you later, an' ta for the lift an' bringin' in t' shoppin'. It were a big 'elp."

That trip to Shepley happened several years ago, long before I employed Maureen as a cleaner. At the time it was no more than a brief encounter, seeming to have no lasting significance. After that, Maureen and I had bumped into each other now and then in the Co-op with a passing, 'how do you do you do?' between us.

Maureen's reminder had brought the whole event back to mind as clear as a bell, however. A great deal of water had flowed under the bridge since then.

CHAPTER 3

A LASTING AND CREATIVE FRIENDSHIP

Soon after that chance encounter in The Pink Teacup, Ernest made the trip to visit the Hepworths and their talented daughter.

The Grange was a house built in the 1930s in a style quite out of keeping with the rest of Holsterdale. It was some distance from the centre of the small town, so Ernest drove there in his Armstrong Siddeley. He was warmly greeted by Mrs Hepworth and shown into a spacious and expensively furnished drawing room, where a well-polished baby grand stood to one side.

Minutes later, their maid Vera came in bearing a tray of tea things and a selection of biscuits.

As Vera poured, Mrs Hepworth asked, "You live alone, I take it."

"Yes, my wife died in 2002. I moved here shortly after her death and intend to remain here until my dying day. I have settled in very well and am making plans to launch myself into society. The MacDonalds have taken me to their bosom."

"Any family?"

"No, my lovely daughter died in an accident. She was promising to be a good actress but that ended abruptly. She was only twenty-two. We called her Connie or Con, rarely by her full name Constance. As she was growing up we laughingly called her our big Con. Once Margery, that's my wife, called her Concon and I said don't call her that. It's clumsy."

"Nicknames are curiosities aren't they? We like to go in for variations of Felicity: Flicka, Flixie, sometimes even Fixit. She does not like to be called Flitty and gets cross if we drop it in now and again."

"You hinted in the café that you think Felicity has a promising musical talent?"

"I do. I won't say more; I'd like to let her talent speak for itself when you hear her. She will be arriving home from school any minute now."

As if on cue, Felicity bounced in and said, "I'm sorry I'm late, the taxi was stuck behind a tractor!"

"Never mind, darling. This is Mr Silver, he'd love to hear you play the piano."

"Oh, okay. Can I have a biscuit first? I'm starving – it was fish for lunch and I hate it! What would you like me to play, Mr Silver?"

"Anything you enjoy playing."

Ernest had half expected 'Chopsticks' or 'Oh can you wash your father's shirt', but Felicity sat down and played 'Fur Elise', perhaps a little slower than Beethoven had intended, but with beautiful phrasing for a child of her age.

"My word that was lovely, Felicity."

"Can I go now?"

"Of course you can. Go and change, then you can go for a ride on Horace. Ask Vera to come and watch you whilst I finish my tea with Mr Silver."

"Alright, Mummy. G'bye, Mr Silver."

"Goodbye, Felicity. It was lovely to meet you. Goodness me that was impressive, Mrs Hepworth. She must have a very good teacher?"

"Yes, at school she has lessons with Miss Lavers, who reckons she's her star pupil. But I'm no musician myself so I needed, shall we say, a second opinion. Should we be doing more for her?"

"At the moment I would suggest you 'go with the flow'. Don't push her, but give her all the encouragement you can."

"Thank you so much, Mr Silver. Good advice is best sought and then pondered over. Before you go, please would you tickle the ivories for me? Some people say tinkle the ivories – I find that irritating, don't you?"

Ernest happily obliged and played Chopin's 'Minute Waltz'. He found that the piano was rather unresponsive in tone, and a couple of black notes stuck, which rather spoilt the flow. This had not affected Felicity's playing, but he knew that if she progressed, as he expected she would, a better instrument would be needed.

"I hesitate to mention this, but I'm going to suggest that this is not one of Bechstein's better models. As she improves I think Felicity will deserve a better piano."

"Well, I appreciate your honesty, we will have to see what we can do. I'm afraid Flixie may have to choose between a new piano and a new pony!"

Ernest said his goodbyes and left.

He became a frequent visitor to The Grange; Mr Hepworth struck up a strong bond with Ernest as they chatted after dinner about many topics, 'putting the world to rights', as they liked to describe their conversations. Mr Hepworth could talk endlessly about wines and their vintages, and Ernest thoroughly enjoyed the fruits of his extensive cellar.

Felicity often came and played for them before she went to bed; she loved it when Ernest came and sat on the piano stool with her to turn the pages of her music. One evening she had brought a duet home from school and they had great fun working on it together.

Many times after school Ernest would have tea with the family, and then Mr Hepworth would retreat to his study and Mrs Hepworth to her room, leaving the two musicians happily playing duets, sometimes even composing variations together.

"If you two are going to ignore me, then I'm going to leave you to it! I've an article to finish, so I'll be down again when Vera calls us for dinner." Mrs Hepworth was a prolific writer, and wrote stirring pieces about country affairs for *Country Life* and *The Lady*.

There was much rejoicing when a new Steinway was delivered; it was Felicity's twelfth birthday present. She and Ernest played on it, uninterrupted for over two hours.

A highlight of their work together was a concert they gave in the Church Hall in aid of the organ fund. Felicity played her grade eight pieces and Ernest and she played several duets together. The organ benefitted by a modest sum, but the audience of music lovers from Holsterdale and the surrounding villages were warmly appreciative.

When they worked together, at first Ernest had helped and corrected Felicity, but as her ability readily improved he found that the tables were occasionally turned as he made mistakes. They would laugh together over their slips and rejoice together over their successes. Felicity's parents loved to hear them play and the sound of the laughter that came from the drawing room as they practiced together.

CHAPTER 4

RECRUITMENT AND POTENTIAL

It was a couple of years after Laura was born that Ernest and the Hirsts really got to know each other. They had since become friends – close friends, largely thanks to Laura. How he really came to know Laura was the result of a conversation with the rector, Rev. Norris Porter, after morning prayer. Ernest had been in the choir for some time and was well established therein. On this occasion he had been delayed by putting the psalters, hymn books, and anthems in order in readiness for evening prayer.

"Good morning, Mr Porter. I wonder if I could have a word? Have you a minute or two?"

"Fire away, Ernest. No problems, I hope?"

"It's a domestic matter really, and I think you or your wife may be able to help."

"We'll do our best. What is it?"

"As you know, I moved here two or three years ago. I had the house equipped with all the latest gadgets in hope and expectation that I would be able to manage all domestic matters personally, but I'm finding it harder to keep things in order. Frankly, I need help with the housekeeping. I'm a pretty good cook so meals are not a problem, but it's the vacuuming, polishing and tidying up and such that are getting a bit beyond me. Can you recommend a reliable cleaner? My demands will be small at the start."

"Have you spoken to my wife, Aileen?"

"Well, no, I haven't. In fact it only occurred to me just now as I was sorting the choir stalls; I asked myself why I was doing chores here when I really could do with help of a similar nature at home."

"Come round with me now. Aileen has gone ahead to prepare lunch. In fact, come and have a bite with us. Pot luck. No guarantees!"

"Aren't you entertaining the archdeacon? Won't I be in the way?

"Not at all. You might indeed act as a useful buffer zone. The Archdeacon might be glad of a word with you. There's no second-guessing archdeacons, let me assure you. I wonder where he is? He may have gone ahead with Aileen, sneaking an early sherry."

"If you're sure Mrs Porter would welcome an extra mouth to feed."

"Loaves and fishes, dear man! Of course I'm sure. You're welcome to our version of porridge."

"Porridge, for lunch? Surely..."

"Our joke – that is oat cuisine. Porridge. Haute cuisine? An eye opener, if I may say so: the experience for you is worth the risk."

Jokes that need elaborate explanations usually fall flat. This one did – as a pancake. Ernest had taken time to understand the joke and decided to laugh at it. He said, "I thought perhaps you were referring to a jail sentence – doing porridge, as the saying goes."

"Ha, ha, though undertaking Aileen's cooking is to be likened to a jail sentence. Tush, Norris. That is not fair to my dear lady. And she is bound to have cooked up something special for the archdeacon. Come on. It's worth the risk."

As the two men walked across the churchyard to the rectory

front door, the Hepworths walked past and called out, "Good morning Ernest! No time to talk."

Ernest waved as they hurried on, and Norris ushered him in through the front door.

"Join the archdeacon in the drawing room; help yourself to the sherry."

"Thanks, I will."

Ernest opened the drawing room door and, as expected, there was the archdeacon mouth deep in Amontillado, sitting on the sofa with *The Sunday Times* colour supplement open on his knee.

"May I join you?"

"Of course, dear man. Help yourself to the sherry."

He did so.

"Have we met before?" the Archdeacon asked as he put aside the supplement. "I seem to recognise you."

"I was in the choir; you may have noticed me among the tenors."

"Of course. Fine tenor voice, if I may venture to say so."

"A nice compliment. Thanks. I joined the choir about a year ago."

"Well sung anthem. 'O Taste and See'. Handel, is it?"

"Not really. Out by a couple of centuries. It was Vaughan Williams actually."

He laughed. "Dear me. Not used to hearing anthems of any sort; out of hearing, out of mind."

It was hard work making small talk with archdeacons.

"You must trip over many aspects of Anglicanism in your parish visits."

"I do. And many parson's lunches, which in general are more hazardous than their multifarious versions of the service. Have you dined here before?"

"No, first time. On the spur of the moment I was offered pot luck and took it."

"Well now, you'll see how gracious the Lord is." He laughed at his jest as if it were necessary to point out that it was a joke.

Porter bustled in. "Have you two introduced yourselves?" he demanded.

"We're getting around to it," replied the archdeacon as they both stood.

"Michael Knightly, archdeacon, and Ernest Silver, man of many parts."

They shook hands, said a formal 'how do you do' and sat down again.

"Your glasses are both empty. Refreshers?" He reached for the decanter but both men declined. Sweet English sherry is not to everyone's taste.

"In that case, pray join us in the kitchen."

Mrs Porter was presiding at the Aga. Spoon in hand, she directed, "Sit where you like. No sitting on ceremony. You both like brisket, cabbage, string beans, and mashed potatoes, I hope."

Both of them indicated that they had hearty appetites with an overstated 'yum-yum' and a mimed rub on the tummy. Mr Porter sat on a stool at the end of the table.

"So easy, brisket; just pop it in and leave it," Mrs Porter said as she doled it straight from the pans.

She must have put on the cabbage to boil at the same time as the brisket went into the oven. It was overcooked, watery, and flavourless. The beans were well-named as string beans; there is nothing more difficult to handle than a mouth full of string. The mashed potatoes were obviously furnished from a packet, and more than the required portion of milk had been added so her version of mashed potatoes poured like a lumpy custard. There was little opportunity to talk as the three men wrestled politely with the strings wrapping themselves round their tongues.

"Delicious darling, as usual. Well done," gushed Porter as he spooned the last mouthful. "Aileen really is a marvel."

At the church's table one cannot lie and it is impolite to tell the truth. As they paused between courses, Porter told the archdeacon that Mr Silver here had been a godsend.

"He joined the choir about a year ago and has transformed it."

"I must say I was impressed by the singing. The anthem was a delight; the girl soloist was very confident and talented."

Ernest intervened, "It was a boy, actually, and yes, Clifford has admirable potential; he's not the only young person in Holsterdale with a musical talent. Felicity Hepworth – you may have noticed her parents in church this morning – has a remarkable gift on the piano. She also has a lovely singing voice, but no time for the choir."

"How lovely to have young musicians in the town. It was a change to hear confident congregational singing of the canticles and psalms – most unusual to find this these days, more's the pity. Many of my churches shy away from singing psalms."

"All due to Mr Silver here," replied the rector.

"But Mr Tweddle the organist is, and has been for years, in charge. Surely he rules the musical roost?"

"An exceedingly accomplished organist he is, and we are very lucky to have him. FRCOs don't grow on trees, but he has been more than happy to leave the singing and even the choice of anthems in the more than capable hands of Mr Silver here."

"Mr Porter. Enough of these undeserved compliments please," Ernest remonstrated.

"But I am interested. By the way might I ask what pointing you're using? It's unfamiliar to me; how did that come about?"

"The old psalters were very ragged, hung their sagging heads sadly and were frankly neglected. They had lain in the back of a cupboard undisturbed, undusted and unused. In fact, we had stopped psalm singing as a lost cause. We had resorted to metrical versions"

"Some of which," Ernest said, "are beautifully written with popular tunes, of course."

"Indeed. Silver here unearthed these tattered remnants and rightly suggested that these old psalters be chucked out and that we should return to singing psalms and canticles. What pointing did we decide on, Ernest?"

"The Oxford makes more rhythmic sense so I suggested that, and without further ado you and the PCC authorised acquiring a complete new set." (And no wonder; he had offered to foot the bill! Porter didn't see the need to reveal this detail at this time.)

"Yes, Silver invited the whole congregation to come to about half a dozen choir practices; quite a number complied and you see, or rather hear, the most excellent results."

"I have to agree that the congregation coped more than adequately, bravely led by the choir."

Mrs Porter shouted from the scullery, "Have you all finished? Collect the plates, Norris. It's rice pudding for afters. I hope you are all happy with that."

Neither the archdeacon nor Ernest dared say no. It was served straight out of the tin, cupboard cold, not chilled, with a minute spoonful of what might have been raspberry jam and a dollop of pink yoghurt of unidentifiable flavour. Ernest resolved that he'd be careful of accepting pot luck at the rectory in future. At the end of the meal he volunteered to help with the washing up. After all, it was to speak to Mrs Porter about home help that he had come, and this would give him the chance to broach the subject.

"Thank you, Mr Silver. We'll leave you, Norris, to your archidiaconal deliberations. If you two retire into the drawing room I'll bring your coffee."

As the washing up proceeded, Ernest felt he had to say something vaguely complimentary about the meal and commented that the brisket was tender (omitting mention of the gristle, which was not) and cracked a joke about rector and ambrosia at which Mrs Porter guffawed enthusiastically.

"You really are a clever man, Mr Silver. Good joke: rector and ambrosia in the rectory. Do you suppose the ancient gods ate their nectar in a nectary? Norris has the Greek. I must ask him. He may not know but he will enjoy the joke – rector and ambrosia! Food for the gods on high and for us mere mortals on low in the rectory!"

Clearly the joke deserved literary expansion and explanation. Ernest's waggery had fallen even flatter than the rector's.

"I wanted a word with you about getting some home help. I asked the rector about it as I left the church this morning; he said you would be more help than himself, invited me to pot luck and here I am."

"And did we pot black?"

Ernest didn't want to stray into snooker pleasantries so he didn't answer, but steered the conversation back to his quest for a cleaner.

"What sort of help are you aiming for?"

He outlined his limited needs and undemanding demands.

Mrs Porter continued, "I know Maureen Hirst. Do you know her? She cleans for Colonel and Mrs MacDonald. They speak highly of her. She has a little girl who is shortly to go into nursery and she may have time to spare just now. I'll speak to her and, if she seems willing to take on a little more work, I'll bring her round and introduce her to you. Does that seem like a plan?"

"Very much so indeed; where do you want me to put the plates when I've dried them?"

"Just pop them on the side. I'll en-cupboard them later. The cutlery goes in the top drawer to your right."

All that was Ernest's harvest; the archdeacon and the rector never got their coffee.

CHAPTER 5

TO TELL OR NOT TO TELL: WHAT IS THE QUESTION?

Maureen said it was *allus nice to chat while yer doin' a job.*

"By Go', Ernest, tha tells a good tale. No wonder the kiddies like your stories. And our Laura looks forward fer yer bedtime stories every time when come to sit wi' 'er. I don't know what she likes special about birds but she all says they're 'er favourites."

Polishing done, she stood up and held her hands out to Ernest and said, "Just look, my mucky 'ands is right black. I'll wash in't sink wi' soap. That'll tackle it."

"I'll join you. I thought I'd done a good job on my hands but there is still black round my nails."

"Good idea. You give my 'ands a good scrubbin' an' I'll tackle yours."

And so, two contented people laughed together as they shared the same soap and water and came out clean as new pins. Ernest dried his hand on the towel hanging on the Aga rail and sat back.

Maureen did not face Ernest but said, with eyes averted, "Can I ask yer a question?"

"Fire away."

"You must think I'm bein' a bit nosey, but long though we've known you sin' you cem 'ere, in some ways me and 'Arry don't seem to know you proper at all. Not about you, I mean. You 'ave lots of brass to spend; you 'ave two cars; yer big 'ouse is lovely

"... we like you very much. But ... f'r instance, what did you do afore you settled 'ere? In 'Olsterdale, I mean. You've nivver told us an' I dare say we've nivver asked. Ee, I feel right daft askin' yer, but we don't know about what went on afore you set foot, do we?"

"Why do you want to know? Does it matter where or how I made my money? I pay my bills on time. I've made some very good friends since my caravan rested: first of all the Hepworths and Felicity, and you and Harry of course, and not forgetting Laura. I'm on very good terms with the rector and his wife who first introduced me to you. I look upon my work with the choir as a second job and the choir members seem to like my approach – more importantly, Mr Tweddle, the organist, doesn't object. So does it matter what I did before?"

"I did say you might think I was too nosey. I feel right embarrassed in askin'. You're a bit of a mystery man, you are – as I say, nice 'ouse, fancy car an' money to burn. You don't go on long 'olidays that much, though. I don't think you've slept out of 'Olsterdale all that oft sin' we got to know you."

"Oh, come now – I have had holidays, not often admittedly, and not long ones. I must have sneaked out when you weren't looking."

"You're a right dark 'orse, you are, an' no mistake."

The telephone rang. Maureen, who was nearer, asked, "Shall I answer it?"

"Leave it. I'll get it on the answerphone later."

They let it ring until it stopped. It rang again almost immediately.

"Someone's anxious to speak to me. It could be urgent. You'd better pick it up and answer it this time, Maureen."

"Mr Silver's residence. Can I 'elp you?"

She listened for a few seconds and then asked, "Who do you say you want to speak to? Mr Piercy? There's no one 'ere by that name. You must 'ave a—"

Hurriedly, Ernest grabbed the telephone. "I'll talk to him." And he retreated to the middle of the room. After listening for a few seconds, he angrily shouted, "You must be mistaken. This is a case of false identification. Where did you get my name, address, and telephone number from? Someone sold you it without permission. ... No, I do not want to book a holiday. No, I have not entered into any such contract with you, whoever you are. ... I owe you £299? Nonsense! Send me a copy of your contract, if indeed you have one. I'll show it to my accountant and if he agrees, which he will not do, I will pay up. I have no recollection of making such a long-term contract. ... Until 2019, you say? Rubbish. Don't ring again. Keep friendly with your neighbours and goodbye."

With that, and very red in the face, Ernest violently slammed the receiver into its cradle.

"Sorry about that, Maureen. I am plagued with too many nuisance calls."

"I wasn't listenin' an' I couldn't catch what they was sayin', but I seemed to 'ear singin.'"

"It was just background noise – a terrible nuisance, sometimes."

More than a little rattled, Ernest shifted back into his chair.

"Now what were we talking about before that rude intrusion?"

"You, an' where you come fra."

"What was it that made you ask? Was it off the cuff? Or did Harry put you up to it?"

"Nob'dy else. Me an' 'Arry was talking last night, an' we all of a sudden bethought that we didn't know all that much about you, even though you've spent hours an' hours in our 'ome', an' you've etten at our table loads and loads, an' we've asked you, must be a thousand times, to bathe Laura an' put 'er to bed, ever since she were a right little 'un. You talk lots about Laura but, about yourself, you nivver let on. I mean, this mornin' when you were talkin' about your dad an' that, were a bit of a surprise to me that you've nivver spoke about suchlike afore. Me an' 'Arry were talkin' about you last night, because some folks i'n't town are beginnin' to talk. We stand up for you, I promise you that, an' we try to ignore the gossips, but we're beginnin' to wonder if we're daft not payin' attention to what they 'ave to say. Now do you see what I'm on about?"

"I do indeed. I hear what you have to say and it distresses me, very much. Can I answer your question by saying that my past is a long story, but you have nothing, absolutely nothing, to get het up about? What I did before I settled in the north. … I closed that book years ago or, to put it another way, my past is a foreign country, even to me. I have packed it all away, I had hoped, for good. It all took place a long way from here, much of it in London and has no relevance to my present state. Until this distressing moment, the door to the past I have kept firmly shut and locked, blinds down and shutters shut." Then, with a laugh, "My word, I am rather overdosing on metaphors, they are giving me indigestion."

Maureen didn't share his laugh. "You've not bin i' prison or owt like that, then?"

"Goodness me! Is that what people are saying?"

"Not ezackly, but they say where there's smoke there could be a fire burnin' underneath."

She looked at him intently and waited.

"All I will say is that there was nothing out of the ordinary in my former life – that is before I settled in Holsterdale. I'm not a mafia mastermind seeking safety and anonymity in a small northern town. I made my money legitimately."

She still said nothing but stared at him straight in the face – truth or dare fashion.

"I hope this doesn't mean that you are regretting your confidence in me with Laura, that your trust in me has been a mistake? I couldn't bear to think that. What are people saying?

Do they tell you to be more careful when you let me look after Laura in your home? I assure you that you have nothing to worry about. Are they saying they'd rather I didn't go into school to be with their children, to listen to their reading and to tell stories? Have your friends said anything of this to the head teacher? Mr McCullough's never mentioned any worries on such matters to me. Are you losing friends because of me? Now there are a handful of questions for you to answer. You've challenged me with your questions; now it's my turn to challenge you."

"I won't speak for other folks. Laura wouldn't talk to me an' 'Arry if we stopped you comin' to our 'ouse an' that. She can be that okkard when she wants. I'm tellin' you she loves you, she says so. An' she says so tons of times. I daresn't think what she would do if we shut you out."

"Surely you weren't thinking of shutting me out? I do truly hope not. Did you think twice before coming here this morning to clean for me? Did Harry tell you to ask these questions? I'd never dreamt that you could be worried in the slightest about me and Laura. Being together so much, I mean. You've given me a great deal to think about."

Maureen had nothing further to add as her eyes turned deliberately away from him to the cleaning things still on the table.

Ernest had no option but to insist firmly, "You'd better go now, Maureen. The rain has almost stopped so … Your money is in the usual place. Your coat will be quite dry and I dare say your shoes will have dried out too. I would be grateful if you'd wheel the bins to the corner for me before you go. Forget about the Co-op, I'll go myself in the morning. We can all hope by then this storm will have blown over."

As Maureen struggled into her coat, tears streamed down her face. Down Ernest's face too. Neither of them spoke.

To Tell Or Not To Tell: What Is The Question?

Maureen swiftly picked up her money and hurriedly left, trundling the bins as she went. The rain had almost stopped.

The poor man tearfully pondered, *I don't suppose my answers and assurances will satisfy her or Harry, but it's all I want to reveal at the moment.* He wholeheartedly wished he hadn't said 'fire away', but he had, and no genius could take it back, not even by turning back the clock.

There were two storms going on: for one, the weather outside, and for another a storm Maureen's interrogation had stirred up.

Now was not the right time to reveal to Maureen where Mr Piercy fitted in, or what part Mr Piercy played in his life. He had made sacrificial pretences to preserve his true identity, and was in no way going to enact the moment of revelation under any sort of duress. It needed careful planning and detailed choreography, which he had only recently been considering.

The call was from a man he used to know many years ago. How the hell had Pete got his home phone number? Ernest decided he would leave sorting all that out. No urgency so far as that was concerned.

CHAPTER 6

WHY IS LAURA? WHAT IS SHE – TO ME?

For many minutes after Maureen had gone home, Ernest remained seated in the kitchen; his breathing was irregular, his heartbeat fluttery. He stared, unseeing, at the back door. Tears coursed down his cheeks, which he now and then wiped away with the back of his hand.

He began to think of all the lovely times and many hours he had spent with the Hirsts and their daughter. Ernest reflected on them and stored them against the bleak years he would now be faced to spend without ever being with her, with her laughs, her cuddles, and her weird imagination. All this summation of happiness and contentment was threatened, he knew that. The tide had turned and he was adrift without anchor. He might even have to leave Holsterdale, his adopted town, which had welcomed him unquestioningly, had made him feel so well liked and so highly regarded.

Laura's company, on his knee – never again.

One night in particular struck him as special, and he recalled every detail of it. He had bathed Laura, washed her hair and had been downstairs in the sitting room reading her nursery rhymes out of her favourite book. This particular rhyme was his favourite:

The North Wind doth blow
And we shall have snow,
And what will poor robin do then, poor thing?
He'll sleep in the barn
And keep himself warm,
And hide himself under his wing, poor thing.

"I think that is a silly poem – I don't want you to read it to me again."

Ernest was surprised at her swift reaction.

"What's wrong with it? I think it's a lovely poem."

Laura responded, "Robins are not poor, they're brave little birds. They come out in all weathers, the wet and windy, and in heavy snowstorms. Don't you dare call them poor, Uncle Ernest; in our nature book it says they are fighters. They'd never hide in a barn and keep themselves warm. It's a silly poem. I don't want to hear it again. Read me another, please, Uncle Ernest."

"Righty-ho then. Simple Simon, do you like that better?"

"Yes. Go on then. Don't stop to talk about it before we've heard it."

Some mothers and fathers would tell their kids not to be cheeky to their elders and betters, but not so Ernest. He loved every syllable that precious child uttered.

Simple Simon met a pie man, going to the fair.
Said Simple Simon to the pie man – May I taste your ware?
Said the pie man to Simple Simon, show first your penny.
Said Simple Simon to the pie man, Indeed I have not any!

Ernest hadn't time to read the next verse. As soon as he had read this, Laura asked, "Is Charlie Nattrass simple, Uncle Ernest?"

"Why do you want to know?"

"Because the big lads tease 'im an' call him a barmpot. Barmpots are simple, aren't they?"

"That's not a nice thing to say about anybody. I hope you don't call little Charlie a barmpot, Laura."

"No, I do not, but the big lads do. When he tries to join in football games, they kick the ball at him and he can't dodge fast enough and they laugh if it hits him and knocks him over. That's cruel, isn't it, Uncle Ernest?"

"It certainly is. Children can be cruel because they don't know how not to be. Life can be cruel too, Laura."

"How do you mean?"

"Well, let's see. When you are older, you'll understand that some things happen that are disappointing or sad. Maybe you'll want to cry when your pet dies. You'll think it's unfair."

"I cried when my cat got run over."

"Exactly, life was cruel to you then. And sometimes we can't stop people doing unkind or cruel things to others. Sometimes they do it when they're angry, or jealous or thwarted; now that's a good word for you to learn about. But you do your best for Charlie Nattrass. And we all love you for it."

"Does love mean the same as like?"

"They have similar meanings, but love is stronger."

"I thought love was being soppy and kissing and that, like the boring bits in films."

"That comes into it but there's more to love than that."

Was this a suitable conversation with an eight-year-old girl? It was hard to know when to stop and how to give credible examples, even for one so worldly wise as Ernest. He knew how he felt about this inquiring little girl, but this interrogation by Laura might lead him to awkward territory and to telling her in so many words how he felt about her, and she about him. The direction of her chatter made him jittery. He must steer the chat to matters affecting Charlie Nattrass.

"Look at it this way. You say you like Charlie Nattrass, but what you do for him takes you a bit further and gives you a nice feeling that you've done good, that you more than just like him."

"I'm not going out with 'im. Charlie and me are not courting or owt like that and I don't kiss 'im. Eurgh!"

"I wonder if you're old enough to understand the term 'shades of meaning'? I'll try and explain. There are different levels of liking and loving. I like Yorkshire pudding but I wouldn't go so far as to say that I love it."

"Mum says she loves Yorkshire pudding."

"Oh dear. We are getting into deep water. Another time. Let's call it quits for now. Back to talking about Charlie, please."

"Is Charlie simple, though?"

"Charlie takes time to learn things. For example, he is maybe not as good a reader as some of his classmates. We're all made different. Some of us are good at sums, some can draw nice pictures, and we all learn good and bad habits from our school friends and our mums and dads. Some parents use bad language and their children don't see anything wrong with using it too. Some children are kind by nature, others learn to be kind by example. You're lucky, Laura, you have learned to read very quickly and you read very well indeed. You don't use bad language and I think you are a very kind young lady. Perhaps Charlie is not as lucky as you in some ways, but he is lucky that you are kind and stick up for him."

"I like Charlie. I look after 'im. I take him for walks when I see him crying. We have a secret hiding place where we can shelter from the rain. It's under a big bush what flowers in the spring. It has big shiny leaves that keep the rain off real well."

"It's time for bed. You are dry now. I'll brush your hair to stop it getting entangled into knots. And, I might ask, where's your nightie?"

"Upstairs under the pillow, silly man! You must be soft in tha 'ead if you don't remember that. It's always under my pillow, in't it?"

She was off his knee and upstairs before you could say Jack Robinson; she was down again as swiftly, nightie on and brandishing her hairbrush. He brushed her hair and took her upstairs where she leaped into bed, duvet pulled tight under her chin. He kissed her good night, her eyes tight shut and within seconds she was sound asleep. It was all over in the twinkling.

Many such thoughts came and went; happy recollections that were in danger of never again being allowed. Tears reappeared through the smiles.

CHAPTER 7

THE ORDER OF THE BATH AND OTHER HONOURS

Swiftly following that lovely bedtime recollection, another image took its place that really made him smile, though he knew in his bones there would be no possibility of repetition.

Maureen and Harry had been training for the Great North Run. They had arranged for Laura to stay with her Uncle Arthur, who Ernest had never met, but the plans fell through when the uncle became ill. All right then: one of them would run, the other stay at home.

Ernest had become a favourite visitor and was once a week treated to delicious meals. Maureen was a good cook, and an invitation to eat with them was never to be turned down. Not just for the food, they were good company too. Every week Ernest put Laura to bed, usually on Tuesday nights when Ma and Pa Hirst were out training. Tuesday nights always, and some weeks more frequently.

Laura liked these special bath nights with Ernest and he was equally delighted to get his sleeves wet as she 'swam' up and down the bath with a whoosh. It was during these times that he started to tell her stories in bed and was thrilled when she made unusual and unexpected twists to the story. He eagerly looked forward to these evenings alone with this strange but bright little girl.

Ernest, overhearing the Hirst's discussion about who should

run and who stay at home, tentatively offered to step in so that both could run. "Might Laura like to stay with me in my house? It would seem like a holiday, wouldn't it?"

Laura was only six years old, and the suggestion that this child should stay with an old man in his own posh house was little short of outrageous, even if it was to be in a posh bedroom of her own. It would solve a problem for the Hirsts of course, but would it be ruled out of order? Indeed, *should* it be ruled out?

Harry said they would ask Laura first; Maureen agreed and she knelt down and sweetly asked Laura if she would like to have a nice 'oliday with Uncle Ernest. It would be in a strange bedroom and in a strange bed, they had to point out. Ernest painted an imaginary picture of a lovely night. Laura's reply amazed them all. She said that she always wanted to have a holiday in Uncle Ernest's house. Little Miss Independent strikes again.

And so it came about that Ernest and Laura were upstairs in his house, 31 South Street, getting the spare bed ready for her. Maureen had come round and uncovered from the kist a pretty duvet cover with colourful peacocks on it. She had said Laura would love it.

On this special day, before they set off for the north, Maureen and Harry had taken Laura round to Ernest's, said goodbye to her and told her to be a good girl. Much to their mixture of delight and disappointment, Laura had given them both a quick kiss and raced off into the house – no tears or regrets in sight.

Stuffing the duvet into the peacock cover was an entertaining challenge solved when Laura climbed inside the cover and pushed the ends of the duvet into the corners. He sat on the open end of the cover and briefly trapped her inside. She giggled as she struggled to get out of it. Ernest put a hot water bottle in the bed to air it. It had not been slept in for ages.

When it was time for bed Laura had a shower, which she said she preferred to a bath. Ernest washed her hair. Laura tried unsuccessfully to dry herself ready for bed. Ernest took over and towelled her thoroughly upstairs. Downstairs in the kitchen he made her a quick drink of hot chocolate. Laura sat on the kitchen table to drink it, before finally going up to bed. Two minutes conscientious tooth brushing followed in the bathroom, then the usual speedy ritual of jumping into the bed. No story this time: she said she was too tired. Ernest couldn't resist a quick kiss. In minutes she was asleep.

A further kiss goodnight could not be resisted and then Ernest crept downstairs, happier than he had ever remembered being.

As he made ready for bed, he peeped in and saw Laura fast asleep. She was sprawled on the bed, most of the duvet on the floor. She must have been restless. Carefully, Ernest replaced the duvet over her, gave her another kiss and whispered goodnight. She didn't stir.

At about two o'clock he awoke in response to gentleman's purposes and was startled to find Laura in his bed snuggled up beside him, one leg over his chest. She must have crept in, perhaps frightened by the unfamiliar creaking in this old house and in a dark room. Ernest had purposely left the landing light on and it had lit her way into his bedroom and into his bed. He tucked her into his bed where she lay apparently undisturbed, went to complete his night-time pee and then crossed the landing into her room and bed where he restlessly tried to sleep until morning.

Such and similar happy events would never happen again if what Maureen had said about the gossiping neighbours was true. Maureen and Harry might never again leave her alone with him.

CHAPTER 8

THE AFTERNOON OF A PHONE

When Ernest was fully awake, he thought he really should call Pete to ask why his former colleague had rung him, and to find out what unrecorded message was behind the call. He wasn't all that keen to speak to the man, had never really liked him, but he was curious to know why Peter Freeway had rung.

Ernest dialled 1471 and was told: A long string of numbers "called today at 11.17 hours. To return the call press three; there is normally a charge for this service."

He pressed three, half hoping that the number was engaged. He hoped that Pete had changed. Pete answered immediately. Ernest quickly explained the fictional £299 and asked what on Earth he wanted. Pete replied that he had traced some survivors of former players from the Riddell Theatre Company – from those long and best forgotten fit up days in Scotland. Pete added that it must be sixty years since Fettercairn and that a golden Jubilee was in order before they all took their last curtain call!

"Not for a long time yet for me, Peter. I have long distance plans and I've much to look forward to."

"Yes, well, we can all hope. Good luck, mate."

He continued that he'd advertised in *The Stage* and found two or three tattered remnants to gather in the name of past glories. Between them, they had cooked up a plan to push the boat out and meet for dinner at Browns Hotel, Mayfair in early December. Date not exactly fixed yet but if he, Ernest, was interested, Pete would add him and to the list and get in touch again to tell the when and how and so forth.

Ernest could hardly concentrate on what Pete was saying. His mind was flooded with other things, but he said, somewhat reluctantly, that yes, he'd come. He then asked Pete how he had found his home phone number. Pete replied mysteriously that he had his contacts, but gave no names, no pack drill. Ernest wondered who the contacts could possibly be but didn't press for an answer. Pete added that he knew that Margery and Ernest had married and that he had seen her death in *The Telegraph*. He was sorry he wasn't at her funeral; he had been touring in the north and didn't see the notice until it was too late, or he certainly would have come, 'cross my heart and hope to die'. When was it exactly, he wanted to know? Ernest replied that she had died eleven years ago.

"My God, so long! Eleven years! How time passes when you're having fun."

Before he rang off, Pete, almost as an afterthought, asked if Ernest had seen anything of Reg Page recently. He knew that Reg and Ernest had worked up a double act.

Ernest answered that Reg and he had toured together for a couple of years with only moderate success, but they had split years ago when TV effectively dismantled music halls and the like. Reg and he had bumped into one another now and again since those long-lost years, but not at all recently. He added that he'd had no up-to-date contact with Reg, didn't know even if he was still alive and, frankly, didn't much care. He made no promises, one way or the other.

Pete said, "Nice to have a chat, pussy cat. See you in December, remember. Don't be a square – be there. Life has its ups and downs. See you at Browns." On that jocular note, Pete rang off.

Pete's phone call, with its irritating *renaissancede temps perdus*, had startled him. For over ten years in Holsterdale,

Ernest had successfully hidden his stage name and acting career, not only from others but even from himself. His theatrical career had been no great shakes at its best and nothing to write home about. He had made numerous TV appearances in bit parts (none of them memorable).

He had drowned this part of his past, and in his memory it had sunk without trace. Even in his quieter moments he never brought those pointless years back to mind. The timing of that conversation over the brass polishing had not instinctively been the right time to prompt Ernest to reveal all. If he had responded as Mr Piercy to Pete, all his past would have spilled out with the necessary explanations in tow. He would have had to come clean, to reveal to Maureen that he had indeed been an actor, confirming their suspicions. He could have come clean when she asked but he didn't, and knew he was not anything like secure enough in his adopted role as country squire in Holsterdale.

Maureen and Harry were, to all intents and purposes, his closest friends in the town. The Hepworths, especially Felicity, were very close to his heart of course.

Even so, he could not confide in them and hope that the secret would remain a secret. Once the Hirsts knew, the cat would certainly be out of the bag. He wasn't ready for that just yet. He had always congratulated himself that he had made a remarkable success of this adopted role as country gent. It was possibly the most completely rounded characterisation in his long career, one that would have the critics, if they knew about it and recognised it for what it was, on bended knee in admiration. He wasn't ready yet to own up and spoil his performance.

At least over those theatrical years he had never had to descend to serving at petrol stations or behind cocktail bars or waiting at tables in Pizza Express. He had only once slept in a cardboard box on the Embankment. He awoke chilled to the very marrow. He had often slept wrapped in stage curtains. That was dusty and did nothing for the bronchioles. Throughout his career he had kept body and soul together as a professional actor without resorting to such rescue missions adopted by most of his fellow actors in the dicey theatre trade. He congratulated himself that avoiding these economic tricks and other such tactics could be rightly interpreted as success.

Ernest tried to shake off these disturbing thoughts, stirred himself, mechanically scrunched up the Brasso blackened newspaper and tossed it into the bin. He had no appetite for lunch, not even a bowl of soup. He walked into the cold sitting room and threw himself into his chair, closed his eyes and determined again to try to sleep. He had nothing to do. He turned on the television in the hope that Countdown would lull him to sleep – it usually did – but its soporific magic failed to do the trick: his mind a buzzing, angry swarm of bees bringing home little honey. He had done nothing all day but clean a few brass objects, yet he was totally exhausted.

He must have sat there motionless for over an hour when the doorbell rang emphatically. Only the Rev. Porter rang it like that, in a stentorian fashion that demanded attention. He roused himself, wiped his damp eyes and went to the door.

"Come in, dear man. What brings you out in this mad autumnal day?" This weak attempt at jocularity failed to make its mark.

"Thanks, I will," replied Mr Porter.

"What's to do now?" Ernest asked.

"It's two things really. First, Mr Tweddle is going to be away at this, of all weekends, the Feast of All Saints, so I wondered if you would be kind enough to, erm, 'preside at the console', so to speak? I know a three manual organ isn't your instrument, but I *just thought...*"

"Go on, for heaven's sake! I'll do it. You have the hymn

numbers, I presume. I hope 'Jerusalem' isn't one of them. It's tricky enough on the piano!"

"No. Nothing elaborate."

"What was the other thing?"

"The other thing? Oh, yes, I'd like you to read the Old Testament lesson. Judges chapter 16, *'And Samson said let me die ...'*, Samson destroying the Temple. Dramatic. You do it so very well."

"Right then. If I must."

"I knew you'd do it. Aileen thought you might not want to do both, but I was sure you would oblige. She is forever telling me I put on you too much; you're better than Barkis for being a willing horse. I can take you to water and I can rely on you to swim. Ha, ha! I said, 'I know a likely horse when I see one.'"

"Mm. ... Is that it, then?"

"Yes, I think so."

"Thanks for calling."

"Oh? Are you all right, Ernest?"

"Yes, why shouldn't I be?"

"No reason. I just thought..."

"I mustn't keep you. You're a busy man."

"Yes, I suppose I could be so described. Goodbye, then."

With that Porter departed, no handshake, nothing further said.

As he left, Norris heard the door behind him bang shut immediately. He hurried home, deprived of the expected cup of Earl Grey and a buttered scone. He looked at his watch and thought, *Well, that's a rum do*. He would tell Aileen all about it over a cup of tea.

Aileen expressed no surprise at the reported rebuff at the hands of the willing horse and, without warning, she asked, "Have you ever regretted inviting Silver to join the choir? He seems to have taken over. It amazes me that Tweddle puts up with him."

The Afternoon Of A Phone

"Nat Tweddle is very easy going, but he enjoys playing the organ – indeed he is a very competent organist. You don't find many FRCOs to the pound outside cathedrals; we are lucky to have him. He spends much of his spare time practicing his Bach fugues. His variations, as he accompanies the last verse of all the hymns, are the envy of other parishes in the area. As you know, many churches no longer have an organ that works, let alone an organist who can play it. At Christchurch in Shepley, they play accompaniments to the hymns on CDs, Karaoke style. It sounds quite good but it's not like the real thing. So if someone who knows what he's doing comes along and helps with the choir, Tweddle, and I might say I too, welcome them. You have to admit that the choir is bigger and in better fettle since Ernest stepped up to the plate. The archdeacon commented upon it, remember?"

"Yes, that's all very well. He *is* good company, but everything he does appears to me to be a performance. I mean, that time when he asked if you would put on a memorial service for his late wife. What was that all about? Her funeral, at her request, was a humanist celebration. What on earth would she want with a Christian memorial?"

"Well, he has undergone a transformation here in Holsterdale, and he said he'd feel more comfortable if he knew she was in safe hands in the hereafter."

"Sounds more like a line from a play."

"Aileen, have faith in his human nature, for God's sake."

"Anyhow, you sensibly put the kibosh on that. Her wishes had to be respected, you said, and quite right too."

"He'd got the service all worked out; hymn, *'The day thou gavest Lord is ended,'* and a piece Elgar wrote in 1914. I t was called something like Aspirin – I don't remember exactly – an orchestral piece with a prominent part for the harp."

"There you are. Hearing a harp in heaven – should be a comfort for her, if that's where she is."

"He even had a tape of it to be played at the end of the service."

"However, you don't need to bother yourself about that anymore. The Elgar was probably one he'd heard at a concert somewhere. The fact that he chose it reinforces my ideas about the man. Every action he makes is so very proper, the right thing for a man in his position to do. If I didn't know better, I'd say he plays everything by the book, as if he'd researched it."

"You've never mentioned this before, Aileen. You're saying that he's a phony? I've never even suspected that for an instant. He knows his way around the prayer book and can quote from the New and even the Old Testament."

"Well, look at that dinner party he held for us, Colonel and Mrs MacDonald and the church wardens and their wives. Everything was exactly as it ought to be: matching cutlery, china and so on, wine glasses of the right shape and size and in the correct place. He admitted he had hired caterers to provide and serve the food; he couldn't have created that menu in his kitchen, well equipped though it might be. His seating plan round the table was meticulous and fully thought out. He even asked me to take the ladies into the drawing room – idiotically calling it the withdrawing room – whilst you men stayed at the table to pass the port. Like act two of an Alfred Lunt and Lynne Fontanne comedy. But did you notice the dead giveaway?"

"No. What was the dead giveaway? Pray tell."

"He held his knife as if it were a fountain pen. He didn't pick that uncool habit up from a textbook. Nobody who *is* anybody would dream of doing that."

"Aileen, my dear, you're a terrible snob."

"I know my strengths."

"Snobbery is no strength; it's a trespass. We all suffer from them and pray daily for forgiveness."

"Indeed we do. Your trespass, Norris dear, and I've pointed this out to you frequently, is that you can always find something good to say about every scallywag you come across."

The Afternoon Of A Phone

"Ernest is no scallywag. You're not equating him with Fred Jones, the drunken failure, surely."

"Certainly not! I wouldn't have Jones cross our threshold, and I didn't mean it like that, as you perfectly well know."

"Aileen, dear, you are a marvel. But where does all this lead us?"

"That Ernest is a phony! And did you notice the flowers on that piece in the middle of the table – what do they call it?"

"Epergne, I think it's called. Yes I did, but what of that?"

"Set dressing, that's what it was; like they do at the Little Theatre when there's a banquet going on. Nobody but amateur directors ask for epergnes these days. Life is too short."

"Darling, you do surprise me."

"I keep my eyes open and my mind uncluttered too, for that matter! And you would do well if you were more watchful too. And another thing; you remember when he asked me if I could recommend a cleaner? I suggested Maureen Hirst. Look what's happened there. He's swallowed the Hirsts whole. He's never off their doorstep. Frankly, I wish I had never introduced him to the good-natured Hirsts."

"You exaggerate, darling. Maureen is a thoroughly good sort and a trustworthy cleaner. Ernest turns out to be an ideal and trusted babysitter – not that Laura is still a baby, but you know what I mean. I have to admit he does talk about Laura quite a lot. She's in the junior choir and he says she sings very well for her age. But he sees her in school too, along with all the other children he's come into contact with. The young ones in reception think he's great, and you must agree that he and his open-top car trips are a major and very popular attraction at the parish fete."

"Has his name never cropped up when you make your parish visits to the school? I presume you do talk to the head teacher?"

"McCullough and I do talk often but there's no reason for Ernest's name to crop up. Why should we talk about him? If there was a scandal surrounding him, then we would have to talk about him, but there isn't. Not even a whiff. So in general, McCullough and I have no call to mention Ernest's name. I do hear from the reception teacher, Eileen Flowers, and from many parents, that he's very imaginative at making up impromptu stories for the younger children, and that he is endlessly patient with listening to the kids who are struggling with their reading."

"Do you know what I'm thinking? You've hit on it, bullseye. His whole life and lifestyle are just another made up story."

"Stop it, Aileen. You're making me dizzy with these, as I see it, unfounded speculations."

"Yes, well, here's another thing. How is it that he's so good at it? Most country squires (and I'm sure that's the role Ernest is playing) couldn't do it, wouldn't even want to. The toffs in your congregation read so badly, can't read for toffee and what's more, they wouldn't have the foggiest notion how to teach reading or the patience to listen to a four-year-old's halting attempts. Just listen to the posh end reading the lessons in church – hopeless."

"What on earth do you mean by toffs? Names, for heaven's sake?"

"You know perfectly well who I mean!"

"Aileen, dear, all these speculations don't alter the fact that Ernest is a thoroughly decent, well-meaning chap. However, I must get on with my homily for Sunday. I've got to reread Judges for the umpteenth time and come up with something new. We'll talk about all this later. Making a new sermon out of Samson's destruction of the Temple will take just a little thought."

"Do you remember what Ernest said when I suggested he should have a cat for company?"

"No, I don't. Is it relevant?"

"Perhaps not, but his detailed description of an event that took place over seventy years ago was little short of miraculous and it showed graphically that his mother had no time for him."

"Go on, then; sermon on hold for the time being. Tell me what he had to say…"

"I got up early because I had heard Topsy in the kitchen meowing like mad half the night. … I went down to see what was up and she was sitting in her box and licking a kitten. The box was just a cardboard soap box that groceries had been delivered in. I'd put a blanket in it to make it cosy and there she was, licking this little black kitten. I dragged her box, which was near the back door and a bit draughty, to be near the cooker. Then I ran upstairs to tell Mumsy what had happened.

"'For God's sake, what are you doing up at this unearthly hour. Go back to bed, you stupid boy. It's only just after seven o'clock. Be off with you.'

"I did go back to bed, but I was itching to see Topsy and her kitten. I couldn't wait until the clock struck eight. It was half-term holiday so there was no school to go to that day. I dressed as fast as I could and ran downstairs. There was just one kitten, and that had anchored itself to Topy's tummy and was sucking away like mad. Then, all of a sudden Topsy rolled over on her side and out shot another kitten, wet and black like the first. Topsy started licking it all over. I was so excited that I had to tell someone, so I ran upstairs to tell Mumsy.

"'Another kitten? And will you please stop calling me Mumsy. It's a ridiculous name. I am your mother, God help me, so call me Mother. Have you brushed your teeth?'

"I didn't answer.

"'Well, have you?'

"'Pops likes me to call you Mumsy.'

"'That's all well and good but it's Mother from now on, do you hear? No matter what your father says. Teeth – have you brushed them?'

"'No, I forgot.'

"'You'd forget your head if it were loose, you idiotic child. Well, go and brush them now, immediately!'

"As I went she shouted after me, 'And get your own breakfast. There's Force in the cupboard and milk in the larder. And remember to put the milk back in the larder with the cover on when you've done.'

"The Force packet was unopened and as I struggled to open it, some spilt on the table. I brushed it off into the bowl with my hand and went into the larder with the bowl to get the milk. The jug was full and I poured too much into the bowl. I tried to suck it out with my lips but the bowl tipped and some milk and Force dripped onto the floor. I carried the half-empty bowl clumsily back into the kitchen, leaving a trail of milk and flakes in my wake. I sat at the table to eat what was left and then my feet crunched through a minefield of Force flakes on my way to the sink. I put the dish into the sink and found a dish cloth. I returned to the larder to clean up as best a six-year-old could.

"After all this kerfuffle, there were two more kittens, one with white paws like Topsy. I rushed upstairs to announce the big news. Mumsy, sorry, I mean mother was at the dressing table doing her make up. She was wafting her hand in the air to dry the nail varnish.

"'What do you want now?' she asked impatiently. I hated her plucked eyebrows. They made her look silly and she used too much dark-red lipstick that stuck to my face if and when she kissed me. I kept my thoughts to myself as I replied,

"'Topsy's had THREE MORE kittens!'

"'Tell your father when he comes back. He'll deal with it.' She didn't quite share my excitement and continued wafting. 'Go away, and make sure the kitchen is tidy before I come down. Have you had your breakfast?'

"'Yes,' I replied.

"'Go away then, and don't bother me again. I'm playing bridge *this morning with the Marton-Moores and I don't want you making me late.'*

"I went downstairs hoping to see yet another kitten, but there were still only four, all pawing Topsy's tummy, sucking like mad. I pulled a chair up so that I could sit and watch them. Topsy looked tired but she let them have a go at her. I heard Mother in the hall. She was going out of the front door, thank goodness. Phew. She wouldn't see the mess. But she suspected and deliberately came into the kitchen to inspect.

"'What in God's name has been going on here?'

"This was her first onslaught. Before she could continue the attack, the back door opened and in strode Pops, fresh from battle exercises as he calls them. 'Oh, good, you're back. You make sure he gets this mess cleaned up. I'm off to the Brotherton's for bridge and I'm late, thanks to this crass simpleton. There are some kittens in that box: you know what to do!'

"Thank heaven she was gone. Pops saluted ironically (I didn't know what that meant at the time, but I do now) and Mother departed through the front door.

"'What's been going on here?' he asked gently.

"'I spilled some Force flakes on the table when I opened the new packet and some must have fallen onto the floor. I didn't notice and I must have trod on them. But Topsy's had four kittens and one of them is just like her with white paws.'

"'Indeed, let me have a look.'

"'I saw some of them come out of her tummy. They shot out like bullets.'

"'Look, I must get cleaned up. You run upstairs and run the hot water into the bath, while I mop up the kitchen and the trail of milk to wherever it leads.'

"'Thanks, Pops. You're not cross then?'

"'There's a time to be cross when it really matters. Now you run the bath, there's a good lad.' I noticed he didn't look at the kittens when he went for the mop.

"I ran upstairs, turned on the hot tap in the bath and then, just for safety, I did brush my teeth. When I went down to the kitchen, Pops had cleaned up the mess, including the milky trail to the larder. Topsy's box was again where it's usually kept, by the back door. As he went to put the mop away, he said, 'Now, I want you to find one of those sacks we buy potatoes in. They may be in the wash house, I think. Then I want you to pick up a couple of buckets, they're definitely in the wash house, take them and the sack to the back yard. Fill both buckets about half-full of water. When you've done all that, you can come back here to be with Topsy and her brood. I won't be half a tick, but this face paint takes a bit of getting off.'

"'You slap makeup on as thick as Mumsy does and it takes her HOURS to take it off.'

"'We use face paint for different reasons – but I won't go into that now. Do you understand what I've asked you to do? A potato sack and two buckets half-full of water. Back yard. Yes?'

"I hadn't forgotten, but I didn't know why he wanted it done. I did as bid and was crouched watching with Topsy and her brood.

"At about eleven-forty Pops emerged, clean and shiny. I was gazing fascinated at Topsy with her kittens, which were still in the box by the back door. Captain Silver, that was my father, who had a job to do and knew how to do it, marched straight out of the back door and called me to follow him. He was thinking that some things in battle are unpleasant, unwelcome and yet demanding. Discipline was the order of the day. Grit your teeth and get on with it.

"'Ernest, I see you've done what I asked. Now which is the smaller bucket?'

"'This one.'

"'Yes, but I think it needs a bit more water, about half as much again. You do it, Ernest.'

"The tap was in the wall over a stone sink so it was easy-peasy.

"'Now what, Pops?'

The Afternoon Of A Phone

"'You found a sack. Good lad. It's a bit bigger than we need but it'll do. Now go into the kitchen and lift the kittens gently into it and bring it out to me, cargo loaded.'

"I did as I was told. The kittens were by now warm and dry. I had to pull them gently off Topsy's tummy, where they were firmly anchored and busily sucking. I'd never done such as this before and I was surprised how much I had to tug them off their mum. Topsy didn't seem to protest, she just let me get on with it.

"As I put them gently into the sack they squeaked noisily. When all four were in I took the sack full of what Pops had called 'cargo', into the yard.

"'Here they are, Pops. Now what?'

"'Now I don't want you to cry, lad. There are some things that have to be done in life and this time you and I are doing it together. Now listen, we couldn't have the town overrun with cats, could we? That wouldn't be right, wouldn't be sensible would it? What you have to do today will teach you that not all things in life are nice – that some things are unpleasant. Some dreadful things have to be done, like wars and so on. Nobody truly wants to do these horrid things, except politicians perhaps. Only in stories you have happy-ever-after endings. One just has to grit one's teeth and—'

"'Are we going to drownded them?' I'd heard about the young man who drownded himself in the boggy pond on the moor last year, and that's the word I had heard in the village.

"'Yes, we are going to drown them – drown, that's the right word by the way. We are going to drown, not drownded them, and you are going to do it. There are some lessons in life that we never forget, and today is one of those. I don't think you will ever forget what you've learned today.'

"'Couldn't we sell them or give them away?'

"'Not in Catterick Camp. Sorry, but they've more than enough already and to spare. No definitely not. Now drop the sack into the larger bucket, quickly now, and put the smaller bucket on top.

Quickly now, don't dilly dally.' I dropped the sack into the bucket and straight away put the smaller bucket on top. Their squeaking quickly stopped, and I ran upstairs and hid my head in my pillow. I cried and cried – my pillow was wet with my tears. I could still hear their pitiable squeals long after I knew they must be dead – and I had drowned them. Pops came up and sat on the edge of my bed and put his hand gently on my shoulder.

"'It doesn't matter; if you want to cry, go ahead. I used to cry a lot as a boy about all sorts of things – getting my bottom smacked, being told off in front of the whole school, being late, getting a low mark for homework, I could go on – but I've had to teach myself not to give in. Crying doesn't help; sometimes it makes you look silly or childish. It's a hard lesson to learn but the sooner you learn it the better. Be a man, Ernest. Men don't cry. When you're ready, dry your eyes, come downstairs and we'll think of something nicer to do. We could go for a lovely walk, if you want; the weather's picking up, and the hazelnuts might be ripe for eating.'"

"You're quite right, Aileen. It is an interesting story. I wonder if I should preach on Noah, instead."

"Stick to Samson, dear. It's safer." Aileen always liked the last word.

BOOK TWO

THE FLOODED RIVER HORST MOVES TO CENTRE STAGE

CHAPTER 9

A TIDE IN THE AFFAIRS OF A MAN TAKEN BY THE FLOOD

As soon as the rector had gone, Ernest fell into his most comfortable chair in the drawing room. When he had half-nodded, half-slept he looked out of the window and saw that the rain had eased. Submerged, indeed trapped, by all these disturbing thoughts, he had felt himself a hostage: stifled in this house. He considered what he could do to release the strain on his jangling nerves. Time enough before Sunday to look up the Samson lesson, and in any case he didn't feel like rehearsing the reading just then.

He donned his heavy overcoat, one more suitable for shepherding than for tripping off in the car, and picked up the keys of the Ford. Decision taken, he'd drive to the Horst Falls which would be spectacular after all the rain. Blow the cobwebs off and enjoy the spectacle.

It was a short drive through the town, past Water Street where the Hirsts lived and up to the top of the green. Through the heavy cloud that had descended he could just make out the river in the near distance; it was in full spate, brown and turbulent; it was lashing the banks, many feet above the level of the river bed. At the top of the hill, he pulled up and climbed out to watch as many as a dozen children playing football. They were some distance off so it wasn't easy for him to pick out individuals. He knew, however, that Laura was bound to be amongst them, though he couldn't spot her among the melee. The field they were playing in was too close for comfort to the raging torrent.

Ernest ruminated as he watched. *Look at those children, letting off steam after a whole day cooped up inside.*

He could make out Maurice in his bright red anorak; he was a quiet one in class but he certainly knew how to kick a ball.

Whoops, splash, right into a puddle. More laundry for Jamie's mum, there'd be a ticking off him when he got home. All the boys were the same, clean in the morning but by lunchtime covered in muck. *There's mud and muck everywhere today,* Ernest thought. He wondered where Laura was, sure that she would be in the thick of it. He loved that child, and pictured her windswept face, muddy and laughing at the rain.

Yes he did adore that lively, energetic and unpredictable young lass. Was that too strong a word? He didn't think so. She'd always come up with the weirdest ideas when he was storytelling in Reception, which were even stranger and more outlandish at home in bed now that she was older.

She had been rather a plain Jane at four, and she had not improved in looks. In fact she was just as plain now as an eight-year-old, plain as a pike staff. But behind that unremarkable face, he thought, there was a mind that was truly astonishing, with an imagination as quick as mercury; she'd not lost any of that four years later. Beauty is in the eye of the beholder and he beheld her lovingly – to him she was beautiful.

And how does a four-year-old develop into such a kind and thoughtful child at the age of eight? He thought. Parental example no doubt – both Maureen and Harry are good, well-meaning sorts, but how else? She still demands bedtime stories, which is a wonderful bonus. These bath and bed nights with storytelling have become a bond between Laura and I. But how and why does she seek my company? I don't know what magic links us together.

It can only be magic, inexplicable and mystical. I am the luckiest, most fortunate man alive.

These were his thoughts, but what were hers?

There's no reason on earth why we two, separated by over seventy years, should have such a bond. Clearly she looks up to me, yet she treats me as an equal. She often ticks me off and tells me I am silly. These good-natured reprimands never upset me, rather the opposite; they amuse me. She could twirl me round her little finger, yet her persuasions are kind and friendly. She cuddles up to me without saying a word and the warmth of her nearness needs no words to give me intense pleasure.

Textbooks may find explanations for my thoughts and feelings, not all of them complimentary, but what of hers? Ask her why she loves her Uncle Ernest and she'd struggle to understand the question, let alone articulate an answer. So have I bought her love in some way? Certainly not by buying expensive gifts.

What have I bought her that's out of the ordinary? A doll's pram when she was four? Maybe it was a touch more expensive than the pushchair her parents could have splashed out on, but not extravagant. A doll's house when she was five? But she had to save up to buy furniture for it. I can't immediately recall her sixth and seventh birthday gifts and this latest one, on her eighth, was of no great monetary value – not that Laura would calculate in such terms anyway. My Christmas giving amounted to my buying the family tickets to see the latest show at the Yorkshire Playhouse, in better seats than Harry would have wanted to pay for. But again, Laura wouldn't understand that I had paid the extra, or why they were sitting in splendid seats near the front.

Where do I fit in with the family? Laura has no living grandparents. She has two godparents, Mabel Nattrass, who lives in the same street and sees her most days, and Harry's brother Alfred, who lives in Spain and always forgets his duties as present giver. Then there's Uncle Arthur – I believe he is brother to Maureen's late mother. They don't see him all that often, though he lives fairly near in Gargrave.

So where do I fit in? As a surrogate grandparent perhaps? That would be my best guess. Harry and Maureen treat me very lovingly and see me more often than many grandparents. I know of grandparents who are not allowed to see their own grandchildren. This sort of injustice is a wounding deprivation to children and their seniors; another nail in the relationships coffin. Such preventions, in my experience, are caused by unreasoning parents, who come between and separate the generations. There are more than enough semi-official warnings presented to children:

"Don't accept sweets from strangers."

"If someone offers you a lift in their car don't get in."

"If you fall and hurt yourself don't let a stranger comfort you."

'I know full well the reasons for such warnings. I'm so glad Harry and Maureen treat me as I am, a willing and dependable friend, trusting me to babysit for their amazing daughter and reciprocate her fondness for hugs and kisses.

It was occasions like this, when he was watching the children at play, that prompted such musings. These and similar thoughts made him feel at ease and comfortable in his own skin.

It was about 5 o'clock, and soon the children would run home for their tea, Laura amongst them. When they lost their ball in the river, many of them had already gone home and were no doubt busy with their laptops, watching CBBC or pestering their mums for a biscuit to put them on until teatime. The few children remaining on the green were too far off for Ernest to pick out individuals. They appeared to be squabbling, possibly about whose fault it was that they had lost their ball. Laura would be among them, most probably trying to calm them down. She was a born mediator even at the age of eight. She was usually the last to leave the field of play. If she wasn't among the few remaining, she would by now have gone home. She was a pretty good timekeeper and she had a new watch to flourish in front of her friends who were still waiting for theirs to come in their Christmas parcels.

There was no further activity worth watching anymore and, thinking he had delayed going to the Falls, Ernest was about to climb back into his car when he was astonished to find Laura standing very near him. She had little Charlie Nattrass in tow. How on earth had they arrived there unnoticed? How had he not seen them coming?

"Now, how did you get here without my seeing you, Laura?"

"You were looking the other way, silly! An' we crept up behind you for fun. We were going to say boo but you turned round and spoilt the joke."

"And you, Charlie, are a long way from home."

"Yes, I know," he mumbled.

"I looked out for you playing football, Laura, but I couldn't spot you in the mist."

"Me and Charlie thought it were safer out o't road so we've come up 'ere to look down at the river. It were too dangerous larking wi' t' ball so near the river. An' I thought Charlie might do somethin' daft wi' excitement if 'e joined in."

"You're right – a flooding river is very dangerous. That was very sensible of you, Laura. Well done."

"We go for walks lots, don't we, Charlie?"

"Aye, we do that."

"I love watching the flood, but at a safe distance. But just a minute; isn't it nearly your teatime, Charlie? And yours too, Laura?"

"Yeah," muttered Charlie, master of monosyllables.

"I think you'd better take him home, Laura."

"No, I can get there by mesel'." And with that, Charlie hobbled off down the road.

A Tide In The Affairs Of A Man Taken By The Flood

"Chase after him, Laura. You brought him all this way up here and it's only fair that you should take him home."

"No need. He's nearly there by now. Look at 'im. He's off like the clappers. He'll be right. Just look at 'im go." Indeed he was almost out of sight, running clumsily.

"So you came out to look at t' river? It gives me a big thrill when it's fast and rushing like that."

"Me too. As a matter of fact, I was on my way up to see the waterfall; it must be pretty lively up there. Then I slowed down when I saw you all playing football."

"'Ave you noticed the gulls and the rooks dippin' an' divin' in the wind. Just like in your stories about Ali the Albatross. It must be great to be flying up there in this gale."

"Ah yes, but Ali the Albatross flies over the big seas."

"You don't need to use childish words. I know all about oceans. Atlantic, Pacific, Arctic – some daft folks call it Artic without the C – Indian. I could go on but this isn't a test."

Then, with an unexpected change of subject, Laura said, "It says in our science book that the river's that fast because of gravity, but I think it's better to think that it's rushing home for its tea. I think its racing 'ome. Maybe it's peaceful there? Is it peaceful in the oceans, Uncle Ernest?"

"Well, the biggest ocean was called the Pacific, because when the first men saw it it was calm and peaceful. Pacific means peaceful, you should know. But all oceans can be very rough and dangerous. Men have bravely sailed on them to trade, to make themselves rich."

"I know all about it, and pirates and that. But we're not in school now so let's talk about something else."

All this time Ernest had been sitting on the driving seat, half-in and half-out of the car, and Laura had been leaning against the back door with her damp hair blowing across her face.

"Have you any other names, Uncle Ernest. Apart from Ernest, I mean?"

"What a strange question. Why do you want to know?"

"I was just thinking, some people have more than one forename. What's the point of having extra names? Is it because they're posh?"

"Not really. I have two names."

"So have I!"

"I didn't know you had two names. What's your other one?"

"Hirst, silly! I'm Laura Hirst, remember me?"

"How could I forget? I thought you meant you had two Christian names."

"Well, I haven't. Just the one. Anyway, you're not supposed to say Christian names anymore, you're supposed to call them forenames, now."

"I stand corrected. Actually I meant to say I have two forenames. My first name is after my father, Martin. My initials are M.E.S. That's why I was nicknamed Messy at school, but that's a long time ago and I don't want to talk about it just now."

With another swerve in her conversation, Laura asked, "Why have you come out in your car? You could easy have walked it up here."

"I've just told you; I was intending going further up the valley to look at the waterfall. I bet it's spectacular after all this rain. But then I stopped to watch you kicking the ball about, except I now know you weren't down there with the lads."

"Can I come with you? In the car?"

"No, sorry, not this time. Isn't it your teatime?"

"Mum and Dad won't mind. It's not all that far to the Falls an' it won't tek all that long. In any case, they know you've done it afore. Me in your car, I mean."

"No, I agree it's not far, but I really think—"

"You could tell 'em on your mobile that we've gone to see the waterfall. They'll not mind if I'm a bit late."

CHAPTER 10

LAURA IS NOT HOME FOR HER TEA

Earlier, Maureen had trundled Ernest's bins to the roadside for emptying. The rain had almost stopped, but her face was wet with tears. She'd been to the Co-op and then straight home; she'd rung the MacDonald's to say that she wasn't feeling well and asked if they wouldn't mind if she didn't clean for them that afternoon. She'd made herself a cup of soup and sat at the kitchen table to drink it. She had bought the toilet paper and Brasso for Ernest, which were all in a plastic bag by the back door ready to take round. She wished she hadn't mentioned the rumours circulating in the town about Ernest and their Laura. What would Harry make of it when she told him what Ernest had answered?

She later woke with a start. A glance at the kitchen clock told her that she slept far longer than she'd intended. The soup was clap-cold and she poured it down the sink untouched. Maureen thought she had heard Laura bounce in, take an apple and bounce out again. It was time to make tea. She was mixing the ingredients for toad in the hole, a family favourite. Her husband, Harry, worked for an IT group in Shepley. His hobby was gardening and the allotment, his pride and joy, provided fresh veg more or less all year round.

The table needed siding to make room for the family to eat. Siding was Laura's job: siding first, then setting the table after.

She heard the door go and called out, "Is that you, Laura? Wash your hands, and then you've your jobs to do."

"It's not Laura, it's me."

"You're 'ome early, 'Arry. What are you doing 'ome at this time of day?"

"Flooding in the valley. They thought we ought to get home. There's a danger that the roads will close. No danger for us up here, we're well above the flood water line, but some of the others might be in for a wetting. However, it's stopped raining now so maybe it was a false alarm. Where's Laura?"

"She's out with the kids, playing football. She cem in after school, I'm not sure she changed out of uniform and if she did I'm not sure what she put on. 'Er uniform will be all ovver t' floor – she is a monkey. Any'ow, she grabbed an apple and off she went. I were that sleepy I didn't tek no notice."

"Did you go to Ernest's this morning?"

"Yes, it were teeming it down, but mi coat dried out afore I left 'im to come 'ome."

"Did you ask 'im what he'd done before comin' 'ere?"

"Yes I did, I said we'd been talking and reckoned we didn't know much about 'im."

"What did he say? Did he admit it?"

"No, not exactly; 'e nivver let on 'at 'e were an actor."

"Did you tell him why you'd asked him, about what folks were gossiping?"

"I did... An' that 'ad 'im fair capped. 'E were right upset."

"Did you tell him we were on his side – that we didn't pay no attention to what folks have to say?"

"Aye, he were right glad to 'ear it. 'E asked if it made a difference to 'im comin' to look after Laura. I said no. I telled 'im 'at Laura wouldn't speak to us if we stopped 'im comin'. 'E were right chuffed to 'ear it an' all."

Maureen poured the batter over the sausages in the tin and

shoved it all in the oven. She went on, "Anyway, it's time she cem in and set t' table."

"I'll fetch her."

Harry put his coat on and went into the already dark streets. Not much hope of finding her in this. The rain had started up again and was torrential. Very soon Harry was soaked. He went along Water Street and out to the field. He could have easily made out the sounds of children shouting if it was calm, but over the noise of rushing water and howling gale that was nigh on impossible. Laura would as usual have been among the over-excited goings on, but there was nobody about. The children must have left the green; too dark to play obviously. There was no sign of Laura. A hooded lad Harry thought he recognised shouted as he ran past, saying that the kids' ball had blown into the river and they'd lost it. The hoodie had no idea who or where Laura was.

"Prob'ly gone 'ome!" he shouted as he raced off.

There was no temptation to remain long in the bitter weather and, thinking that Laura was bound to be home by now, Harry returned after only a few minutes. No need to panic.

"She's not out there. Their ball had blown into the river and the kids'd all gone home. Has our Laura come in?"

"No, she's still not back. I hope nobody tried to jump in to get the ball. Laura wouldn't, even she's more sense than that. All the same, I don't want her staying out any longer. It's closing in. And she knows what time we 'ave tea. She took 'er birthday watch to school this mornin'. We don't want it wet. Go and have another look for her, please, Harry, and tell her tea's ready."

This time Harry was anxious, and more determined than before to find her. He looked over garden walls. She wasn't the sort to hide or do silly things like that.

Empty handed, Harry announced on his return, "Laura's not out there."

"Then where the hell is she for God's sake, Harry? You just 'aven't looked proper."

"She might have gone round to Ernest's. She'll be okay," Harry asserted with much less conviction than he really felt.

"Go round and see. If she's there surely he'd have rung up to say so. Oh Lord, Laura, where are you?"

"I'll go round to Ernest's and fetch her back. She's sure to be there. He'll look after her. Hang on, I won't be a tick."

Harry went round to Ernest's and found the house deserted. There were no lights on in the house. He tried the front and back doors and both were locked; he could see in the garage that Ernest's blue Ford was not in its usual place beside the Armstrong Siddeley which was, as usual in the winter months, covered in a white dust sheet. He convinced himself that if Laura had gone off with Ernest she would be safe, no doubt about that. Some things in life are a good bet and Ernest was a good bet, no messing. And it would not be unusual that Laura could be with him. All the same, there was something fishy that both Laura and Ernest were missing, either together or separately.

Harry ran back home with more than a trace of unease. Laura wouldn't go missing on purpose. She'd never find a nest and stay in it, and Ernest could look after himself. She's safe, he reassured himself. On his way back Harry bumped into a few men scurrying home and asked them if they'd seen Laura. Nobody had, but none of them seemed all that bothered.

"She'll turn up, don't you fret," was the best they had to offer.

On his return, their house lights were not on. "Don't say she's gone out herself."

He tried the door: it was locked. He realised – damnation – that his keys were in his other coat pocket. He couldn't get in. Harry paused for a couple of seconds and went round to the back door. It was also locked. He asked himself where the hell she had gone to. Maybe the church hall where they regularly went for keep fit.

The lights were on in the hall and there were a few foursomes playing badminton.

"Has anyone seen Maureen?" he shouted.

Alan, one of the players, replied as he stretched for a high smash, "She was here two or three minutes ago. Looking for Laura, she said."

"That's what I've been doing since about half-five," Harry replied.

"Lots of others are out even now, looking for Laura. Some players thought she's maybe gone to see Ernest Silver. She's pally with him, we all know that."

"She's not there. I've just been round and his house is in darkness. That's the first place Laura would have gone to." Harry was beside himself.

"Cheer up, old chum. Laura will be safe somewhere. Maureen must have found her by now."

The players had stopped the game and were gathered round Harry, all showing concern.

"I'm off to look for them both; stopping here kalling isn't getting us anywhere," shouted Harry as he went out into the darkness.

"I'll come with you," Alan called out. "Half a tick and I'll get my anorak. Somebody take my place in the game. Take over where I left off. It's my serve, by the way. Don't go by yourself, Harry."

But Harry was already halfway down the street. Alan ran to catch up with him.

"Where are you going to look now?" Alan shouted, out of puff as he came level.

"I've no idea, Alan. I've been down every street and alley in the town, into all three pubs, which I know is pointless because Maureen never goes into any pub on her own, and Laura would never go in a pub anyway. The shops were all shut except the corner shop, and they hadn't seen Maureen all day."

"I expect you've been down to the green where the kids were larking," Alan enquired.

"I have. It's worth another look though."

"Let's go then."

They half ran as they hurried on. It was totally dark by this time as the full moon was completely hidden by the lowering clouds. The pair splashed through numerous deep puddles. All of a sudden they stopped in their tracks.

"Is that her?" Harry said. They strained their eyes and in the distance and in the gloom saw a lone figure standing and staring at the river. It was Maureen. They both shouted her name as they raced towards her, but she either didn't hear over the roar of the river or she had blanked all hearing out. Even as they reached her she failed to notice them as she stared bleakly at the swollen river. Harry clasped her round the waist.

"Come away, Maureen. Thank God I've found you. Laura is safe, I'm sure of it. She's not here, that's for certain. Come away, love. Come back home. Come on. We're doing nothing by staying here."

Maureen turned towards him with an empty, unseeing stare; he caught her safely as she slumped into his arms.

"Help me, Alan. Let's get her home. There's no point in staying here."

They half carried her limp form. Harry reached into her coat pocket for the key. Once inside, they eased off her soaking anorak and lowered her gently onto the couch. She had said nothing all this time and said nothing now. Just a blank stare: that's all she was capable of.

"I'll brew a cup of tea," said Alan as he went into the scullery. "You go make Maureen comfortable."

Harry turned up the thermostat, took off his own coat and

hung it up behind the door, leaving Maureen's coat over her knees. He then wandered into the scullery.

"There are mugs on the rack," he said.

Alan replied, "Does she take milk and sugar?"

"Just milk, but they say a cup of sweet tea does the trick so a couple of spoons in hers."

Alan added, "Go and look after your missus. I can manage in here."

"Sugar's in the red tin..."

"I'll find it. Not rocket science, making a cup of tea. Go on; give 'er a cuddle – she needs it."

Harry did as he was told, took her wet coat off her knees and replaced it with the rug that hung over the back of the sofa; he then gently eased himself down beside her and carefully pulled her into his arms. She didn't resist, but her shivering body was rigid. He kissed her forehead. They both stared blankly with unseeing eyes and uneasy minds full of the question, *where is she?*

CHAPTER 11

SAFE AS HOUSES

Wednesday flood day one, later that afternoon

For a while, Ernest and Laura said nothing at all. Being close and comfortable was enough for them both. Her warm body next to his was all that Ernest wanted. The rain had started up again ferociously, and driving would require concentration.

"We're a bit too exposed to the wind here. I think it would be better if we sheltered under the trees."

Ernest started the car and drove just a few yards, then stopped and switched off the engine. The car was well hidden by overhanging branches. He had no intention of going further upstream, but he was happy enough to enjoy the quiet comfort of this astonishing girl. They sat in the car without moving. It was safer to do that than to venture on to the Falls. Her warmth overwhelmed him with joy. He was idiotically fond of this little madam. He enjoyed her company, her confidence and energy. But more than fondness, he adored this strange personality in a fashion he'd never loved anyone else. Not ever, in all of his life. Of course he had adored his daughter, Constance, but those feelings had been shared with Margery.

That kind of sharing of love for a daughter was different. Were his personal, unshared feelings for Laura ridiculous – the vast difference between Laura's eight years and his eighty making nonsense of what he felt about her? Of course he shared with Harry and Maureen the love of this strange young lady, but they were parents. He was not her parent or even related to her in any way. Was it strange that such affection should be experienced? Is it unusual. He felt such warmth inwardly whenever in her company, even if this didn't show in his face. These feelings ran through him like a river now, in his car with her by his side in this dreadful weather.

Ernest had never told Maureen or Harry in so many words how much Laura meant to him, though they must have guessed.

Neither of this strangely mismatched pair had spoken in the car for about five minutes, then out of the blue Laura asked, "Why are you smiling?"

"Was I smiling?"

"You sure were. You smile with your eyes. I like people that smile with their eyes. Mrs Ward-Walker, who takes us for PE, smiles with her mouth and not with her eyes. When she smiles she looks like she's a tiger about to eat us up. I don't like mouth-smilers."

"Well I never. So I'm an eye-smiler, am I? I didn't know I was smiling. I was just thinking to myself."

"And it made you smile. What were you thinking about?"

"Plenty! You never fail to amaze me."

"Miss Flowers in Reception smiles with her eyes; that's why the kids like her. She smiles with her eyes even when she's cross because they aren't tidying up at the end of the afternoon. Mrs Thornley, our class teacher, smiles with both but she's ever so strict. I like her though because she makes us work and won't stand no nonsense."

The car was rocking from side to side in the ferocious gusts.

"Will it be hard steering?"

"I will have to concentrate or we'd be blown off course."

"Let's not talk about that. It's boring."

"All right then. So what shall we talk about?"

"Why have you come out in your car just to look at the flooding river? You could have walked it to the top of the green."

"I've already told you: I was on my way up to see the waterfall. It's a bit upstream from our picnic place. The river was hardly a trickle in the summer, but I bet it will be spectacularly exciting now after all this rain."

"So let's go and have a look. Start the car and let's go, PLEASE!"

Reluctantly, Ernest started up and drove his car with the satisfied Laura safely seat-belted and snuggled in close by his side.

"You're very persuasive, Laura."

"That's the way. Good for you, Uncle Ernest."

He drove for a while in silence, struggling with the steering wheel. After they had gone a very slow mile or so, Laura said, "I'm glad you didn't make me take Charlie home. I'd have missed the excitement if I'd gone with 'im."

"So would I, but if I'd realised how difficult driving in this weather was going to be, I'd have gone home too. I should have turned round before we got going and taken you home."

"You're not blaming me, I hope?"

"Good gracious me, no! It's my fault and I should have had more sense. In fact, I'm going to be sensible right now." And as he said so he stopped the car, preparing to turn round. "I'm taking you home."

"No, you're not."

"Laura, it's not safe to go on. You should be at home, safe and sound, and so should I."

"We're not going back now. Not seeing as we've come this far!"

"You really should have taken Charlie home when I asked you, you know, Laura. In fact, I should have popped you both in the car and taken you both back to where you belong."

"But you didn't and we're here now and that settles it. We're going on."

"Laura, please, darling!"

"Start up again. We're nearly there. PLEASE! You promised."

"I did no such thing."

"As good as, you did. Please, Uncle Ernest. Please?" She hugged him tight so he couldn't resist.

And foolishly he didn't. Ernest restarted the car and drove on. It was true that they didn't have much further to go. They would see the Falls and return home. A child's logic is a powerful tool in the hands of the likes of Laura. And Laura, unaware of the danger, confident in the old man by her side and satisfied that they were still going on, settled to watch. She watched, and he prayed, Laura comfortably huddled down in her seat next to the old man who should have more sense.

"Have you opened your window, Laura?"

"Yes."

"Please close it, it's very cold. And you'll be wet through in no time."

"Why? It's great having the wind blowing in your face like this."

Ernest stopped the car, reached over and closed the window without a word being said.

The engine conked out.

"Thanks for nothing. You're cross with me now."

"No, darling. I'm not cross."

"Yes, you are. I can tell. You go red when you're angry."

"Well, I'm not cross with you; I'm cross with myself for letting you get into my car. I should have turned round and abandoned the whole idea of going to the Falls, and you should have taken Charlie home to Auntie Mabel's and then gone home yourself."

"Too late now. We're on our way and there's no turning back the clock."

"Time waits for no man and never gives us time to catch up."

"What does that mean?"

"It means that I'm a silly old fool. That's what it means."

"I don't understand what you're talking about. It's boring. Get the cat started, PLEASE!"

Ernest pressed the starter and the engine roared into life. He began to turn the car, but Laura grabbed at the steering wheel.

"You're not meaning to turn round, are you?"

"Yes, I am. It's not safe to continue." For her age, she was very strong, and Ernest's tired arms were not strong enough to resist.

"No, you're not. We're going on." And she held the steering wheel firmly gripped.

"Laura, you're not being fair."

"Same as you! You said we were going to the Falls and now you're trying to break your promise."

"But still—"

"A promise is a promise. We're going on. Yes? Say yes."

"You win, you impossible rascal. We're going on. I've said before that you're very persuasive."

"I know. It feels good that way. Go on, please! You can't stop now."

Two minutes of silence followed. Laura was snuggled comfortably against Uncle Ernest in his car and she was confidently expecting to speed towards the waterfall. Speed was a relative term; the foul weather had made driving dangerous for Ernest. Safe driving, even at a crawl, was virtually impossible. The rain was again heavier and the wind was gusting more savagely than before. Laura rejoiced with every second as the car swerved at every buffeting gust, ignoring or unaware that lovely Uncle Ernest was struggling to keep the car on the road. Visibility was hopeless; the headlights scarcely made an impact. Torn leaves were sticking to the windscreen and, to make matters worse, the edges of the road were ill defined and irregular, shaped more by nature than by design; the white painted edges which were only just clear enough to see on a bright summer's day, were even less visible because the worn shadows of the painted lines were buried under debris.

Dead leaves and torn branches were whipped off the trees that densely over hung the road.

Ernest heartily regretted coming out at all, the more so with the precious cargo nestling comfortably against him, apparently unaware of the perilous situation they were in.

"We should turn back."

"Not again! What for?"

"I'm finding it hard to drive. My arms are really hurting and my eyes are stinging, so I can hardly see the road under these shady trees."

"Well, I can. It's dark and it's spooky here and I love it. Anyway, we're nearly there, aren't we?"

"Not far I, suppose. Let's not talk for a minute so I can really concentrate."

Too easily persuaded, and with huge regrets, Ernest struggled on.

CHAPTER 12

WAITING

All the time that Ernest was otherwise engaged, the Hirsts were at home, ill at ease and anxiously waiting for news of their daughter. Maureen had dozed in Harry's arms. He extricated himself from under her sleeping frame, to ease the pins and needles and cramp in his arm. He had been sitting unmoving and silent for ages, and as he swung his arms to restore circulation he spoke to Alan.

"Thanks for stopping, Alan. You should have gone home long since. Your missus will wonder what you've been up to."

"That's okay. While you were both asleep, I took a look outside but there were nowt going on, no signs of nobody. It's not the night to be going out like, so folks'll be at 'ome in front of telly. Anyhow, I came back in and sat here and said nowt. Sorry."

"That's okay. Thanks anyway."

"I've made a fresh brew of tea. I thought that might be welcome when you wake up."

"Brilliant."

Maureen and Harry hadn't moved after Harry had nestled up with her on the couch. Alan came in with two mugs of tea. "I've put extra sugar in hers. It'll help bring her round."

"Ta, Alan. Give it here. I'll hold it for her. Come on Maureen, just take a sip." And he held it gently to her lips.

Waiting

"I tell you what," said Alan thoughtfully, "I think you should call the police, Harry."

"I don't want no police," Maureen shouted, fully roused by the very suggestion.

"Alan's right, Maureen love. The police can start looking. We've 'ad no luck and they'll find her. They know how to get going."

"Look sharp then. If you're goin' to ring 'em, gerron wi' it," she reluctantly agreed.

"Thanks, Alan, you're spot on. Can you dial 999 for me and then hand me the phone?"

Alan dialled.

"Police, ambulance, or fire service?"

"I'm not sure. It's about a missing girl and there's a flood in Holsterdale."

"I'll put you through."

Seconds later, a voice enquired after details about the girl: full name, address and description. Alan gave the details efficiently.

"What was she wearing, they want to know?" He asked Maureen, who was trying to listen in to what was being said at the other end.

"I think she could 'ave changed out of 'er school uniform straight after school. I think she is wearing a sweatshirt, the red one with the tower on it she got in Blackpool in the summer. On top she prob'ly 'ad her old light green anorak and she might 'ave changed into her jeggings, but I didn't notice when she went out, I were that sleepy."

"Was she wearing wellies or her school shoes, they want to know?"

"I'm not sure. I'll see if 'er wellies is by the back door."

"She's just gone to look," Alan said over the phone.

"'Er shoes aren't there by the back door, prob'ly in her bedroom but her wellies have gone."

"We think she's wearing wellies. Is that all?"

"Leave it to us. We'll take action just now. An officer will be round as soon as we get organised. Probably early tomorrow morning, that will be Thursday, October 14th. Meantime, try to get some rest if you can. Don't worry. Most of these disappearing acts turn out okay one way or another. And most important, if you learn anything more, or if the little girl turns up, let us know straight away. That will help us *and* save valuable police time. We don't want to be looking for someone who has already turned up now, do we?"

"Did you say someone'll call round tomorrow morning?"

"A DC, likely"

"What's a DC?"

"Oh, sorry ... a DC is a detective constable."

"Okay, ta." Alan rang off.

By the time Alan put the phone down, the Hirsts had calmed down considerably. The reassurances about good outcomes had settled their nerves a lot. Nothing was said for a few minutes.

Then Harry said, "Have we done the right thing?"

He settled back on the settee with Maureen, and Alan made yet more fresh mugs of sweet tea and brought them in. There was little they could say and nothing they could do.

While Maureen dozed fitfully once more, Alan nipped out to see if there was anything going on. But there wasn't. All the folks who had been seeking Laura had gone home; it was too dark now, like looking for a black cat in a coal cellar.

"There's nowt goin 'on out there," he said as he came back in.

"You might as well go 'ome, Alan, lad."

"Well, if you're sure, I think I will"

"Thanks for all your 'elp, Alan, Goodnight."

"It were nowt. There's nowt more I can do 'ere, not now. I'll pop round in t' morning before I got to work. See if there's any news. Good night."

CHAPTER 13

A REAL ADVENTURE

Laura was comfortably safe and perfectly sound in Ernest's car. Uncle Ernest could do no wrong, she thought, so what was he complaining about? Uncle Ernest was a good driver; her mother had told her so. She was excited like never before. Car rides in the sun with the roof down in Uncle's posh car, with her hair streaming in the wind – that was magic. But that was nothing to this. This was epic, a real adventure, not a made-up story; it was actually happening.

Ernest thought this was bloody ridiculous. He really should have paid no attention to this slip of a girl with her infantile demands. He was being foolish and goodness knows where that fetches you. He just wanted to see his precious cargo back where she belonged, at home in the bosom of her loving family.

"This is really exciting," squealed Laura. "Can you see where you're going?"

"Of course I can." A nonsensical lie. Then he said, "Laura, just fish my mobile out of my pocket and ring your mum."

"Where is it?"

"In my coat pocket, I think."

"Got it! How do you switch it on?"

"I thought all you eight-year-olds knew how to use a mobile."

"We do. I do. But yours isn't like ours. It's old fashioned. I bet it doesn't work."

"Of course it works. Give it here, I'll do it."

He slowed down but continued to struggle one handed with the steering wheel. He tried to call. The rain was now torrential and the wind was howling – would he be able to hear even if he got through?

"Mum says you shouldn't drive an' use your mobile. Dad does, and she gets right cross if he uses it when she is in the car."

"Quite right, please teacher. I'll stop if it makes you happy." But against all common sense he continued dialling on the phone and wrestling with the steering wheel. He drove on.

"Damnation – the bloody thing's flat," he cursed under his breath.

"Can't you get through?" she asked.

"No, afraid not. The battery's flat." He flung the damned thing onto the dashboard.

The Belton Tower was one of the few identifiable landmarks on the deserted road. The shadow of its bulk loomed over the road, making the dark night darker. The road from that point was overshadowed by tall trees, their branches meeting overhead to form a dark and seemingly endless tunnel which made steering difficult, even on a sunny day. In that black night, the ability to see the road in the tree-lined tunnel was like entering a dark and mysterious cave. And Ernest's eyes were not as young as they used to be. As he drove past the keep, Ernest realised thankfully that they were nearing their journey's end where this torture would cease. The waterfall was some short distance upstream of an old bridge which crossed the river and led to the field, where a couple of summers ago the Hirsts and he had picnicked.

"Do you remember that beautiful, sunny day in the summer when we had a picnic in a field? It's just over there on the other side of the river. We can't go over the bridge now; the river's too high."

"I wouldn't want a picnic in the rain, anyway," replied Laura.

A Real Adventure

"I wish I wasn't even driving in the rain. Once we've seen the river in all its glory, I'm taking you home, no arguments!"

CHAPTER 14

STILL NOT FOUND

Meanwhile, Harry and Maureen were at home, worried beyond belief about their daughter who had still not been found. Harry urged Maureen that they must try to get some rest and went upstairs. Maureen didn't follow immediately, but sat gazing at a school photo of Laura. She had taken it in its frame from the mantelpiece to hold in her hands. She kissed it. Her tears dripped onto it. It was a comfort just to hold it, to gaze at it, as though Laura was there in her arms.

Harry came down maybe half an hour later and took his grieving wife gently upstairs. She didn't resist his firm yet gentle grip.

"I can't sleep. I don't think I'll ever sleep again. To think she should be I' bedroom next door. Where is she, 'Arry?"

"I can't answer that, love. Let's try to get some sleep. Get yourself into bed and put the light out." Listlessly, Maureen climbed into bed. Harry switched off the light by his bedside.

He was dozing when Maureen sat up all of a sudden and said,

"Harry, did we tell the 999 man what Charlie 'ad telled 'is mum? Did we forget or am I dreamin'?"

"Bloody hell, Maureen, how could we forget that? Did we or did we not?"

"I'm thinkin' we forgot. There were that much going on in mi 'ead 'at I didn't think on."

"I'll ring 'em up now. I'll dial 999."

He ran downstairs two at a time and dialled 999. He explained who he was and that a young lad had seen Laura by Silver's car. He didn't know exactly where but he thought it might help. He was thanked and told that he could expect some action in the early morning.

"What did they say?"

"I left the message and they said we could expect something to start in the mornin'. Now go back to bed and this time with no alarming thoughts to set us off again."

Neither could sleep, and Maureen said, "Let's 'ave a mug of tea. That should settle us."

"I'll make it," said Harry, as he lurched out of bed. Ten minutes later he came upstairs carrying two large mugs of sweet tea. As he entered the bedroom he announced, "Here we are," and stubbed his toe. Both mugs went flying. Tea all over the carpet and one smashed mug.

"You gurt warp 'ead! You 'adn't yer slippers on; sometimes, 'Arry, you really make me mad. You are a stupid, stupid man. I'm allus tellin' yer to put yer slippers on. You nivver tek no notice."

"I'll mop it up. I'll get a towel."

"You'll do no such bloody thing. I don't wash best towels to mop the carpet with. Besides it'll be sticky wi' sugar in. It needs more than a moppin'; it wants a proper job."

She was out of bed and pushed him. "Out of mi way, yer clumsy clot. Get back into bed and shut up. Don't say owt or I'll clatter thee."

Harry didn't say anything; there are times when silence is golden and this was clearly vintage. He climbed back into bed, pulled the sheets over his head and left an angry Maureen to get a bucket of hot water and all the necessary accoutrements for a proper job. The quarrel had briefly pushed Laura into the background. Laura didn't stay there for long.

* * *

As he was losing grip on reality, Ernest prayed with all his heart that another random tree branch would carry him away too. The awesome drama had drained every morsel of his strength. A black cloud enveloped Ernest as he desperately tried to cling on to he knew not what or why. He passed out.

He lay there unconscious, wet and muddy. When, at length, he regained consciousness, he was very cold. He shivered uncontrollably. He had no way of knowing how long he had lain there. As he came round, the hideous sounds of the scene still drummed in his ears. With great effort, he stumbled up that same grassy slope he had so recently staggered down. He tripped and collapsed onto the road which was now a running river. The shock of this latest fall stunned his very being and he was violently sick. The entire contents of his stomach erupted and were washed from him by the fast-flowing torrent he was lying in.

Ernest lay there stunned physically and mentally for what seemed to him like hours. He slowly gathered himself together and staggered to the car. He must get away from this fateful place, but where could he go? Mechanically, he switched on the engine, turned the car round and drove. He neither knew nor cared where so long as he was leaving the Falls well behind him. His eyes were swollen with tears, his knee was torn and bleeding and hurt like hell.

The rain was lashing down, the wipers were unable to cope with the torrent on the windscreen and the headlights were hardly effective. It was dark as night. He could not go home; he didn't know how to say what must be said to Maureen and Harry. His arms ached and were unsteady, his grip infirm and his driving erratic. He shivered so violently that he could barely hang on to the steering wheel, and his consciousness hung by a thread.

The road he had driven up would lead him back to Holsterdale, to his home and to the Hirsts. What could he say to them?

The truth; unvarnished, incomprehensible, unbelievable? He could not relate to them the simple, yet horribly complicated truth, that their lovely Laura had been casually dragged from his arms, had drowned and that he had tried his best to save her. No, relating all that was impossible. He took a right turn leading to a road that at least, mercifully, did not take him back to Holsterdale. It was unfamiliar territory to him. The turning was near to Holsterdale but it was not one that he had explored before. He was driving into the unknown and that suited him in his awful situation.

He had no idea how long he had been driving through this unfamiliar territory, but his exhaustion was extreme. He must stop and rest in the hope of gathering strength. He pulled into a clearing near a stone stile. His front wheels crunched into a pile of limestone chippings, set there in readiness for winter's icy roads. The car stalled. Ernest eased on the brakes and turned off the lights. An overwhelming tiredness engulfed him and he passed out. Thankfully he had managed to park his car where it would be safe and, he hoped, unseen. He didn't want a helpful soul to come to his aid, to ask him if he was all right. Interference from a stranger was the last thing he needed. No padding but unwelcome St. Bernard – though the brandy would have been appreciated.

When he regained some semblance of wakefulness, he was seriously cold, and his shivering was out of control. Stiffly he eased himself out of the car and bashed his arms together, trying to restore his circulation. He stamped his feet and tried to march round the car – all this would get him going again if anything would. At last he felt alive enough to climb back into the car and, with numb fingers, turned the engine over. After a few feeble goes, the engine roared into life. Ernest drove off, not knowing where he was or where he was heading. The weather had somewhat eased; driving was not so much of a torture as it had been earlier on with Laura snuggled comfortably by his side. Oh Laura ... Laura ... Harry ... Maureen ... Horst Falls ... trees ... Laura. His thoughts revolved but always returned to Laura: his beloved Laura, his no-more-Laura, this disappeared, phantasmal Laura.

The roads were deserted and no wonder. This was no night to be out. He tried to puzzle out where he was but there were no familiar landmarks, no lights and no cars. He had driven into the unimaginable maw of hellish darkness. At last in the distance he could make out lights. Was it a farm? Was it a home with kind folks who would offer him shelter and a night's rest? As he came nearer he could make out that it was perhaps a hostel of some kind. His spirits soared as he arrived at what he could only describe as a road house.

CHAPTER 15

REFUGE

'The Painter's Arms' was emblazoned on a board in need of repainting. Clearly this was not exactly a high-class establishment, but any port in a storm would be welcome in his exhausted situation. He could see in the car park that there were only two or three cars. There were lights on in the building – at least some people were still awake. He parked on a shallow slope near two cars. Not a crowd to face evidently – he would be safe and anonymous.

He climbed the dimly lit steps leading to the front door. On entering he found himself in a panelled hall with a reception desk. On it was a bell, which he rang. As if by magic, a young man, who looked in need of a good meal, appeared from behind nearby smoked glass doors. He had obviously been waiting in the wings for this precious moment. On cue, he said the well-rehearsed line, "Yes; can I help you?"

"I don't suppose you could find me a bed for the night?"

"We surely could, sir. It's £45 per night, bed and breakfast."

"Do I pay now?" he asked, as he groped for his wallet.

"No, sir. Pay in't mornin' 'll do," the lank youth replied.

"I'm afraid I haven't any luggage. I was intending to drive home tonight but the stormy weather rather said otherwise."

"No matter, sir. You look a bit wet an' yer shiverin'. I reckon you could do with a nice hot bath."

"Is there a bathroom en suite?"

"Shower room."

"But you mentioned a bath, didn't you?"

"I said you could do with a bath. I didn't say we 'ad one."

"A shower will have to do."

"It will, sir, if you're stoppin' 'ere for the night."

"Thank you, young man. But I haven't a change of clothes. All the clothing I have with me are those I stand up in. As I say, I intended driving home, but there was a puncture and had to change the wheels. It's a messy business at the best of times, but in this weather – well, you can understand why I am so wet and muddy."

"We 'ave a drying room, sir. We're used to folks 'at come in soppin' and needin' to dry out."

"You're not the angel Gabriel by any remote chance, are you? Am I in heaven? You offer me gifts rich and rare."

"I've been called some things but I ain't no angel, sir. I like a bit of – yer know ..." The accompanying wink completed the sentence for him.

"I must sit down. I'm feeling dizzy. I've had rather a dreadful night and I'm exhausted."

"Yes, sir, but on a wooden chair if yer don't mind. We don't want us soft furnishin's wet like, do we?"

"No indeed. I understand."

As Ernest sat down, the talkative youth said, "Sign in the visitor's book, please."

"Now, do you mean? My hands are so stiff I couldn't sign the pledge if I had to."

"No, tomorrer mornin' will do."

As Ernest sat down on the nearest wooden chair he asked, "Can you show me a room, please."

"Yes, sir. Room number seven, upstairs and second on your right. You can find it for yourself. I'll give you the key." He reached it from a hook behind him and handed it over in one

Refuge

smooth, well-practiced movement. "Here it is, sir, your key to room seven. It's on the first landing."

"Thank you, my good man."

"If you knew me better you wouldn't call me that, sir. The name's Francis, sir."

As he rose to take the key Ernest asked, "I don't suppose there's the chance of a bite to eat, Francis."

"Y're stretching a point for something to eat this time of night. The kitchen's closed and the chef 'as gone 'ome, but you can order snacks at the bar. "

Ernest rose, hobbled over to the bar and again rang a bell. The same engaging Francis popped up behind the bar and asked, "Can I 'elp you, sir?"

"Goodness me, Francis, you're everywhere: receptionist and barman too."

"And sandwich maker to the Queen. Not that I'm that fussy about who I serve – man, woman or in between, I'm not fussed. Multitasking, sir. It in't only women as can do it. What would you wish? You can 'ave any sandwich you please, as long as it's 'am and in brown."

"A ham sandwich will do nicely – and a pint of stout, please."

"Guinness, sir?"

"Is there a choice?"

"No, sir, but it sounds better if I ask."

"In my room perhaps?"

"Nay, you're askin' for the moon. I'm not a waiter too, sir. Downstairs, in the lounge by the log fire; you'll be comfortable enough there."

"Is there a log fire? Great Caesar's Ghost, I have fallen on my feet."

"No, sir, it's electric but it looks good."

Ernest was quite warming to this young starveling's banter, which for a brief spell had made him forget ...

"Now you just pop up to room seven, slip yer top coat off,

wash yer 'ands and face. There's a towelling gown in the shower room. Pop that on, and if you want you could bring your wet coat down and I'll shove it in the drying room. Come an' sit by the fire. Yer supper will be ready. I'll see to it myself."

Ernest did as he was bidden and descended from his room in a white bath robe. As promised, the supper was ready. The Guinness was too cold and the sandwiches too dry, but he was hungry and it all went down.

After partaking of this satisfying but unsatisfactory repast, Ernest shut his eyes and relaxed into the floral cushion, designed more for decoration than for comfort. The fire emitted little heat; the welcoming glow came from an orange tinted lightbulb, which made scant contribution to the comfort of the weary traveller.

No sooner had he dozed off than he was awakened by a loud exclamation. "Bugger me. It's Rosy."

Ernest opened his eyes and beheld towering over him an overweight man so totally bald that his pink face seemed to start at the chin and was destined to end at back of his neck.

"I'm sorry, were you addressing me?"

"I certainly was. You ARE Rosy. Don't tell me I'm mistaken. You're Rosy, or I'm a Dutchman."

"Maybe, but who in the name of Beelzebub are you?"

"I'll give you two guesses. First clue: I wasn't always bald. In fact, I once had a fine head of black hair. Not fantastically blond and curly like yours used to be, but I was proud of the hair I had way back then."

No answer.

"Second clue: why did the chicken cross the road in the depth of winter in Sandringham?"

"You can't be Reg Page?"

"I am that very person, and what are you doing in these out of the way places? Escaping from the law or what?"

"Sorry, Reg. I've had a very trying day."

Ignoring this warning to keep off, Reg continued, "Do you still sing? We ended our act with a song; your tenor to my bass. Can you still sing? My voice has gone caput."

"A bit – in a church choir."

"What are you doing in church, let alone in a choir?"

"Singing." A laconic response might be the best way to shut the irritating man up.

"Don't tell me that Rosy Piercy has become a God botherer!"

"Sorry, Reg. I'm too exhausted to entertain your faintly amusing questions just now."

Ernest heaved himself upright and half-ran, half-staggered to the stairs. He tripped over a bar stool and fell headlong at the feet of a couple who were also making for the stairs. He screamed in real agony, "Shit, shit, shit!" In falling he had further bruised his already damaged knee and grazed his leg against the bottom step. Without apologising, he scrambled to his feet and made a hurried and undignified exit.

His numb hands made several wavering attempts at manipulating the key in his door. Safely in his room, he burst into tears: tears of self-pity, tears of self-loathing, tears for Laura and tears that he had bumped into Reg Page. Of all people, Reg was the last he wished to encounter.

He flung himself on the chair and tried to see what damage he had done to his leg. He could hardly see in the light of the single bulb in the middle of the ceiling. His leg hurt like hell. His whole body hurt. There was nothing he could do about it, no bandages. His handkerchief was wet and muddy – it would have done more harm than good to bind his leg with that.

He slumped onto the bed and buried his head in the pillow trying to blot out ... but with no effect. In this position, exhaustion took over and he fell asleep, perchance to dream. How long he lay there he couldn't tell but he heard footsteps outside his door and a whispered, "Goodnight, Rosy."

He tried to consider what to do. He couldn't face Reg in the morning, that was certain, so he resolved to leave before that oaf had got out of bed. He'd have an early breakfast if Francis would oblige, and then he'd make his getaway.

Ernest roused himself and sat for a few more minutes. Reg would now be out of harm's way in bed. He resolved to leave right now at this instant.

He took off the towelling robe and put on his soiled and soggy overcoat, glad now that it had not been put in the drying room; quietly Ernest opened the bedroom door and instead of turning left towards the front stairs, he turned right in the hope of finding a back door somewhere or somehow. He had made up his mind not to stay another minute; he would get into his car and drive. Groping along the dimly lit corridor, he came across and descended some back stairs, at the bottom of which was a single door which he guessed would lead back into what might be the bar or storeroom. Was there a back door to the outdoors – for delivery men or parking or whatever? None that he could see. No alternative but to open this single door and creep through. No point in turning around and climbing back up the stairs. Through the door he could hear the sounds of some last-minute tidying up. He waited impatiently until these sounds ceased. Miracle of miracles, nobody had come through the door and discovered him cowering there. At last there was total silence. He carefully opened the door; its hinges creaked but no matter. He found himself at the side of the public bar, dimly lit by security lights. He strained his eyes and noticed that the main door to the hotel was opposite. Hoping it was not locked, he tiptoed stealthily towards it.

"Going out, are we, Mr er...?" It was a loud voice, one he had not heard before. He discerned in the gloom, barely visible, a heavily built man.

Startled, Ernest hurriedly replied, "Just going to the car to get something to sleep in."

The voice replied: "I was just sitting for a few quiet minutes at the end of a long day before locking up. Won't be long, will you?" The voice must belong to the landlord.

"I don't really need to go if it's inconvenient."

"Go ahead. Two minutes won't make no deal of difference."

Ernest hurried out down the steps, slid into the car and let off the brakes without switching on the headlights; the slight slope allowed the car to roll silently backwards until Ernest could make a decent turn. Then he switched on the engine and roared off into the night.

"Why on earth did I do that? This is ridiculous, but I have to get away."

The night was unusually dark. There should have been a half moon, but the thick clouds obscured it. The road was unlit and narrow in places. Branches brushed against the sides of the car and he swerved to avoid a thick hedge. Car headlights in the distance were getting nearer. They dazzled as the car swept past. He caught up with a milk lorry and had to drag on for miles behind it until it stopped to pick up a churn. Ernest could pass it at last. Another set of headlights were getting nearer, but what was probably a light van suddenly swung left into a side road. In the distance, another set of headlights alternately appeared and disappeared in front of him. The road was an undulating switchback. The effect was mesmerizing and puzzling. As this latest car heaved past, the uncaring driver did not even bother to dim his lights. Ernest had to swerve into a farm gateway to avoid a certain collision. More branches brushed against his car and the engine stalled. At least half a dozen more cars whizzed by, on their way home from a roistering party no doubt. He was thankful to be stationary as they passed. With them now out of sight, he started up the car and revved off.

"Thank God for that gateway."

He was now on a gradual slope upwards with these same occasional undulations which had puzzled him only a few moments earlier. The switchback effect on him was nauseating.

As he reached what he hoped to be near the summit, the car engine faltered.

"Oh, bugger," he cried out loud. "I'm out of petrol. I can't stop here."

He prayed that the petrol would last until the top of this slope. That far-from-silent prayer was unanswered, and the car ground to a standstill, conked out. Ernest tugged on the brakes. A stray moonbeam momentarily lit the landscape opening up before him. "The North Yorkshire Moors? It must be." The clouds almost immediately closed again. The moonlight switched off and the briefly illuminated scene before him vanished. He released the brakes briefly and rolled the car forward into what must be one of the few passing places. It would be safe there until morning. He tugged on the handbrake and had just enough presence of mind to switch off the lights. Ernest had only a muddled idea about where he was, with no moonlight and no identifiable landmarks. He was too tired and too confused to try to work out or worry about it now. He'd find out in the morning; time enough to think through the what, when, where, which and whys. Totally exhausted, sickened, weary, and past caring, Ernest finally drifted into unconsciousness.

CHAPTER 16

HELP IS AT HAND

It was half past six on the morning of Thursday, October 14th.

The alarm, with a bell loud enough to waken the dead, had roused Harry, after a restless night, into instant wakefulness. Every morning he was first to rise, out of force of habit. As he slipped out of bed he saw that Maureen was, unusually, awake. He usually brought her a cup of tea after he was showered, breakfasted and dressed before he left the house for work. Normally this gave her time enough to get herself out of bed and waken Laura for school. That oft repeated activity was routine.

This time, still in T-shirt and pants, Harry went downstairs and found Maureen standing, staring out of the window. She didn't stir or say anything when he asked her, "How long have you been down here?"

Straight away he crossed and put a gentle hand on her shoulder. Reassuringly, he added, "She'll be back safe and sound, you mark my words. She'll be with Ernest, probably tucked up in a nice bed somewhere."

He was not convinced by his own words, but what else could he say? He too stared out of the window. It was still dark; dawn an hour or so away. The police floodlights were lit and there were signs of activity out there.

Unknown and unexplained last night to Alan, his 999 message had initiated and alerted a massive and immediate response. The sooner the police started, the better the likelihood of a favourable outcome. It took some time to assemble the personnel and equipment to set up an incident room. The best place was within a public building, a town hall or a sports hall. In the event, the decision was taken to send a readily equipped van with a trailer to Holsterdale and to put in on the green, near to, but a safe distance from, the flooding river.

There was a large van and a trailer with all the equipment and personnel needed for the coordination of efforts. In terms of telephone, computers: you name it, they had it. It was still dark. Floodlights were set up overlooking the river and frogmen were ready to make a start in and around the river. Dog handlers were to hand. Loads of townsfolk, in spite of the rain, turned out to see what the fuss was all about.

All this police activity took place after the 999 call and mostly after Harry and Maureen had gone to bed.

They turned on the radio and after a few minutes of national news they heard:

"This is Thursday, October 14th, at seven o'clock. A child has gone missing, feared drowned, in North Yorkshire. Here is John Whitwell with the details. ..."

"'Holsterdale is a small town in North Yorkshire. It's a tight-knit community on the banks of the River Holst. Yesterday afternoon an eight-year-old girl went missing. The river Holst was in serious flood and there are fears she may have fallen in and drowned. Further details will emerge when Detective Inspector Worth makes a statement later this morning. Last night, friends and neighbours searched until darkness fell at about half-past six. Volunteers are saying they will continue the search at daybreak today.'"

They switched off the radio.

"They've got on to that real quick. 'E said, 'feared drowned'.

Who told 'em that? How did they get to know about it so quick anyhow? Oh, 'Arry, what shall we do if she's … ?"

"She'll turn up, you mark my words. Safe as houses in Ernest's hands – none safer." After a while he added, "Look, I'll ring the police and find out what they know."

He did so and returned to say that they hadn't found any signs of Laura, and that they'd be round in about half an hour to speak to them.

"We'd better get ourselves dressed before they get here."

Maureen, without a word, dragged herself upstairs. Harry put the kettle on and popped a couple of slices of bread into the toaster. He ran upstairs to get dressed and said, "Look, I can't go to work with this hanging over us. I'll stay here with you – if needs be all day."

He rang the firm to tell them he wouldn't be in that day. Holding his electric razor in his hand, he shaved as he went downstairs. He brewed two mugs of tea and took them up.

"Here you are, lovey. Drink this. It'll do you good."

She took hers and silently sat on the edge of the bed to drink it, cupping the mug in her trembling hands.

Harry ate his breakfast alone and cleared the table. That half hour seemed interminable until he saw the police coming to the door.

"The police are here, love." He shouted up the stairwell.

"I'll be down in a sec," she faintly replied, as she heard the door open downstairs.

"Let me introduce myself, I am DC Susan Ingram and this is PC Wilf Harris."

"May we sit down?" DC Ingram asked. "I think it best if we sit round the table. Is that okay with you?"

As she came in from the stairs, Maureen demanded, "'Ave you found our Laura?"

"Not so far, I'm sorry to say," replied the DC.

"Well, it's time you did. You've 'ad enough time."

"We are doing our best. It's early days and it was too dark last night for a detailed search, but we have frogmen already in and around the river; thankfully the water level had dropped so they can make a thorough search. The dog handlers are ready to make a start. In that connection, I wonder if we could briefly borrow a piece of Laura's clothing, preferably not laundered, so we can give the dogs a scent to work on."

"There'll 'appen be summat in the laundry basket, 'Arry. Go and fetch ... Do you want top clothes or underwear?"

"It doesn't really matter," replied the DC.

"I'll come with you, sir, if that's ok? Help you choose something suitable?"

"Yes, of course. It's this way."

Both returned shortly with a pair of Laura's pants in a clear plastic specimen bag. The DC told Harris to take them to the incidence van and come back straight away.

"What I'm here for is to check that your daughter has really gone missing. She hasn't turned up, has she?"

"We'd've told you if she 'ad, in't that enough for you?" Maureen's impatience was already beginning to boil over.

"Children do strange things, Mrs Hirst, for fun or a bit of mischief," DC Ingram replied patiently. "With your permission, we'd like to make a thorough search of your house and garden and, if you have one, your allotment. Children reported lost frequently turn up either in or near their homes."

"Do you think we—"

Harry interrupted, "They have their job to do, Maureen." He then addressed Ingram. "Let's get on with it and get it over with. Where do you want to start?"

"Thank you, Mr Hirst. Downstairs first, then upstairs in the bedrooms and bathroom. Have you an attic? They're favourite hiding places."

"No, there is an under-drawing over the landing, but Laura

couldn't get up there even if she wanted to, without we were there to pull down the ladder. She'd never be up there."

"She's not gormless in't our lass, and we aren't neither," Maureen pointed out angrily.

"I'll lead the way."

They inspected every room, under every bed, in wardrobes and cupboards. Their searches drew a blank.

At this point PC Harris returned.

"There, what did I tell yer," Maureen said as they came downstairs.

"Next the garden and allotment, please, Mr Hirst." Harry led the way, but again all searches came to nothing.

"I want to see who's in charge."

PC Harris replied, "It's Detective Inspector Worth, and he's in the incident room we've set up on the green."

DC Ingram added hurriedly, "There's no real point in seeing him just now. I have given you all the information we have at this time and the Inspector would only repeat what I've told you.

"Well I want to see 'im all t' same." Maureen was not satisfied.

"I will speak to him on your behalf when I go back. But in the meantime, I have some further questions to ask you, if we could all stay calm and sit down."

"What else do you want to know?" Harry asked. He, like Maureen, was getting impatient.

"Is there anywhere else you think Laura might be?" Ingram asked.

"There's Uncle Ernest's, but 'Arry went round and she weren't there."

"Who is Uncle Ernest?"

"Close friend. 'E spends lots of time 'ere. 'E comes for tea and looks after our Laura when we go joggin' an' that."

"How do you know him, Mrs Hirst?"

"I clean for Mr Silver. We call 'im Ernest, informal like, and I can tell you he was at 'ome yesterday mornin'. Between us we cleaned 'is brasses together. But he wasn't there at teatime and neither were Laura. Neither of 'em were there. That's right, in't it, 'Arry?"

"Yes; he definitely wasn't there. Ernest has two cars and his blue Ford wasn't in the garage," replied Harry.

"How well do you really know this Mr Silver?" asked the DC.

"Like the back of our hand. We are friends, I'd like to say close friends. As I said, 'e comes round here lots to look after our Laura when we go to the gym and such like. Most times we give him a nice tea – he likes his food – and he stays, gives Laura a bath. He's good at washing her hair. Then he puts her to bed and he listens to her read, before he tells her his magical stories."

"That's very interesting. Did you get all that down, Wilf?"

Wilf replied that of course he did – no need to ask.

"They're very thick on, those two, 'im and Laura," added Maureen. "Laura in 'er way says she loves 'im, an' I dare say if you ask 'im 'e'd say t' same. 'E comes 'ere at the drop of an 'at. Often drops in for a cuppa even when she's not at 'ome an' 'e's welcome."

"And you trust him with all that?" said DC Ingram. "You give him an awful lot of leeway with her. You don't think—"

"Look, we've known him a long time. When was the first time, Maureen?"

"E'd only been living 'ere for a few months, mebbe six month. It were just afore our Billy died."

"Who's Billy? Laura's brother?"

"Yes, but Laura was born after Billy died so she never knew him. He was just turned three," said Harry.

"So, last night you went round to Mr Silver's house to see if Laura had gone round. But she hadn't."

"I'm not saying she didn't go there. She might 'ave."

"She might have," Harry repeated, "but neither of them was there and, as I say, his blue Ford wa'n't in the garage."

"Do you know the number plate?" asked the PC

"Do you remember, 'Arry? I'm not good at numbers."

"I'm pretty sure it's YG13 at the start, but I don't recall the rest."

"Thanks, that's helpful. A blue Ford, YG13 will be easy to chase up," the PC said as he made a note.

"You don't think them both being missing is connected in any way, then?" asked the DC.

"Well, she regular goes for rides in 'is fancy car but she allus telled us."

"It's an Armstrong Siddeley," the PC pointed out helpfully.

"I don't think she's ivver bin in 'is Ford, except per'aps when e's given us both a lift," said Maureen.

"So you really trust Mr Silver?"

"Why shouldn't we? E's kindness itself. If she is wi' 'im she's in good 'ands an' safe," said Maureen.

"Folks have been talking 'bout them, though we pay no notice," Harry said.

"What do you mean by 'talking'? What are folks talking about?" Ingram demanded.

"You'd better ask 'em," muttered Maureen.

"We certainly will. Have you heard anything, Wilf?"

"Not much. Not enough to pay attention to. You know what folks are like; if there's something that seems a bit peculiar, they pounce on it like a cat after a rabbit."

"Rest assured we shall continue searching for Laura. Have you any questions you'd like to ask, Wilf?"

"There is one thing we haven't covered; if she didn't go round to see Mr Silver, where else might she go, in such 'orrid weather and in her school shoes?"

"Good point, Wilf. Any ideas?"

"You know better than I do what she's usually up to after school, Maureen," said Harry.

"She might 'ave gone to the Nattrasses; Mabel's 'er godmother, but Tom didn't say she'd gone there last night. Sometimes she goes for a walk by herself. She's strange that way. But we don't mind; she's safe enough like any other kiddie 'at lives 'ere in a small town like this. She loves wild weather, the wilder an' windier the better, an' I've known 'er walk in the wind for the excitement of it. She might 'ave done that, but where she goes I'm not sure. She 'as some favourite 'idin' places," Maureen offered, "but don't ask me where they are."

"We'll give everywhere round here a good going over – no stone unturned – and we'll note what you say about hiding places. Under our police directions, there's a whole crowd of volunteers already out searching systematically. We'll make sure they give the town a good going over."

As they left, DC Ingram asked, "If Laura did get into Mr Silver's car, did you say that it was okay? Did you give him permission to drive her in his car?"

"Not permission, no, but why should we? It's allus been okay with us."

"I mean this time though, Mrs Hirst. Did you give specific permission yesterday for your daughter to go in Mr Silver's car?"

"No. I've telled yer already; there's no need!"

"If she is with 'im, she'll be safe. 'E'd look after 'er if it was 'is dyin' day. 'E were a bit soft on 'er an' she often said she loved im too."

"No permission then. Not yesterday specifically?"

"No, but you could say Silver an' Laura is pals. 'E's over eighty and she's nobbut eight. Why they're that close is fair cappin'."

"Interesting, very interesting," mused Ingram. "Could she be in his car with him? Has he ever given her rides in his car before?"

"Oh, aye," Harry said, "But usually in the summer in his Armstrong Siddeley with the top down."

PC Harris added information from his local knowledge. "His big car is often on the road in summer. I don't think 'e licenses it in the winter. He gives rides to lots of kids in it at the church fete. Very popular 'e is with all the lads and lasses, and lots of 'em call 'im Uncle."

"Thank you, Mr and Mrs Hirst. Now in your second call to 999 you told us that a young lad saw Mr Silver with Laura yesterday. Who is the lad? We'll need to talk to him."

"Oh, aye, that's the Nattrass's lad, Charlie. Tom, his dad, said we could talk to him after 'e'd had his breakfast."

"That is going to be very useful. You obviously know the lad's parents."

"Oh, aye, we're good pals and, as I say, Mrs Nattrass, that's Mabel, is Laura's godmother."

"Can we contact them from here?"

"I'll give 'em a ring," said Harry.

He did so, and within ten minutes the police, with the Hirsts, arrived at number 35.

CHAPTER 17

A TALE TOLD BY A PAGE

Same Time, The Painter's Arms

It was breakfast time in the dining room of The Painter's Arms, and Reg Page had showered generously with the hot water and the courtesy shower gel. He had emerged from the shower pink as a rosebud, dried himself, dressed and gone down to the dining room.

There was no need to order breakfast. They knew what he always had – a full English but without the mushrooms. He helped himself to a dish of prunes, a matter of necessity, and tinned grapefruit, a matter of taste, from the buffet table. When he returned to his place, the manager, Carl Stevens, approached him and said, "That pal of yours left without paying his bill."

"Really? He must have got up very early."

"He did that. I was just locking up when he came in through the door behind the bar. I spoke to 'im as 'e tiptoed across the room. He said he was only going to the car to get something dry to sleep in, but he did a runner. When 'e didn't come back, I went to the door. I could see 'is car 'ad gone and I thought I'd heard a car roar off into the night. That's the last I've seen of him."

"Well, I'm blessed."

"'Ow well do you know 'im?"

"We used to be colleagues, but that's a long story. I hadn't set eyes on him for years until last night."

"Will you pay 'is bill for a night's lodging? 'E left 'is room in a right mess – watter all ovver't shop."

"I hardly think it is my job to do that. I am not my brother's keeper."

"Is 'e your brother then?"

"No fear. That was a biblical ... Oh never mind."

"What is 'is name, anyhow? 'E didn't sign the visitors register."

"Oh hell! Let me think ... I called him Rosy. It's a long time since he adopted his stage name ... No, I can't get it. You could find out if you could Google 'Equity' though."

"Right then, I'll 'ave a look!" At that point Francis came in with Reg's cooked breakfast.

"Your full English, no mushrooms. okay?"

"Fine, thank you." To the manager he added, "I'm sorry about the name. I'll wrack my brains after I've eaten."

The manager left the dining room, just as Mr and Mrs Drew entered. As they helped themselves to cereals from the buffet, Mr Drew said brightly, "Good morning, Mr Page. Nasty day yesterday; walking was out of the question. It looks as though it might brighten up later today, though."

As they sat down at a nearby table, Mrs Drew asked, "Was that man in the bar last night a friend of yours, Mr Page?"

Mr Drew added, "He seemed in a tearing hurry to get upstairs. He tripped and fell just as we were coming down for our nightly snifter."

"He wasn't drunk, was he? His language was, shall we say, fruity."

"No, not drunk, but something seemed to be bothering him more than somewhat."

"Was he a friend of yours?"

"Friend is too strong a word, but I had known him on and off for the past sixty years."

"Really? How intriguing. How did you first come across him?" asked Mr Drew.

"That's a very long story, but if you have an hour or so to spare I should be only too glad to share some happy, and a few not so happy, memories of him with you. It is quite an interesting and, I might add, dramatic tale; worth a biography, if one had the time. Are you intending to walk today? The weather will, as you say, be brightening up later."

"Well," said Mr Drew, "We had intended to walk today but you offer a tempting morsel. You've caught me hook, line, and sinker." Then to his wife, "What do you think, Doreen?"

"I'm game. My walking boots could do with a further chance really to dry out."

"That settles it then, Mr Page. That is, if Barkis is still willing?" he said.

Reg agreed, and later that morning they settled down to a rather long-winded reminiscence. Both agreed afterwards that it had been worth it. Intriguing was their favourite word.

Reg had agreed to tell the Drews about how he first met Rosy, and had gone back to his room to make a few necessary notes. He could have started earlier instead of delaying, but he wanted to do a spot of thorough memory searching, not so much for the Drews' benefit but because seeing Rosy had reawakened him to his own past.

During breakfast early that morning he had forgotten Rosy's family name and hoped that a touch of brain-wracking might supply the answer. He'd also tried to recall the names of people he had completely forgotten about, all the young, aspiring and, some of them, hopelessly hopeful young actors and actresses who had been in the company. On a scrap of paper he had listed most of their names after a struggle – well, the names they went by then of course. Some, including Marjorie, might have adopted a stage name with the approval of Equity, and perhaps others had found reasonable success in other unrelated walks of life, such as interior decorators, plumbers, beauticians, or as middle managers in advertising companies and so on.

A few, in the hope of retaining contact with the theatre, might have turned to becoming professional makeup artists or stage managers. One thing he did know was that Marjorie Dawson was the notable exception. She, he knew, had adopted the stage name Margery Dawe and had made something of a name for herself as an actress. He wasn't used to, and actually didn't approve of, the current misguided custom of referring to stage practitioners, both male and female, as actors. He preferred to use the feminine 'actress', because it was appropriate and, personally, he thought was distinguishing rather than diminishing.

This is the list of names he had garnered in his room. He would produce it and use it as a prompt copy when the Drews returned to the lounge, appetites whetted for an insight into the arcane realms of theatre:

Janet Riddell – owner of The Riddell theatre company and director of plays (middle sixties)
James St John Stevens – partner of Janet Riddell (sixties)
Rosy – surname? Family name?
Reginald Page – myself, no need to mention age!
Marjorie Dawson – aka Margery Dawe.
Peter – surname?
Phil Rawsthorne – incompetent pianist.
Morris Twirlpin, Moz – tap dancer and bosom friend of:
Oswin Makepiece, Oz – tap dancer
Brigitta Flaverson – pretty young thing
Faith Dunway-Culbertson – butch, heavy (aged – middle thirties)

Reg ordered coffee and biscuits at eleven, and took up position in the lounge. The Drews were prompt, following a motto of their own devising: promptness is the politeness of Drews.

"Good morning again," they said, as they seated themselves.

"Shall I pour?" asked Mrs Drew and she did so without waiting for a reply. "Help yourselves to milk and sugar." (She pronounced it 'shugger' to rhyme with bugger.)

"I'll start at the very beginning."

"A very good place to start," sang the Drews *cum cantibus in choro*, with a joyous laugh.

"But we mustn't interrupt, Doreen," said Mr Drew in self-admonishment as he slapped his wrist in mock punishment.

"Thank you, Mr Drew."

"I first met Rosy – I still can't recollect his civvy name, so I must continue to call him Rosy – I first met him on the station platform at Laurencekirk. He had come to join The Riddell Theatre Company, of which I was an acting member. The joint owner, James St John Stevens, had passed round a photograph the night before to help us identify him as he got off the train. As he did so he added, 'This new young man will take your parts from under your feet if you don't look out. Isn't he divine?'

"Divine was an understatement. He was truly scrumptious – no songs please – fresh complexion, a mass of blond curls and slim as a rail. His travelling trunk was by ordinarily standards massive – I'll describe it in detail later, if we have time. He greeted us mere mortals with a cultivated 'How do you do?'

"We loaded ourselves onto the local bus and went off to Fettercairn. The others who had come with me to meet this paragon were Peter What's-his-name and Marjorie Dawson, who held hands, gazed at each other, and never spoke between kisses."

Mr Drew intervened at this point, to share his knowledge that Laurencekirk and Fettercairn were small towns in Scotland. Fettercairn House, he told them, was famous because some of Boswell's writing had been found there recently. Reg had planned to tell them that and was a little put out to have been stumped at first ball.

"Anyway, we all fired questions at this Adonis: 'Are you a quick study? You'd better be. We put on a different play every night. You're not on tonight: *Alice in Wonderland* is already cast and we have to get back to rehearse.'"

Mrs Drew interrupted, "You surely don't mean you did a different play every night."

"I do mean that exactly. We demolished the set and got the scripts for the next night, learnt our lines before going to bed, setup the scenery in the morning and rehearsed as soon as that was done, and then again in the afternoon. Didn't half keep you on your toes. Small part to start with but if you'd been in a play once, you were in for a bigger part next time. We were usually in a town for, say, four weeks, and then we'd move to another town and start again.

"Isn't this interesting, hubby?"

"Indeed, Doreen, but do let the man get on; proceed, Mr Page."

"More questions for the poor man, 'Can you play the piano? If you can, you'll be playing tonight. Philip is hopeless. He is some relation of the composer Alan Rawsthorne but he doesn't have a musical bone in his body.'"

"Rosy had time to reply. 'Yes, I can play the piano but only to grade seven.'

"'We've survived on grade three, so you'll pass.'

"Then another searching question: 'Are you queer? You look as though you could be.'

"'Does it matter? Why do you want to know?'

"'Just look out for Jimmy. He'll try to sit next to you in the bar. If his thighs massage yours, get up and find any excuse to get away. That's a signal to beware of – unless you're interested, of course?'

"'Who's Jimmy?'

"'He's the part-owner – James Stevens. His wife is Janet Riddell. The company's named after her. She doesn't care what he gets up to – we all think she's the other way too. What do you think, Marjorie? Has she tried it on with you?'

"Marjorie was preoccupied and mumbled 'Mm,' without letting go of the back of Pete's tongue.

"'Why is it called The Riddell Theatre Company? Is it her money that keeps it going?'

"'Probably. She tots up the takings and banks it. Jimmy gets pocket money to pay for his beer. He consumes gallons. That's why we joke about Jimmy Riddle. He's always looking for a lavvy.'"

"Why is that a joke, Mr Page?" asked the lavatorially innocent Mrs Drew.

"It means going for a wee-wee, Doreen," The long-suffering husband informed his wife.

"Does it really, Anthony? How very intriguing."

Reg went on, "The question was repeated: 'So are you queer? If you are, don't try it on with Morris and Oswin. They're as queer as coots but so wrapped up in each other they've no time for anyone else. We call them Moz and Oz. No chance of breaking in and stealing Moz from Oz or *vicky-verky*. Leave well alone. They're tapdancing partners. Janet tries to give them a routine even in the darkest tragedies! They're pretty good dancers and always bring the house down, which is good for trade.'"

"Why Janet?" interrupted Mr Drew this time.

"Because she directed all the plays; she'd probably written most of them. They were mostly rewrites or ill-disguised copies of familiar domestic comedies with altered titles. Or we put on some plays about national tragic heroes like Edith Cavell, Florence Nightingale, or Woolf of Quebec. If the original was called 'Black Tulip', her version was 'Purple Iris' and the characters names were altered to suit the company."

A Tale Told By A Page

"What about royalties?" Mr Drew asked.

"Silly question! No decent playwright would draw attention to themselves by associating with these well-thumbed cyclostyled imitations."

"But surely this denies the originator of his dues."

Mr Drew must be a solicitor, thought Reg, a trifle irritated at these interruptions.

"Hardly worth the cost of a postal order. Taking them to court is out of the question – uneconomic. Tickets were half a crown, two shillings and sixpence. With a typical audience of about thirty people, total takings only amounted to four pounds ten shillings, in today's money that would barely be enough to buy a packet of Smarties!"

"It's a shoe string existence, then?"

"It certainly was, Mr Drew. Ernest had signed— Oh, look at that, I've tripped myself into recalling his name – Ernest! Now what the hell was his surname? It'll come. Anyway, you're right, Ernest had signed up to living in poverty. Yet we all were expected to bring our own dinner jacket and trousers, black tie, white shirts, a day suit, a tweed jacket, slacks and an assortment of ties. And two pairs of shoes – black and brown. That is why Ernest's trunk was so massive. And we all had a trunk with all our wordlies in them. I tell you, writing home for extra 'readies' cost a bomb in stamps, and the readies weren't always forthcoming."

"Are you going to tell us about the rest of the company?"

"I could go on. I have a longer list here, but not now. Surely you've had enough. I can tell you about the stage set up and then we'll have a rest."

The Drews' nodded eagerly, so Reg carried on.

"We had to rely on whatever stage happened to be in the Masonic Hall or Parish Room, wherever it was we were playing that night. We had our own set of front curtains and they had to be fixed so they didn't fall down. Then we had a set of five back cloths to set the scene: two interiors, cottagey for poor characters and palatial for rich; two exteriors, heathery moorland and deep, dark woods. They became sets for scenes as diverse as a battle in the Crimea, to Prince Charming's castle in the panto at Christmas. The fifth was sort of neutral which could stand for a waiting room, a hospital ward or railway station. All of them had been painted years ago in crumbling paint, so the effect of them all was as if seen through a mist. Every time they were put up or taken down, a cloud of paint dust arose. Hard luck if you suffered from chest problems.

"When the greeting party reached the Masonic Hall in Fettercairn, rehearsal was in progress. The music manuscript was wrenched from Philip Rawsthorne and was handed to Ernest who took over accompaniment mid-rehearsal, without any instructions. Marjorie detached herself from Pete's adoring lips and gave Ernest his cues. The chorus was made up of local children. They had been practicing at Phil's pace and couldn't keep up with Ernest. The dancing went to pot. Janet was not fazed and signalled to carry on.

"James 'call me Jimmy, please' moved over to lean on the piano to gaze fondly at the golden-headed Adonis who had descended from heaven into our midst. He was well satisfied with this inspiring product, and offered Ernest a crushing handshake with both hands, tantamount to an embrace, when the rehearsal was over.

"Ernest thanked Marjorie for keeping him up to snuff. He saw her as unremarkable at that time, and in any case, Pete clearly had a prior claim. Marjorie was what could best be described as a comely lass, round and rubicund, dressed in a belted flowery print. Her legs were unstockinged, her feet in plain sandals with ankle straps. I've described her in more detail than any of the others because she would have greater significance in Ernest's life than appeared likely at this first encounter.

A Tale Told By A Page

"I really can't go on," Reg said to the Drews, "but I hope you get the picture?"

Another gusher from Mr Drew: "Quite, quite intriguing. Thank you so much, Reg. I hope I may call you Reg?"

"Whatever suits you is fine with me, and how about a snifter before lunch? Sweet sherry for you, Doreen, and a malt whisky perhaps for you, kind sir?"

"That'll suit very well. Glenmorangie if they have such on the premises. If not, a Bell's will do."

Reg ordered the drinks at the bar where Anthony and Doreen Drew joined him and hitched themselves awkwardly onto bar stools.

After lunch, and mellow with two double malts, he offered to take the Drews further into Ernest's rather more realistic career, if they would care to listen. Reg's well produced and easy voice, with a hint of his native Lancashire twang, had the Drews hooked and, after a short walk, they prepared to settle down to listen to the further adventures of Ernest … Reg still didn't remember the surname.

CHAPTER 18

HIKE AND YE SHALL FIND

SAME TIME AT THE B & B

Thursday, October 14th. It was breakfast time in a bed and breakfast establishment at the foot of a long hill known locally as Long Harry. A family and some friends were preparing to set out across the North Yorkshire Moors, to hike later that day to a similar place, another B&B some miles distant. They had stayed the night and sheltered from the stormy blast in this well-regarded B&B some thirty miles north-west of Holsterdale.

The stone building had at one time been a tuberculosis convalescent home. It had been designed to take advantage of the southern aspect. It nestled unobtrusively in the hillside, with fells above it and a gentle slope down towards the valley below. When such nursing facilities were no longer recommended for TB sufferers, it had not been demolished like many other similar homes had been. The late Mr Cyril Charlesworth, with a lifelong experience of B&Bs, bought it and converted it into a quality service for hikers, climbers, bird watchers, and the like. It had become a popular venue, making the most of the moors and wildlife, especially birdlife.

The south-facing loggias were smartly picked out in white, and almost all the remaining woodwork was painted deep green. Thus it presented a welcoming face, and had been well used since Charlesworth took it over.

The previous day's bitter weather had exposed a group of southerners to the worst Yorkshire could fling at them, and this bedraggled party had arrived soaked to the skin. They thankfully made the most of the generously provided drying room.

The party constituted of John and Mavis Keating, their eleven-year-old son Oliver, Mavis's brother Tim Brooking and his partner Joyce. They were all from Essex. To them the north was wild and forbidding, cluttered with dark satanic mills, but worth a try. Central to the party was a mutual friend, Al Teal, who had organised the trip. Al knew the terrain well, being a native of these parts. He was the one with the map, compasses and a fully charged mobile phone, which was the last word in sophistication. He, without consulting Google, could state with authority that ferns were decorative and welcome and that bracken, which to the untrained eye looked much the same, was the scourge of mankind.

This tall and lanky man was more than a bit of a know-all; he was a pain in the neck. His all-knowing personality could not be relied on in an emergency, but that didn't matter – in his capable hands emergencies didn't happen, even while hiking. That was his view. The party were all safe as houses. That was his view too.

After a hearty supper, this exhausted crew flung themselves into bed. Their hope of sound sleep was ill founded for reasons quite different from the harrowing circumstances that had disturbed the Hirsts or the Porters. Here their attempts to sleep were thwarted by physical, not psychological causes. They had been allotted single-story rooms with glazed roofing, which was battered during the night by massive hailstones that descended from the heavens. The incessant drumming from on high meant that none would sleep quietly that night. 'Nessun Dorma' rendered in a broad Yorkshire accent.

Breakfast was more than a little entertaining to the bog-eyed travellers. They ordered a full English breakfast from a waitress by the name of Alice, who took their order and spoke in an alien and incomprehensible tongue.

"Na then, then. There were no liggin' abed wi' you lot as mornin' then. 'Appen the 'ail on't glass roof med ter much racket. You was that done in when you cem 'ere. I thowt you'd drop off at instant yer 'ed 'it piller. Did yer not sleep then?"

It was difficult for them to respond and it was tedious to ask Al to translate, so they said yes and hoped that would do for an answer. Alice thought they were a funny lot, these southerners.

She continued, "Any roads on, do yer want beans wi' yer eggs and backon, or 'ow?"

The appropriate answer this time seemed to be no, again in the hope that they'd get what they thought they'd asked for. The aggressive tone of the question and her strange use of words amused them vastly, but they daren't laugh until she had disappeared into the bowels of the kitchen. Al translated for them, but it was too late. The damage had been done and no-one would be served beans that morning. They had come to explore the renowned Yorkshire Dales. Such linguistic entertainments clearly had to be part of the northern experience.

As she served them an enormous breakfast of death-defying dimensions she announced, "T' rains passed o'er. I reckon yer'll 'ave a better 'ike terday. By 'eck, it were drenching weren't it when yer come to t'door last night. Yer'll 'ave dried out bi now."

They didn't argue. They couldn't; they had scarcely understood what she had said. But they were hungry enough to eat what was put before them, no complaints.

The party settled up and departed on the next leg of their hike.

The B&B was some distance from the road. The drive passed at one side of the gardens, which in former times must have provided peace of mind and tranquillity to the patients. They were now neglected. A wide but overgrown south-facing lawn was surrounded by what, in its heyday, would have been an elegant shrubbery. Untrimmed ponticum rhododendrons had taken over. There were still a few battered remnants of the pink blossoms hanging there sadly.

When they reached the gate, John asked, "Where is Oliver?"

Joyce answered, "He said he needed the toilet. He'll catch us up."

Oliver took little time to pee. He raced and caught them up, kicking a football. As they headed onto the road he was ahead with the ball, dribbling expertly. A veritable Beckham in the making, so his dad hoped. John had once played in a five aside team under the direction of Arsenal's youth scheme. He really had high expectations that great things were in store for his lively son. He had spent hours in the park encouraging and training this apple of his eye. There really was some promise in the lad, and the whole party admired the lad's skill.

"Is he any good? At football I mean?" Joyce asked.

John replied, "Good enough for the under fifteens, but I doubt he'll ever be a Beckham." He didn't want to boast, so he played his expectations down.

"He hasn't got the figure for it," added the prodigy's mother.

"What the hell has his figure got to do with it?" was the proud father's instant rejoinder.

It was time for Al to chip in. "Has he really got the talent? He's not handling the ball all that well. He'll lose it in this wind if he can't hang on to it better than that."

"Leave the lad alone, Al," said John, annoyed that his treasure was being thus cruelly criticised. "He's less than you."

This argument was not a good beginning to a long and arduous hike. They turned left onto the road. This was the start of a long haul up Long Harry.

The hike was largely conducted in silence.

Soon Oliver was a hundred yards ahead. The road at this point was narrow and held in place by deep banks topped by low walls overhung with high hedges, so there was no danger whatsoever of the ball being lost. There was very little traffic on the road.

Whenever breathing allowed they talked about the view, the plants, especially the heather – even though it had lost its attractive purple hue – the bird life and so on. Al put them wise on matters of dispute as they hauled themselves breathlessly up the incline. They strode along, Al unhelpfully naming this promontory and that. The occasional startling burst of sunlight, when the clouds parted to let it through, cast a brilliant burst of bright green on the hills and was a delight. Now and again they could see through gaps in the hedges that hung over them.

When they came across piles of rubbish or a fly-tipped mattress or litter, they waxed lyrical about irresponsibility and lack of care.

"What on earth prompts an idiot to drive all the way here to deposit a mattress in the ditch?"

"It must be a northern trait, a product of the industrial and commercial instinct."

"It never happens like this where we come from."

Al let it be known that the hill was called 'Long Harry' and all agreed it was well named. The road undulated, but the essential direction was upwards. After about two hours' hike, the road emerged from the walls and hedges and opened on to the view of a wide expanse of moorland. They were now quite high, nearing what Al suggested was the summit. He added mournfully that they should have come last month when the purple heather was unbeatable. The view of the moorland was breath-taking.

Time for a snack, they all decided. There was a passing point where the road was wider, and near it they found a convenient bench. Many a traveller must have used it after the long haul up Long Harry, and why shouldn't they do likewise?

John called out to Oliver, who was many yards ahead, that

they were stopping for a bite to eat and he, still dribbling his blessed ball, re-joined them.

"You'd better be careful with that ball, young man. If the wind catches it, it'll be over the edge and then you've lost it."

Al had uttered so many wise warnings that it inevitably meant they were ignored by all, especially by Oliver who knew better than that silly old fool. "No worries," said Oliver, as he bit into a salmon paste sandwich and a mouthful of fruit loaf. "Can I have one of those chocolate biscuits as well?" Satisfied, if not indulged, he wandered off again with his ball under his arm.

The conversation turned again to fly tipping because next to the bench they sitting on was a waste basket, over-filled with rubbish, and with much litter spilled beside it.

"People really are disgusting!" said Joyce, as she packed any wrappers they had finished with into a plastic bag brought for the purpose. Into the rucksack it went.

"Who is going to come all this way to empty the bloody bin?"

"It's pointless having a bin if it's never going to be emptied." This was John's contribution to the elevating conversation.

There was a view to look at but all they could pay attention to was under their feet. Oliver re-joined them to tell them that he'd seen a car dumped over the edge and it was in the ditch below. They all stood to look.

"Bugger me, so they have." And the conversation on the subject of litter resumed. Just at this point, Oliver accidentally dropped his ball. The wind caught it and whipped it serenely over the edge and it plummeted down into the valley.

"Now, you've lost it," congratulated Al. "I did warn you."

"No worries, I'm after it." And down the hillside Oliver raced.

Part of the slope was easy going, but in places it was much steeper and very boggy, with reedy tussocks to trip the unwary. The ball was clearly visible. It had stopped its wind assisted descent and Oliver could see that it was jammed by the car. If it had bounced any further, it would have been carried off by the fast-flowing, swollen beck. Breathless and muddy, the lad gingerly inched forward to pick it up. The ditch sides were steep so he crawled, bit by bit, to avoid tipping himself headlong into the stream. He saw that the car was wedged above a tree stump.

As he reached for the ball, he spotted someone in the car. He inched forward, retrieved his ball and saw that there was indeed a body slumped in the driving seat, motionless: a man with his head inert on the steering wheel.

Oliver backed away and shouted, "There's a man in the car!"

"We can't hear you. Say again!"

Oliver again shouted, "There's a man in the car and I think he's dead!"

CHAPTER 19

CHARLIE TELLS ALL

SAME TIME AT THE NATTRASS' HOUSE

That morning, Maureen and Harry went to the Nattrasses' house, 35 Water Street. Charlie was up and dressed and was just finishing off his cereal.

"Hi, Auntie Maureen."

"Now then, Charlie, give your auntie a kiss."

Harry asked, "What does Charlie think he knows?"

"Leave it 'til later, Harry," Tom replied. Mabel said she had already told Charlie that a young lady wanted to talk to him.

"What about?"

"She is going to help us find Laura. You'd like that, wouldn't you, Charlie?"

Charlie started to cry. "'Course I would."

Mabel gave him a cuddle. "There's no need to cry, Charlie boy."

"It's my fault."

"What is your fault, laddie? You've done nothing wrong."

Just at that moment the police arrived and Tom let them in.

"Good morning. Let's get to know each other. You, I presume are Mr and Mrs Nattrass. We've already met both Mr and Mrs Hirst. I am DC Susan Ingram and this is PC Wilf Harris. And this must be young Charlie. Hello, Charlie, how are you today?"

"I'm okay."

"We have come to try to find your friend, Laura. Did you tell your mum where Laura was last night?"

"For God's sake; we've already telled yer this morning!" Maureen shouted.

"Charlie, did you see our Laura get into Uncle Ernest's car yesterday?"

Tears burst from Charlie, but no answer.

"Please, Mrs Hirst. Shouting won't help. Please try to remain calm and let me ask the questions."

"Look, my daughter is missin' an' you're faffing around askin' daft questions when we already know the answers."

"Maureen, shut your gob!"

"Thank you, Mr Hirst. Let's all keep quiet when I am talking to Charlie."

After a long pause, "Tell me, Charlie, did you see your friend Laura get into Uncle Ernest's car yesterday afternoon?"

Through his tears Charlie mumbled, "No. I didn't."

"You didn't?"

"No."

"Were you with Laura at all?"

"Aye. Me an' Laura saw 'im in 'is car, but we didn't get in."

"Did Uncle Ernest talk to you?"

"Aye."

"Did he ask if you'd like a ride in his car?"

"No 'e didn't.

"What did he say?"

"'E said it were time for mi tea."

"Nothing else?"

"'E telled Laura to tek me 'ome, but I ran off 'ome on me own."

"Did Laura come with you?"

"No, she stopped."

"Again, I'm asking you, did you see Laura get into Uncle Ernest's car?"

"No. I never looked back."

"Thank you, Charlie. You've been ever so helpful. I think you deserve a sweet, don't you think so, Mrs Nattrass?"

"He shall have one for playtime. Have we finished? It's time I took 'im to school."

"Yes, we have finished. Oh, one last question, Charlie. Where were you when you saw Uncle Ernest in his car?"

"At top of t' green."

After Mabel had taken Charlie to school, DC Ingram said, "I think she must have got into his car up there. The sniffer dogs this morning traced her up to the top of the green, but then the trace went blank. This is usually the sign that the person we are looking for has got into a vehicle."

"She'll be safe, then; safe as 'ouses."

Back at the incident HQ, DCI Worth summed up as follows:
Initial Report

The morning after the 999 calls, an incidence room was set up on the green in Holsterdale, North Yorkshire under the command of DCI Worth. It was equipped with all communication links, computer networking and staffed with a detective sergeant, two DCs, one of whom was DC Susan Ingram, with links to the local PC Wilf Harris.

There was also a civilian secretary/typist who would record onto the computer linkage system all reports and comments from the police and the general public.

Visit to the Hirsts' house at 47 Water Street

DC Ingram and PC Harris have visited the Hirsts at their home, 47 Water Street, and reported on their findings.

Finding that it was clear that the child, Laura Hirst, aged eight, was not to be found in the Hirsts' home and environs. She had come home after school and immediately gone out again. Reason for her doing so was not clear, though the Hirsts said she often plays football with the lads.

She also reported that the Hirsts separately had searched the town and had informed friends that their daughter was missing.

It likely that several people had turned out to help the search. Also, there is a Mr Ernest Silver, close friend of the family and especially close to the girl, who is also missing; they might be together in his car.

The Hirsts had expressed satisfaction that if the two were together both would be safe. PC Harris intervened to say that the car was a blue Ford Focus, reg. YG13 —

An immediate message was sent to all police cars and stations in the area asking them to report if they had seen or knew the whereabouts of this blue Ford Focus car, and to question the driver if the car was stopped.

A follow-up 999 call had been received, late on the night of Wednesday, 13th October, with information that a child called Charlie Nattrass had told his mum that he'd seen Laura Hirst get into Mr Silver's car that afternoon.

To follow that up, DC Ingram and PC Harris called on the lad in his home. The boy said he had *not seen* Laura Hirst get into Mr Silver's car, but they concluded that she probably had got into it. The sniffer dogs had traced her to the top of the green. The trace then ended and this could mean that she had entered a vehicle at this point.

DC Ingram pointed out that the Hirsts were confident that the girl would be safe if she was indeed in Silver's car. They had no further relevant information.

DC Ingram added that Mrs Hirst had demanded to speak directly to the police officer in charge. She and PC Harris had brought the Hirsts fully up to date, and reassured them that they would be informed of any developments as they arose.

Dog Handler's Report

A piece of Laura Hirst's clothing had been provided by the Hirsts for the dog handlers, and they reported that they had picked up the scent of the girl from her house. It appeared that the girl had not gone onto the green. The dogs had followed her scent on the footpath by the side of the road leading to the top of the green, and had gone up the road to the top of the green. Her scent trace stopped there. She did not appear to have returned down the road.

The decision, taken immediately, was that they should search the area at the top of the green for tyre marks which, hopefully, would indicate which direction this vehicle might have travelled.

River search

Floodlights had been set up in the early morning of Thursday, October 14th. The river level had dropped and its pace had dropped significantly, it was safe to enter the water; divers entered the river to search. However, visibility in the water was compromised by sandy brown colouration due to top soil and sand scoured up from the river bed.

They have found no trace of the girl.

CHAPTER 20

RESCUE AND RECOVERY

"You stay here, love," John shouted to Mavis. "Look after our things. Come on, Tim; let's go see what's up."

"I'll stay up here too," Al volunteered. "My mobile may come in handy."

The two men scrambled down the craggy slope as fast as they dared, picking their way carefully through the bog. They were completely clarted up when they reached the car.

Yes, there was a man in the car, but they both agreed it was too tricky to try to get him out, the car being precariously balanced above the stream. Oliver tried to make suggestions, but he was told to shut up.

John shouted to the group above, "Use your mobile and call for help." His voice was carried away by the wind and they didn't hear; at least, they didn't react.

John told Oliver, "Make yourself useful. Clamber up there as fast as you can and tell Al to ring the police on his mobile – and for God's sake, forget about that bloody ball. I'll get you another one if you lose it, so look sharp."

Oliver reached the top very nearly as quickly as he had slithered down. Message delivered, Al called 999.

"Fire, police or ambulance?"

"Police and ambulance. There's a man in a crashed car. It's off the road, down a steep incline near a fast-flowing beck. He's unconscious; we're not sure he's still alive."

Rescue And Recovery

"You say he's not conscious. Are you sure?"

"I don't know. Just a minute and I'll ask this lad who first saw the car and the man in it. Are you sure the man was not conscious, Oliver?"

"I think so. He looked dead to me."

Oliver was excited at being at the centre of attention in all this drama. He'd completely forgotten about his ball.

"Where are you calling from?"

"At the top of a hill called Long Harry, about thirty miles north west of Holsterdale," and he gave the map reference. Know-alls could be useful in an emergency after all.

"There's a picnic bench where we stopped for a sandwich when this young lad here lost his ball over the edge. He went to retrieve it and spotted the car with the man in it."

"Right, you stay where you are and signal to the police to stop when they arrive. Please stay on line."

"I'll do my best but mobile's—"

"Dad's mobile is in his rucksack. It'll be charged." Young lads could be helpful in an emergency, too.

Meanwhile, back at the car, the two men assessed the situation.

"If anyone even disturbs this car at all, it's going to slide into the water – if they even touch it," said John.

Tim replied, "I think I can reach him though, I'm taller than you."

"Why do that? It's too risky."

"To see if he's alive. If he's already dead that's hard luck on the poor blighter, but it makes getting the car out much more straightforward."

"Okay then, but be careful," warned John. "Don't touch the car or any part of it. That tree stump looks mighty dicey to me and that's the only thing that's preventing it sliding into the water."

Taking great care where he planted his feet, Tim stretched

into the car. He could just reach the man's neck. He felt for a pulse and said, "He's still alive. There is a pulse but it's very feeble."

"Good, now get yourself back here sharpish. I don't want two dead bodies on my hands."

It was obviously too dangerous to try to get the man out, and there was nothing they could do to administer first aid. It would have been both pointless and stupid to attempt anything that might dislodge and precipitate the car into the swollen stream.

John thought what to do next, he felt useless just standing about in this quagmire doing nothing.

"You stay here, Tim," he said. "I'll clamber up and advise 999 that they need mechanical assistance: a crane, chains, or something of that sort, to stabilise the damned thing."

"No, I'll go. I can explain the situation better than you" "

"Thanks very much!"

"Well, you know what I mean." Without further argument, Tim set off up the slippery slope.

Breathless, he reached the top, grabbed the mobile from Al, and explained the urgent necessity for a crane or whatever to stabilise the car before any attempts at rescue or resuscitation.

"The man's in a bad way; even so, more lives are at risk if the car isn't stabilised first." He handed the mobile back to Al.

Al guessed that the poor bugger must have run off the road, blinded by the pouring rain last night. Mavis and Joyce, talking quietly to each other as this drama unfolded, felt that the poor man didn't have a chance. "Not in last night's downpour. If he is alive, he can count himself lucky."

Tim sat down on the bench to compose himself and to get his breath back. The women and Al joined him and sat without saying another word. Oliver, overexcited, was already on the lookout. When he spotted a car approaching, he stood in the middle of the road to flag it down. It wasn't the police car, but it was driven by a man who wasn't for stopping.

Rescue And Recovery

"Get out of the way, you stupid idiot!" he bellowed as he roared by, missing Oliver by inches.

It was not surprising that it took some time for the police and then the ambulance to arrive in this remote spot, but Oliver was finally rewarded for his vigilant lookout as first he, then the others spotted them in the distance.

Explanations were speedily outlined: "There's a man in the car but he seems to be deeply unconscious; I was able to feel a pulse in his neck but it's very feeble. I daren't get any closer, or we'd have tried to get him out."

The police, followed by the paramedics, went down with not a little cursing at the quagmire and could see immediately that the car was in imminent danger of sliding into the beck. They made a note of the number plate and rang for mechanical assistance. While they were waiting, it was established that the owner of the car was Ernest Silver of an address in Holsterdale. It was probable that the unconscious man was Mr Silver, but they had to await further confirmation.

Eventually a low-loader arrived with heavy-duty chains. These were attached by a hook to the rear of the car. They decided simply to stabilise the car to make sure it wasn't going anywhere as the chains were tensioned. It was now safe for the paramedics to do their stuff, and they entered the car to examine and treat the unconscious man. They worked efficiently, without fuss, speaking little and understanding each other apparently by osmosis. At length they gingerly extricated the unconscious man from his car, gently lifted him onto a stretcher and then, with much sliding in the mud, hoisted him up to the waiting ambulance.

Oliver was engrossed, indeed fascinated and entertained, as the paramedics worked to keep the man alive. The drivers and the police made a huge fuss of him because he had been the centre of the story, the first to raise the alarm when he saw the man in the car. They had made a fuss of him at school when he scored the winning goal last week, but that was nothing to this! This was true adulation and he wallowed in it. His joy was complete when he was allowed to sit in one of in the police cars; his excitement boiled over. He didn't know and didn't need to know that they had put him there to get him out of the way. He had asked the paramedics if the man was dead and was not a little disappointed when they said the man would live. He'd never seen a dead body before; it would have added to the excitement of the story he told back at school.

After this long hiatus in their hiking trip – eventful and dramatic though it had been – it was clear that the hikers couldn't possibly reach their next B&B in the remaining daylight. Al's mobile was again in demand as he ordered a taxi. He was told it would take up to an hour to reach them so, rather than sitting and waiting, they decided to walk on, if only to keep their circulation going, keeping in touch with the taxi driver to make sure he didn't miss them.

Oliver had lagged behind to watch as first the ambulance, then the low-loader with the damaged blue car on board, and finally the police cars left. He watched the police taking some measurements on the road; what was the point, he wondered?

The records showed that Ernest had been a professional actor; that he had lived in Hackney, London, before coming to Holsterdale; that he was a widower and that his wife had died some years before. It was also evident that he had been routinely DBS checked before starting to work with children, as an unpaid teaching assistant in St. Mary's C of E Primary School. The report Ingram and Wilf Harris had made about their visit to the Hirsts with their particular concerns and suspicions about Silver had been noted.

Ernest's unconscious form was taken by ambulance to Iverdale General Hospital. One of the drivers knew Harry Hirst.

"Have you got you mobile on you, Jake?"

"It's in my pocket, yes. Who do you want me to call?"

"Harry Hirst."

"Have you got his number?"

"Give it here. I'll dial and you speak. Tell Harry that Ernest Silver is being taken to the Iverdale, likely to intensive care."

Jake did this as the driver sped on.

When the ambulance reached the hospital, Silver was put on a life support machine. His clothes and all the belongings on his person and from the car were itemised and stored.

News travels fast in small towns like Holsterdale. Soon there wasn't a house in the town that didn't know that Ernest Silver was alive but not exactly kicking. What gory details they didn't know, they imagined and passed on.

The part young Oliver had played in the drama was never part of the gossip. Some take centre stage for an hour and then are heard no more, and such was the fate of Oliver.

Oliver, who had started the theatrical ball rolling when he chased after his own ball down the slope and had discovered the car with its dramatic contents, had been thrilled to be sat in a police car. He had expected that he'd be whisked off in it at speed with his mum and dad. But he was to be disappointed. There were to be no free rides in a police car, not even for a star witness.

What a let-down after all that excitement – and he now had lost his ball. When the taxi reached them as they marched steadily onwards, he sat in the middle of the back seat and never stopped babbling on about the car, the mud, his lost ball, the dead man who wasn't dead after all, and so on.

What a day to remember! His football, now lost in the mud, was somewhere below the top of the hill stupidly called Long Harry. If, in the unlikely event that this football were to be restored to him, he would have it signed by all the teams who had taken part in the rescue: police men and women, paramedics, truck drivers and crane operators. It would be his football, his prize trophy, and he would be the hero of the hour – a Beckham-style experience for sure. He rehearsed in his mind's eye the story he would tell to Harry Gration on *Look North*. His very own ball had played a pivotal role in an awesome adventure.

His mother Mavis expected that his homework essay on 'what I did on my holiday' would gain him well deserved top marks.

CHAPTER 21

A VERY CLOSE FRIEND

It was late in the Thursday afternoon. Unaware of all the drama that had taken place at the top of Long Harry, the Hirsts were sitting waiting for news, any news, of Laura and any news of Ernest. They had gone out into the town for something to do. Many folks had come up to them to say how sorry they were. Such well-meant offerings were, at the same time, both welcomed and of little comfort. They had just taken their coats off when the phone rang. Harry answered it and listened.

"Bugger me. You don't say."

He put the phone down.

"That's a chap in an ambulance that's takin' Ernest to the Iverdale. He's unconscious and they're taking him likely to intensive."

"I must go an' see 'im. 'E'll know where our Laura is if anyone does. Will they let me see 'im? 'E'll know what's happened to our Laura. They'll let me in. I'm off. I'll tek t' car!" And, grabbing her coat from the back of the door, she left before Harry could stop her.

Maureen was barely aware of the journey, her mind full of confusing thoughts. Arriving at the hospital she didn't ask where Ernest had been taken, she just knew if he was in intensive, that would be where Billy had been, and she knew how to get there. She was right, of course. She half-ran all the way down the endless corridors and turned right into intensive.

Luckily there was no-one there to stop her. Ernest was there; she saw him swathed in bandages and draped with drips and oxygen tubes and various monitors. His face was almost hidden by the oxygen mask. It was hard for her to tell for certain who he was, but the name label above his bed told all. His hands were under the bedclothes. A nurse came in silently and quite startled her.

"What are you doing here?"

Maureen quickly explained that she was not a relative, that indeed he had no relatives, but that she was a very close friend.

"Can I 'old 'is 'and?"

"It's as much as my job's worth to say yes. I'll get into right trouble if they catch you 'ere with me looking on. Only next of kin and close relatives allowed on this ward."

"Please. It's very important. Can 'e speak?"

"No, I'm afraid not. He's in a deep coma."

"Let me 'old 'is 'and. I know it'll comfort 'im. Please let me stay a bit longer? I won't disturb 'im, I promise."

"Just a few minutes, that's all. It may be a long time before he's able to speak. If at all, that is. Trauma to the head can be very severe; he's had a savage bump, and the effects can be long-lasting. I shouldn't really tell you this, but the doctors say that the outcome is unpredictable. We are doing tests to see what damage has been done. After that, we'll know more about his condition and his prospects. You told me you think he has no relatives. I've made a note of it. Are you sure you're right?"

"Yes, I think so. 'E nivver talks about any relations and' there are no photos. I didn't tell a lie to get you to let me see 'im. 'E 'as other friends, but I think we are closest: me, mi 'usband, 'Arry, and our Laura, mi daughter." Tears poured down Maureen's face.

"Oh, go on then. Just for a minute, mind. I'm off. I don't want Sister catching me with you in 'ere. Then, go. Please go."

With that the nurse disappeared. Maureen gently put her

A Very Close Friend

hands under the covers and stroked Ernest's hands. They were very cold.

"Who are you and what are you doing here?" It was the dreaded sister.

"'E's my friend. I just 'eard ..."

"I am sorry for your distress, but I'm afraid it is strictly next of kin on this ward. I'll give you a few moments to say goodbye, and then I'm afraid you'll have to let Mr Silver rest."

"Thank you, I'll leave him in peace." Maureen stroked Ernest's cheek and quietly left.

* * *

Harry had just finished making a pot of tea when the police arrived.

"We're here again because we have some information for you, and we'd like to ask you a few more questions. May we come in?"

"Of course. Would you like a mug of tea? I've just mashed it."

"Ta, but no thanks, we've just had one," said DC Ingram.

After they had reintroduced themselves and sat down, Ingram said, "We have some news about your friend, Mr Silver. His car was found near the top of Long Harry. Do you know it? It's quite a way from here?"

Harry replied, "Aye, we know it. It's a while since we drove that way, though."

"Mr Silver was found in his car – it's the blue Ford you mentioned before, but he was unconscious. It seems that it had run off the road into a steep valley. A young lad spotted the car and his parents called for assistance. They thought he was dead."

"You're not telling me Ernest is dead?"

"No, Mr Silver is not dead, but he is unconscious; in a coma."

"It turned out to be Mr Silver in the car and his car had

been prevented from falling into the fast-running beck by a tree stump. When the paramedics were able to get at him they treated him on the spot, but they were unable to bring him round."

Harry instantly asked if there was any news about Laura; was she in the car with him?

"I'm afraid not, no."

Harry tried to be calm and rational, "Ernest's car had run off the road? That's not like Ernest. He's a very careful driver."

"Accidents can happen, especially late at night. And of course the weather may have played a part."

"Thanks for telling us how he were found. We knew he'd been hurt and taken to Iverdale General and probably into intensive."

"How do you know that?"

"A call from the ambulance that were taking 'im there; Maureen's already gone to see 'im. She could be back any minute."

"Wilf, message Worth and tell him that Mrs Hirst has gone to the Iverdale to see Silver. He'll go spare. There should be police watching that no-one contacts Silver apart from medics."

Wilf complied.

"So, you have no news of Laura?" Harry again asked.

"We're still looking for her," replied the DC. "I'm sorry I have nothing more positive to tell you. We will be questioning Mr Silver when the doctors give us the go ahead. As soon as we have any further news, we'll let you know."

With no further questions, Ingram and Harris departed.

The police had left Harry in a quandary. Were the police connecting Ernest in some way with Laura's disappearance? Ernest would do anything for the girl he doted on. If she was in danger in the river, Ernest would dive in to save her rather than watch her drown. Once it got around that both Laura and Ernest had disappeared at the same time, and may have

A Very Close Friend

been together, all hell would be let loose. Was it possible? No, it was unimaginable that Ernest had somehow hurt their lovely daughter. The man was daft about Laura, Harry was sure of that. But what did he really know about him?

Folks in and around Holsterdale had been saying things about Ernest, even suggesting, or at least suspecting, that he was a pervert; that it wasn't normal for a man of his age to be so close to an eight-year-old lass. He could hardly believe that to be true. He knew that Maureen simply wouldn't give credit to these rumours, but rumours and gossip are powerful and can grow. But it couldn't be true, … could it?

He was sitting at the table thinking these overwhelming thoughts when Maureen returned. He heard the car drive up and he braced himself to hear what she had to say about Ernest.

"'E's very poorly," she said without being asked, as she hung her coat behind the door. "They let me see 'im an' they let me 'old 'is 'and. I don't think 'e knew me. I'm not sure that 'e even knew I was there."

"Did he move when you held his hand?"

"No, not even a squeeze; I've nivver 'eld 'is 'and before and I was shocked 'ow bony it was, wi' lots of spare skin on 'is fingers an' the back of 'is 'and. I've nivver thought of Ernest as an old man, 'e's allus behaved young like, but it seemed as though the accident 'ad sucked all the youth out of 'im. 'E were frail and 'is 'ands was like paper."

"The police have been here while you were gone."

"What did they tell yer?"

"How he'd been found off the road near the top o' Long Harry. And he'd been taken to the Iverdale. They seem to think that there's a suspicious connection between Laura and Ernest going missing at the same time; they'll dig 'til they get to the bottom of it."

"They won't find nowt. Ernest is too kind and gentle to want to do nobody no 'arm, an' 'e loves 'er too much for that to be even thought of. 'E lives for 'er if you get mi meanin'. Any'ow, Laura trusts 'im an' I trust 'im an' all. E's been kindness itself to us, 'specially to Laura, and a generous mate to you an' me. 'E wouldn't do nothin' to 'urt or 'arm 'er."

"Aye, Maureen but you know what they say about perverts, grooming and that. Maybe folks are right, what they say. They can be clever and cunning. Get at folks sideways like."

"Say nowt more! I won't 'ave it. Ernest is as genuine as … well I don't know what, but 'e is genuine. 'E's for real. No matter what's 'appened to our Laura, Ernest 'as nowt to do wi' it. So shut your gob. Not another word. Do you 'ear?"

"Have it your own way but …"

"Stop it, stop it! I won't 'ave it. Say as much as you like, I'm not listenin.'"

There was silence for several minutes, then Maureen asked, "Did the police say if they'd found the secret 'idin' place 'at Charlie Nattrass were on about?"

"No. I don't think they even mentioned it."

"They're 'opeless. We tell 'em about summat 'at might be important an' they tek no gorm."

"I didn't say they'd done nothing about it. I said they didn't mention it, that's all."

"If they didn't say nowt, it tells me 'at they don't think it's 'igh on their thinkin' list."

"They have their priorities."

"Priorities, my foot! I'm goin' round to the Nattrasses an' mek 'em tell their Charlie to cough up."

"Not, now, Maureen, it's too late. Leave it 'til morning."

"Well, you go round and tell them Nattrasses 'at I want to 'ave a word with their Charlie first thing in t 'mornin.'"

CHAPTER 22

A DEEPER LOOK

DC Ingram and PC Harris reported to HQ. Worth nearly went ballistic.

"We had no option. She was up and gone before we even got there."

"Now look, we have sufficient evidence to nominate Silver as a suspect. We'll have 24/7 guard on the ward he is in. Sergeant, detail a man to be at the hospital pronto and establish a rota. Nobody apart from medics is to enter his room. When he comes round, we'll interview him. Got that?"

"Sir."

"Now, what else did you learn with the Hirsts, Ingram?"

"We only spoke to Mr Hirst. Mrs Hirst didn't return while we were there. It's obvious that the Hirsts are on Silver's side. They won't believe a word said against him."

"Clever bastards, these groomers."

"Aye, that's what we thought."

"Right then, go back to the Hirsts and find out how they came to know him. See why they are on his side."

* * *

They arrived soon after Mrs Hirst had returned home.

Harry let them in and Ingram immediately went on to the attack.

"Does Mr Silver have any other friends in the town, apart from you and Mrs Hirst? Or elsewhere for that matter?"

PC Harris intervened, "He's quite well known in the town. Particular with the church folks; I think he's well respected, but how many folks he can really call friends, I don't know."

Harry added, "How many folks actually think of him as a mate is anyone's guess, but we are his friends, right enough. "

"E's lovely with us and special with our Laura."

"He's quite pally with the rector, Rev Porter, and he sees a bit of Colonel MacDonald. I think he's thick with the Hepworths who live in the Grange and 'e's on the PCC, by the way."

"What's that?"

Harry replied, "Parochial Church Council, so he might have pals there. Oh, and he gets on pretty well with Nat Tweddle, the organist. 'E's not close like, with any of 'em, not as close as he is with me and Maureen. That's plenty to be going on with."

"And how about Long Harry, where he was found?" Ingram asked.

"Yer've fund 'im but yer wasting yer time talkin' to us about 'im. You should be out looking for our Laura. Yer've 'ad two days and yer've not fund 'er. Yer 'opeless, you lot. I don't think yer've tried. Not 'ard enough any roads on."

"We are doing our best and Long Harry, where his car was found, might give us the best clues about what happened."

"We've been that way many times by ourselves, but never with Ernest. Ask some of them others if he ever talked about Long Harry and beyond. Oh, and there is another chap Ernest gets on with real well. It's Jacob Smith. 'E's the man what does dry stone walling. I think Ernest sees quite a bit of them, that's Jacob and 'is partner Les Pickles. I think Ernest sups a pint with them every so often. Now, they might know summat. They rebuild walls all over the shop, so Jacob might have an idea what Ernest was doing that way."

"Do you need me anymore?" Maureen asked, "I've got a

sickenin' 'eadache. I'm off upstairs." And she went without waiting for an answer.

"Have you made a note of those names, Wilf?" DC Ingram asked.

"All down in black and white in my notebook," replied PC Wilf, as he licked his pencil.

"Before we go, I'd like to ask how well you think you know Mr Silver?"

"Maureen has told you she cleans for Ernest and gets on real well with him. We were talking the other night, me and Maureen, and we bethought ourselves how we don't know a right lot about him. He's never let on what he did before he came to this town and when she asked him yesterday morning he were a bit cagey, as if he didn't real want to tell 'er what he did afore, like. But, we like im; he comes round our house for tea right often and when 'e babysits we've let him bath and put our Laura to bed."

"And you've never worried about what he does with her. No funny business or anything like that?"

"Our Laura would have told us if he'd tried anything on, like. She tells us she loves him and says so right often. If he'd hit her or hurt her she'd have said as much. We've never seen no bruises on her or owt like that."

"There are other ways of harming children. He wouldn't have to hit her to damage her in other ways."

"You don't think that he'd … No, he'd never do anything like that. You're trying to make me say I think Ernest's a pervert."

"I've never said that. No, I just want to be clear in my mind what sort of man Mr Silver is. If you don't think he's a pervert, that's good enough for me. You paint a very clear picture. Thank you very much, Mr Hirst. Have you any further questions you want to ask, Wilf?"

"No, I think we've got all we need."

"Fine. Well, thank you for your time, Mr Hirst. We'll keep

in touch. We can leave you in peace, now. I hope your wife's headache gets better. Goodbye."

As they left the police talked over what they had learned.

"Were you satisfied that Hirst was telling the truth? I think he was maybe covering up. I think maybe Silver is not the only pebble on the perverted beach. What do you think?"

"Nay, I don't know what to think. One thing, though – you didn't let on that we know from records that Silver was an actor afore he settled in 'Olsterdale."

"Oh. Bloody hell, no!"

"Lost opportunity, there, Susan."

"Yes, well, you didn't mention it either so shut up about that. There are more things between heaven and the round table than are dreamed of, in my thinking. We all know that close relatives are the first to suspect in matters such as abuse … and murder."

"And even parents? Bloody hell! But you're not thinking of murder, Susan?"

"Not out of the question. The lass is missing; she's still not found, don't forget. She may have drowned in the river, but there are other reasons why people go missing."

"Well, I'm capped. By God we have a lot to look for. I thought this were a straightforward case of missing-thought-drowned. It's easy to jump to the wrong conclusions, isn't it?"

"They aren't always the wrong conclusions, but you have to think outside the box, Wilf. We often turn up murky aspects of human nature when we're looking for something less. There's nowt so strange as human nature. Nowt so queer as folks."

"Do we have to suspect everyone?"

"It's part of the job, Wilf. There are more than slugs under stones."

CHAPTER 23

MEET THE PORTERS AT THE RECTORY

On Thursday evening, October 14th, the Rev Norris Porter was returning from choir practice. The choir gossips had been full of the mystery of Mr Silver's disappearance, and the news that he had been found and was in hospital only added to the mystery. Norris had struggled on the piano with one hand to accompany the singing, preferring not to tackle the organ. The absence of both resident organist and Mr Silver was very trying, with the added irritation that neither he nor the choir had the list of next Sunday's hymns. But those issues, usually a cause for grumbling amongst the choristers, were not at the top of anyone's agenda. They just muddled through it, despite many wrong notes and strange chordal misdemeanours.

After the practice, two sopranos stayed behind. Gladys was the first to speak, "On behalf of the choir we have always, always got on well with Mr Silver, but … we've all 'ad us suspicions, nuff said." Moira nodded in agreement.

It was with a heavy heart, therefore, that Norris trailed up the hill to the rectory for what he knew would be a heated conversation, a lukewarm cup of tea and a last go at his sermon. The wind was cold and damp and sadly he could not expect his Aileen's welcome to be warm and dry. His pace was defined by two contradictory needs: the one demanded a sluggish pace, as he thought through what he was going to have to say to his lady wife; the other demanded urgent speed occasioned by his eternally irritating prostate condition: he was desperate for a pee.

An early escape into the sanctuary of his study would be highly unlikely and he had no appetite for the expected and prolonged inquisition that would delay his escape. Aileen was a model ornament to the rectory, in many ways, and a much to be wondered at wife of a traditionally minded incumbent. She presided at Mother's Union meetings with an iron will; she approved of cassocks, surplices and such like; she had never needed to bother with the differences between a chasuble and a dalmatic, though she was meticulous with changing the coloured altar and lectern cloths: green for Trinity, red for martyrs and so on. She had no truck with incense and insisted that two candles on the altar were entirely sufficient, 'six might hint at popery'. In all these matters, Norris and his wife Aileen travelled the same well-trodden middle road and they safely steered a central course.

But she was by no means certain that Norris was well enough practiced in the arcane arts of man management; this uncertainty formed a formidable barrier between them. Total harmony in the rectory rarely went much beyond the choice of hymns.

Norris's study was a refuge whenever strife reared its ugly head. He never argued the toss on such matters as what to eat or where to go on holidays. The question of Ernest Silver was a strife-ridden case in point, and a difficult one for Norris. He was not looking forward to his return home that evening. Aileen's jutting lower jaw would today out-jut – propelled, as it were, into a tiresome inquisition.

"Is that you, darling?" Aileen asked disarmingly, as she heard the back door open and close.

She was reclining on their worn-out sofa of vintage years and was clutching to her bony bosom a pink cushion embroidered with many-coloured flowers. Her teeth were having a go at a ginger nut. A battle of Jutland loomed, with a fusillade of biscuit crumbs.

"Just a tick, darling, toilet first," Norris replied.

She raised her voice, "Your tea is in the teapot on the kitchen table. I brewed only a couple of minutes ago – it should still be hot enough. You might like to pour me another one too. Mugs are on the hooks. No sugar this time for me, thanks, darling. The bickies are here on the sofa, so don't bother to look for them in there."

A few minutes later, Norris entered the sitting room bearing two mugs of tea, with his sermon folder tucked under his arm. As he handed over the tea, he muttered, "I've known where the mugs are kept for the past I-don't-know-how-many years, but thank you so much, darling, for reminding me, just in case I had forgotten."

The ritual of the teapot on the table is as familiar and well-practiced as the rite of Holy Communion. No need for eternal rehearsals and reminders.

"Choir practice went well, darling?"

"Aileen, dear, catastrophe averted. That's as far as I can go, thank you."

"Ernest didn't turn up, then?"

"No. The choir knew better than I what was going on. He's in Iverdale General and they say he is unconscious and in intensive care."

"Oh, that's too bad."

"And there is no sign yet of that little girl, Laura. The Hirsts must be deranged with worry. I really should go round to see them – offer what comfort and consolation I can."

"Silver has had far too unsavoury an influence over the Hirsts. They have always believed in him and trusted Laura to his tender care. Foolishly so, I say. I deeply regret suggesting that Maureen go to clean for him."

"Come now, Aileen. You can be very harsh in your judgments."

"And you too soft in yours. What convinced you that he would be welcomed into the choir and onto the PCC?"

"I felt sorry for him. I've never mentioned this before, but

Ernest at school was confronted with terrible bullying by a senior boy, captain of rugby and *victor ludorum*, that sort of chap. He was much older, and a prefect to boot, admired by the staff and most of the boys for his manliness and his upright conduct. The staff were almost idolatrous where he was concerned, yet he was capable of inflicting the young Ernest with a lifelong injury."

"You mean the prefect beat him? Surely the Head would learn about such matters on the grapevine. Did Ernest not report to anyone in authority about it? Surely he could confide in, say, a young house master or even a junior matron whom he could trust to take him seriously?"

"No, the infliction was not physical. No, it was not a flogging. It was much more demeaning and hurtful than a sore backside."

"You're hinting at abuse, but you're not going to tell me what happened, are you, Norris?"

"No, indeed I'm not. He did tell me confidentially and in graphic detail what happened. But I can tell you that Ernest had been so severely afflicted that he promised himself from that very moment that he would never take advantage of a child. Consequently he considered himself to be perfectly safe with young children; that he would never yield to temptation for, indeed, it would never be a temptation to him at all. And I have to say I believed him."

"It's all very well for Ernest to feel that, and that you should be so understanding as to go along with it, but how about the rest of the world?"

"After coming here to Holsterdale, he spent a little time wondering how he could become a useful citizen of this parish. Church, as well as answering a spiritual need, was a route to getting to know people and, for our benefit, he knew how he could improve the choir's performance. Even you recognise what a good job he has made of that and think of how wonderful his performances with Felicity Hepworth have been. Her parents think very highly of him and always have.

"It was because of their recommendation that he was persuaded to bring his talents to bear on the children of Holsterdale. They introduced him to McCullough, the head of St Mary's Primary School, who asked if he could help children with their reading. He was DBS checked, of course, before he was allowed onto the premises and let loose on the children, as everyone is; that would have revealed any wrongdoing, not only in Holsterdale, but throughout his life. The check gave the all clear and Ernest has subsequently more than earned his keep. McCullough supported him wholeheartedly."

"You mentioned his talents. Yes, he is clearly the possessor of many, but how have they become so well developed? His speaking, his storytelling, and he has the patience of Job. I don't know anything of his background or upbringing. Do you?"

"Neither do I, apart from his awful time at school, I have to admit."

"So where does that leave us?"

"In the dark, but that doesn't mean he can't be trusted. This is getting us nowhere and there is somewhere else I should be – with the Hirsts. My tea is cold anyway. I'll leave my sermon in abeyance and go round there now."

With that he rose, put his raincoat on in the kitchen and departed Hirst-wards. The house was in darkness when he called; he wondered if they were sitting in darkness to avoid unwanted attention. He had intended first to offer sympathy – condolences were premature – and to ask their permission to offer special prayers for the safe delivery of their missing daughter. None of this was possible, so he returned home with a heavy heart.

* * *

Evenings were often quiet at the rectory: Aileen with a book or a bit of light television for half an hour, Norris preferring the quiet of his study. He had a collection of stamps which he enjoyed cataloguing, rearranging and making preparations for swapping at the stamp club in Shepley.

He actually enjoyed the challenge of writing sermons relevant to the modern world. Somehow Noah was too immediately relevant to today's drama and the Bible story had a hopeful outcome. Would a raven or a dove or a circling crow bring good news to the Hirsts? Impossible, he thought. Indeed, he knew it to be impossible beyond a peradventure. Help cometh from nowhere in these situations; Laura's fate must inevitably be sealed by this time. There could be no hope of a joyful outcome for Maureen and Harry. Yet the poor lambs could not begin to mourn until there was absolute certainty that their daughter had died. They were in unenviable limbo, subject to a relentless and hellish torture.

He pondered what he might have said had they been at home when he called earlier that evening. Sometimes the words just arrived, unbidden, and no amount of thoughtful preparation could produce more appropriate words and feelings. Love and comfort had to come from the heart not the head; maybe that should form the basis of his sermon and Norris started to write.

CHAPTER 24

GOSSIP AT THE
GOLDEN UNICORN

The Golden Unicorn was a large family-run inn, just off the main street in Holsterdale. It was the biggest and most pretentious hostelry in the town. It had bedrooms for about twenty guests. You entered straight from the road into a spacious bar. Hill walkers, rock climbers and shoppers were looked after very efficiently and with equal satisfaction. It had a dining room with some pretensions to fine-dining but on this particular night they were screening an important football match; the place was often busy but on account of the match, this night was more than usually so.

Already two or three tables round the fire were occupied by locals with half a mild, a sweet sherry, or a daring G&T, and a bag of crisps to share. The dining room was filling up, mostly with overnight guests and perhaps a group celebrating a special birthday party.

The chatter on the lips of all these people was about yesterday's flood and the most distressing news that a little girl had gone missing. The chatter was noisy, with everyone trying to top the other with better ideas and dramatic interpretations.

"I take it we've all been out looking for the little lass?"

"The' say as Charlie Nattrass saw 'er get into Silver's car yesterday."

"'Ow do you know that?"

"Really, are you quite sure?"

"Oh aye, 'is dad telled me."

"Ay, the kids'd been lakin' about wi't ball, and the' say 'e was watching 'em play. 'E were in 'is Ford, not t' posh un – 'e wouldn't give that an outing i' this weather."

The rain had become little more than a drizzle over the last couple of hours, so looking had not been so uncomfortable as it had been yesterday. It was thought unlikely she'd be hiding.

"She wouldn't be daft enough to 'ide."

"She is a bit of a character as we all know, but silly? I don't think so."

"We've all been looking in our huts and outhouses and so on and so forth."

"I'm not surprised. Poor Harry 'n' Maureen, lossing yer only daughter in't no fun."

"I don't know 'ow our Mavis would tekit."

"Nor me, neither. Our Eileen 'ould go mad, I'm thinkin'."

"I couldn't look today wi' 'Arry until I came 'ome afta work."

"Did you go 'ome wi' 'im an' Maureen at after?"

"No, I di'nt. I were late for me tea as it were."

"I thowt not 'cos I were talking wi' Fred earlier on tonight and 'e said 'e'd gone 'ome wi 'Arry and med em a cup o' tea, like. Tha must 'a' looked round wi' 'Arry earlier on."

"I think she's lost, and I've 'most given up 'oping we'll ivver find 'er," a moaning voice chipped in.

"Me an' all, it's fair cappin' is this. Nowt like this 'as 'appened i' my lifetime i' this 'ere town, and I've lived 'ere, man and boy, for sin' ower seventy year."

"I searched round with 'Arry last night, until it were nearly dark and there was no sign. All we found were Maureen, an' she were right upset." This was Fred, who had quit his badminton and looked with Harry.

"I can imagine. She mun be off 'er 'ead we' worry."

"Aye, she is that. Me an' 'Arry took 'er ome. It were then we phoned police."

"I must say they have been very efficient. Their organisation was tip-top. First rate. A random search would undoubtedly have covered tracks, rendering the chances of our finding this little girl even harder. It really is a mystery that she has vanished without trace even after what amounts to two days diligent searching."

"'Ave yer finished speechifying?"

"This is no time to be offensive. I was merely putting into words what I believe, indeed, that we are all thinking.

"Mebbe not. But it's no time for fancy speechifying neither."

"Let's just stop argufying. If she did get into Silver's car, she could be anywhere. If what young Charlie Nattrass says is reet, there's not much point i' lookin' round 'ere."

"And with 'im up to who-knows-what sort of mischief wi' er."

"Aye, but Charlie in't all there, is 'e? Is what 'e says right? They say 'e's a bit short of change in a sweet shop."

"T' police will 'ave to tek notice, choose what 'e says."

"They've been reet well organised, like, and I doubt any stones've been left unturned. And they say they are already lookin' for Silver's Ford. It can't be far off."

"Nay, well, I scratch me 'ead on this ... but I don't think Charlie'd mek it up, like."

A voice from one of the tables butted in, "Forgive me, I've been listening to what you've all been saying and I've heard, on pretty good authority, that they've found him."

"Fun' who?"

"Silver, yer daft bugger. Is that who you mean?"

"Indeed, it is, Mr Silver. He has been found. I don't know where or any further details."

"'Ow d'yer get 'od o' that?"

"Our daughter Alice works in Iverdale General and she says he is in an isolation ward there."

As this knowledgeable informant was still speaking, a man rushed in from the street and shouted, "Hey, 'ave yer eard the latest? Silver's car 'as bin fund."

"What yer talkin' about? Where 'as it bin fund?"

"Up at top of Long 'Arry, in a ditch."

"'Ow does ter know?"

"Our lad, Tom, were wi't' 'eavy loader what browt it back. It's been taken t' police pound."

"Indeed, this is a mysterious development," said their previous informant. "Was Silver in the car?"

"Oh aye. 'E wer unconscious, though. I 'eard tell that 'e were in Iverdale 'ospital."

"As I said, now tell us what you know about Laura. Was she with him ... in the car, too?"

"No sign. They 'aven't found 'er yet, so they tell me."

"Tell us news, not 'istory. 'E's allus off in 'is fancy car."

"Aye, but it weren't 'is fancy car, whatever they call it. It were 'is Ford."

"Well, 'e wouldn't tek' 'is fancy car out i' this weather."

Another voice announced with some authority, real or assumed, "His fancy car, as you call it, is an Armstrong Siddeley tourer – 17hp – very powerful in those days. I believe it's vintage 1935."

"Worth a bob or two, I shouldn't wonder."

"Yes, indeed. An enviable vehicle."

"'Ow do you know all that, then?"

"I was talking to Silver some time ago after church. Quite a decent chap really, when you get to know him."

"Oh, so you think you know 'im then? So who is 'e, and where does 'e come fra?"

"When I say I got to know him, that is a bit of an exaggeration. But he seemed a decent type. I became better acquainted with him when he joined the parochial church council."

"What did 'e do then, afore 'e come 'ere like?"

"Ay, what were 'e afore 'e landed 'ere?" added another.

"I really couldn't say," said the voice of the man of authority. "He went to some minor public school, which would fit him for anything he would want to do later in life. What that is, as you say, dear man, perhaps a bit of a mystery."

"Yes, well that's another thing. 'E lands 'ere from God knows where and before you know it 'e's ivrywhere. Last summer at the Gala he drives 'is fancy Armstrong-tiddly in the parade with the chairman of t' council at 'is side, waving at folks like as if she were t' Queen of Sheba or summat! Silver was drivin' an' grinnin' like the cat 'at got the cream. When 'e gets to' t field 'e starts givin' free joyrides to t' kiddies in't back of 'is car, no safety belts nor nowt."

"Very generous gesture of him, I'd say, and the kiddies loved it; they had a great time."

"Generous or not, 'e thinks of 'isself a bit of a toff; 'e's in with ivrybody-as-is-anybody, so far as I can see."

"Yeh, but 'oo really knows 'im? I've yet to meet someone as reet knows im, though 'Arry and Maureen Hirst like 'im an' trust 'im with their Laura."

"If I may interject, I don't think it wise to speculate on these relationships at this time," so said the authority figure. "And we must NOT be down in the mouth! Hope springs eternal. They might have been together and somehow got separated. We must just pray that Laura is well."

"I bloody well 'ope so, but I'm not so sure."

"Tha's off tha 'ead if tha thinks owt else."

"Let's not be pessimistic, old chum."

"I'm not thy chum, yer bugger. Silver is just like thee, another smarmy bugger – y're two of a pair, you two."

"This is too serious a matter for that sort of language; there's no call to become offensive."

And with that *Mr Authority* moved away from the bar to avoid further nastiness. He sat thoughtfully on the settle near the fire and out of range. *Though maybe they have a point or two*, he thought to himself. *Two of a pair! Ignoramus! Two of a kind, surely!* And with a hint of a satisfied smile, he drained his pint of mild.

The idle speculation continued back at the bar, without him.

"Yes, well, I don't see what 'Arry 'Irst sees in 'im.

'Im-as-is puts on airs an' 'Arry in't like that, no more is Maureen, not at all, neither of 'em. But they 'ave 'im in't 'ouse and leave 'im there alone wi' their Laura while they go out joggin an' such like. I wouldn't like to think what 'e gets up to. But 'Arry and Maureen seem to think 'e's kosher. I don't."

"Nor me nawther."

"I wouldn't trust 'in wi' a twelve-foot barge pole, but they even let 'im put Laura to bed and them not even in't 'ouse. I wouldn't do that for a bag o' shekels."

"Me nawther; one Silver's enough to last me a lifetime."

"They even give 'im supper an' all. I wouldn't give 'im t' time of day."

"Nor me nawther."

"They say 'e tells a good tale, though."

"E's telling a tale all t' time. What I think, me, is 'e's putting on a' act ivry minute, of ivry 'our of ivry day. Me, that's what I think. 'E just doesn't ring true. All t' time 'e's just telling one big tale after another. A dark 'orse 'e is. Mek no mistake, a dark un is yon' Ernest Silver. I tell yer, that's what I think."

"Me an' all."

Sitting on high stools by the bar was a somewhat unusual pair. At first sight, the 'woman' looked like a witch, wearing a long, black skirt and wide-brimmed black hat, ideally suited to the Halloween evening due to take place at the end of the month (which was already being advertised on posters all around the pub). Closer inspection revealed that her skirt was part of an elegant, lacey gown, and on her head was not actually a witch's wide-brimmed conical affair. No, it had definitely been designed to be worn at a fashionable wedding. Her face was immaculately made up though, with perhaps a little more blue eye shadow than was tasteful and her red lipstick was loosely applied.

Talking to her was a short man wearing a black sweater and dark jeans. The elegant lady and her beau were in fact Jacob Smith and retired geography teacher Leslie Pickles, both well-known and, it must be said, well-liked in the town. This pair, sitting at the bar, had listened to the argument but had not taken part in it. They were also football fans and had turned out to watch the match. Both knew and got on well with Ernest Silver, but they had refused to take part in the general speculation about him and the events of the day. When the football started, they went with the crowd into the lounge to watch and pray.

Jacob and Leslie were both dry stone-wallers, who had fallen into each other's company when Leslie retired. He had always been interested and indeed fascinated by dry stone walls, their history and maintenance. The history of these ancient walls was bound up in the social history of the farmers who had built them. On retirement, Leslie decided to learn how they were constructed first-hand by taking an apprenticeship, so he approached Jacob Smith and asked to be taken on. Smith said if that's what he wanted he could come on in. Smith proved to be a good teacher and Pickles a quick learner. After weeks of heavy work, he could lift the heaviest of stones almost as readily as his master.

They became good friends and, after a while, Pickles moved in to Smith's cottage. Both were to be seen in working gear wherever walls were in need of skilled rebuilding. Sheep and hikers were both to blame for damaging stone walls and there were many such walls in need of care. They thread like lace over the countryside and over the moors. These walls had always been a source of admiration and pride in the district; and the two became as well liked and loved as the walls they worked on.

Ernest had come across them when he was out walking several years ago and had chatted with them as they sat having a break; eating hearty, heavy sandwiches and drinking mugs of sweet tea out of flasks.

"I'm Jacob. That's Les. He was a teacher at the comp in Shepley but 'e took up wi' me when 'e retired, didn't you, Les?"

"Yes, in theory at first, but then I started to help. God did my shoulders ache. Not anymore, though; fitter than I've ever been and not a spare ounce of flesh anywhere."

"It's obviously hard work, I can see that. And in all weathers? Toughens you up, I dare say."

"Better for me than sitting at a desk marking geography homework. What views and the sights we see. I tell you, all history happens here, and you don't have to look far to find it."

"Tha's reet an all. Tha mun come over for a pint or two, if tha wants."

"Thanks, I would love to. I see you've finished your snap, so I won't keep you from you labours."

"Tak 'od o' yond and eft it over 'ere,"

Jacob pointed to a medium sized stone. Ernest bent to pick it up and couldn't get it off the ground. The two men laughed.

"Reet, then, come to our cottage, limestone, by t' bridge next Wednesday after tea, an' we'll 'ave a pint and a reet good natter."

Ernest did so, and from that day a long-lasting friendship grew between these ill-matched but entirely well-suited three. Ernest felt able to be himself in their company without pretence. Back in The Golden Unicorn, Jacob's dress on this occasion was not a precursor to Halloween; Jacob, with his roughened hands, was excited by the slippery feel of silk about his body and face. At home, of an evening, he would dress to suit this unexpected taste. Usually he limited his evening attire to silken dressing gowns, of which he had a collection. On special occasions however, he would go the whole hog, choosing one from a collection of evening dresses, built up over years of rooting around in charity shops, applying make-up surprisingly well to complete the ensemble.

Les did not share this unusual taste and predilection, indeed he found it quite disconcerting initially so it took a while to come to terms with it. But he came to understand the practice and did nothing to discourage it. Leslie thought little of his friend's proclivities but he preferred jeans and a heavy jumper.

Ernest, when he first encountered his silken clad new friend, took much less time than Les to accept it.

For Les, donning an outfit, even for Halloween, was the giddy limit. But he was happy to be seen with Jacob in all his finery and was not bothered that there might be some misinterpretation of their relationship

CHAPTER 25

A SPECIAL REQUEST FOR JACOB

On the many evenings when Ernest went round to the Smith-Pickles entente, he made notes for a serious and comprehensive glossary of all the dialect words and phrases that poured out of Jacob's mouth. There was no need for fancy dress and no desire to go emulate Jacob's unusual crossdressing. Ernest always had a great time in their company and his unscientific approach to linguistics didn't deter him. He was no expert and didn't know the proper way to replicate on paper the sound he heard, so that was a struggle, but their language was so unfamiliar it thrilled and excited him.

Maureen's way of speaking started Ernest thinking about this glossary. He started the list originally when he realised that Laura was not picking up much of this antiquated word usage from her mother, and that most children he met in school were not using dialect words either. The dialect was dying out. Ernest, who had never set foot in Yorkshire until he landed in Holsterdale, felt passionately that it should be preserved somewhere and somehow. He had no intention of publishing his lists, but someone might find them and think them worth an airing.

Jacob's dialect mine was richer than Maureen's and contained precious jewels: it was a major discovery which had to be unearthed seriously, like taking gold from the Incas without killing anybody.

On one occasion Jacob was off work, which was most unusual. What could stop this diligent man from working hard?

In fact, he had a 'boil in't' nick of 'is bum'. Ernest liked this one because it gave a word to a part of the body normally not assigned a name. It meant the crease between the cheeks of one's arse.

When he had stopped laughing Ernest made a note of it and added it to his list when he got home.

Ernest had heard Maureen use the phrase 'wet shod' some years ago and found the phrase useful on many a rainy visit to the Co-op. There were countless contributions from Maureen. As he was writing in the bum episode, he noticed a couple of sentences Maureen had used:

'I'd nobbut a tanner on me' meant I had only a sixpenny piece with me.

'It were summat nor nowt' meant it was something or nothing/inconsequential.

During the same visit, Jacob added to Ernest's list when he was reminiscing about the textile factory he had worked in after leaving school. When the mill closed with the decline of the weaving textile industry he had taken up dry stone walling, which had sustained him ever since.

Jacob had some interesting tales to tell about his childhood. School trips to Golden Acre Park to see the Replica Coronation Regalia in Leeds. Then some phrases from his recounting a trip to Blackpool and how he was sick on the coach home.

One day in mid-September, Ernest called on Jacob with a very serious request: would Jacob please agree to act as executor of his will.

"What does ta want me for? Yer've gotten posher folks nor me."

"Well, I want you to do it. I hope you'll say you will."

"Tha's a fair bit o' brass, I reckon. I wouldn't mek moss nor sand of it – 'andlin' tha brass an' that."

"You won't have to. Your duties will simply be to make sure that what I leave in my will goes to the right people."

"It'll go mostly to yer family, right?"

"I have no family. I may have the odd cousin somewhere in the undergrowth, but I have never seen them or met them and don't know where they might be lurking. Why should I leave my money to them?"

"Well, I'm capped. I nivver thowt owt of suchlike."

"So, will you do it, Jacob?"

"Nay, I'll 'ave to put mi thinkin' cap on."

"Tell him he's got to, Les."

"It's a great honour Ernest is doing, asking you to execute his will."

"Execute? I'm not goin' to cut someone's 'ead off, am I?"

"No, you just have to make sure my so-called fortune goes to the right people. I've quite a bit set by and I want to make people happy by leaving some of my good luck into their hands. To some of them, it will seem like a decent spot of cash – indeed, a tidy sum of money. Your job is just to make sure they are sent it."

"I've not to do it baht 'elp, by myself, like? 'As ter asked somebody else, like?"

"Colonel MacDonald has said yes, he'd do it."

"'E talks that posh I can nivver mek out what 'e's on about 'alf the time."

"So will you do it, please?"

"Can Leslie 'elp if I'm, stuck? I can't do it baht 'elp."

"You can call on any advice you need. You'll help, Leslie, if he asks you?"

"O' course I will."

"Okay then, I'm yer man. I'll tek it on."

"You will? Shake hands on it."

"Nay, it's great to do owt like this fer a mate, and we is mates, in't we?"

"Good man, of course we're mates. By the way, there will be a fee for your pains, Jacob."

"Nay, I'll do it fer nowt."

"I won't be here to insist – I'll be dead – but Col MacDonald will make sure you get it."

"Right then, does ter want a beer to celebrate, while yer 'ere?"

"Thanks. Lovely."

"Les, get the beer like a good lad."

"Certainly, oh mighty master!"

"'E's a right joker is Les. Now Ernest, let's 'ave a bit of straight talkin', where does all tha brass come from? That's plenty on it to spend when yer want."

"Does it matter?"

"Mebbe not, but if I'm to 'and it out like, I'd like to think it were gotten fair and square."

"You're the first person in Holsterdale to ask me that."

"Mebbe, but there's lots 'at I'd like to know."

"Luck, really, I suppose. Look Jacob, can I tell you something?"

"Go on, then. Does it matter?"

"I only feel really comfortable when I'm here with you and Les. You don't make judgements. Everywhere else I sense I'm being tested, questioned, examined, judged even. I feel I have to keep my guard up, but not here."

"You're Ernest Silver. That's all that matters 'ere."

"We tek you fer what you are," Les said, as he brought in three tankards of ale.

"Thanks for that and for the ale, Les."

"So, what's it y're goin' ter tell us?"

"I've never said this to anyone. I was a professional actor before I settled in Holsterdale. Not a very successful one at that, but my wife was pretty good. She invested her money buying a house in a rundown part of London. We got married when we were both about forty years old. Together we bought another house. She died of cancer about twelve years ago and I sold up, at vast profit, and set myself up as a country gent in 31 South Street, Holsterdale. It was my wife's money really. We sort of drifted into marriage but we got on well and it seemed the right thing to do. It worked out nicely until she was ill."

"Doesn't sound very romantic to me, like?"

"No, well, it was romantic and wasn't at the same time. She, that is, Margery, had been quite successful in the theatre and we bought the houses with her money. I did them up and we rented out rooms, mostly for actors needing lodgings in the capital."

"It's reet interestin.'"

This amiable trio sat round the fire over more than a pint or two.

"Just fancy, Les, 'is wife were a star on't telly."

"I didn't say Margery was a star, Jacob. Don't make her out to be more than she really was. She was good though, and got good parts that paid pretty well."

"So, you was an actor an 'all then?"

"Yes, but not in her league, I have to admit."

"Any kiddies?"

"I just said we were both forty when we wed so there was only time for one. Our precious daughter Connie was clever and witty. When she grew up she aimed for the stage but she died in an accident when she was just twenty-two. Don't ask me what happened. Margery was devastated and tried to overcome the pain by working extra hard – doing anything that came her way to blot out the memories that plagued her."

"It was twelve years ago that she turned over in bed and said, 'Just feel my breasts'. You may not believe it, but I couldn't remember when I last did that.

"I said, 'My God, Margery, how long have you known about this?' I tell you, Jacob, there was a lump as big as a tennis ball under her left breast. She said, 'Six months. I first felt it when we were on location in Italy, but I was being paid more than I'd ever earned.' I told her she should have come home. We could have faced this thing together, but she didn't want to pull out.

"It was only a matter of weeks later that Margery told me to get out of the theatre. She said, 'Sell the houses. They'll fetch a lot. Find a nice place to retire.'

"'Where to?' I asked.

"She said, 'Fetch a map and we'll stick a pin in it.'

"I found a road map and with her eyes closed, Margery stuck the pin in Yorkshire. 'Google a nice place in Yorkshire,' she said and when it threw up Holsterdale, she insisted on looking up an estate agent. It was Margery who first pointed to a picture of the house I now live in.

"'Set yourself up as a country gent,' she said. 'It'll be the best role you've ever had!'

"We planned for her to travel north and see it with me, but she never did. It was too late, much too late. The cancer was everywhere and she didn't want to face any more treatment. I found a hospice very near our house in Hackney. The nurses there were incredibly kind and did everything to make Margery's last hours as comfortable and pain free as possible. And, I have to say, they looked after me too, so caring and thoughtful – I was knocked sideways.

"She was very weak but one late afternoon she opened her eyes and said to me, 'Did you ever love me, darling?' She weakly stroked my cheeks, which were wet with tears.

"'Of course I did. I think so, Margie,' I replied.

"'It's difficult to know what love feels like, Leslie, after teenage passion has settled down. I mean, how do you feel about Jacob and vice versa?"

Jacob immediately answered, "We're not ho-mo-sex-u-als." He pronounced the word very deliberately. "We're two men that get on well together; we like each other's company and we like to know there's someone at 'ome when you get back. That's about it, what does ta say Les?"

It was the longest sentence Ernest had ever heard Jacob utter.

Leslie nodded that Jacob had said it all.

"It was about the same between Margery and me. We got on well, we tolerated each other's often long absences, we rarely questioned each other and certainly never indulged in suspicion about late nights. But mostly we enjoyed each other's company. We liked doing things together, buying antiques or choosing wallpaper, going through our books – finances, I mean – and we read aloud to each other. I think we both thought our life together was contented.

"Then she almost sat up and said uncannily clearly, 'Please get out of the theatre. ... It was never your game. ... Sell the houses, promise. ... They'll fetch a lot ... and spend whatever you get on that nice house in Yorkshire.'

"The last words she said to me, so quietly I could hardly hear, she whispered, 'Bye-bye, darling. ... Sleep tight. ... We've had ... some good times.'"

And Ernest said to the two men who were not ho-mo-sex-u-als, "That's exactly what I did, and there was a lot of money left over, which you, Jacob, and the Colonel are going to divide out when I'm gone. You can do it with a clear conscience, Jacob. There is nothing illicit in my background that you could possibly be ashamed of."

CHAPTER 26

MEET THE MacDONALDS'

Colonel MacDonald, the voice of authority, returned from the golden hostelry leaving behind the noisy band of football supporters. The home he returned to was a three-bedroom, pebble-dashed, semi-detached house with once popular but now outdated Tudor embellishments. Its style was quite out of keeping in Holsterdale, though there were a couple of terraces of identical architecture, if such a word could be applied to the speculative building of the thirties. They were old fashioned, but not old enough to be quaint, and stood in stark contrast to the severe, stone terraces in the town which had been built to last.

Chez Macdonald was well maintained to the standards of the many army houses he and his wife Peggy had lived in throughout his military career. Standards must be maintained in a manner suitable to his rank and status.

"Is that you, Michael dear?" Peggy called from the scullery. "Dinner's almost ready," adding a dash of Worcestershire sauce and a light sprinkling of cayenne. "I hope you like it. All present, correct, and in good order. The drizzle still goes on, though mercifully yesterday's biblical storm has said its say."

As they sat at the dining table (they never ate in the kitchen except in emergencies), she said, "It's beans on toast."

Such a supper dish was elevated to the rank of dinner because they drank water with it, unlike the townsfolk who drank pint pots of tea.

"I heard a recipe on Woman's Hour to brighten up the dish, so I have followed their suggestion by t."

"Lovely, darling, you have certainly livened it up," he stuttered, after a startling first bite of the over-peppered concoction. "Perhaps a little less cayenne next time, dear, if I may be permitted to criticise your cooking."

"Oh dear, I'm afraid I have rather overdone it. Would you pour me some water quickly?"

He did so, saying, "I too will imbibe. The cayenne can be particularly fierce at this time of year."

"Never mind, dear, the stewed prunes and junket will cool you down. They slip down so easily, don't you think?"

"Prunes and junket! My word – you have done us proud tonight, darling. I haven't eaten junket since school days. You really are pulling out all the culinary stops this evening, Peggy." The Colonel was not inclined to be sarcastic, and irony was not his forte. He really meant what he said.

After they had eaten, he cried, "All hands to the pump."

The couple repaired to the kitchen to wash up; she washed, he dried and put away. As they enjoyed this intimate, oft rehearsed domestic ritual, Peggy asked if there was any news about the missing girl.

"None at all, I'm afraid. I'll tell all when we sit down in the drawing room."

He methodically placed the dishes and cutlery away – everything in its place and a place for everything – rinsed the sink and hung the tea towel over the rail of a less expensive version of an Aga. Meanwhile, Peggy was making the coffee.

The drawing room was like any other sitting room in a similarly-sized semi. Its furnishing was plain; the walls were cream, mounted here and there with military pictures and, on an occasional table, there were silver framed pictures of their offspring, now grown up and on their way. One photograph which had pride of place was of Col. Michael MacDonald with the Princess Royal, taken at the Palace when he received his MBE. Behind the sofa was a plain mahogany table on which were arranged copies of *Field*, the *Radio Times*, and *National Geographic* magazines all placed in neat piles, face upwards in date order, as you'd expect in an officer's club. They were there to be picked up, read and replaced neatly as if never touched. Evidence of Peggy' presence in the room confined itself to her knitting bag, on top of which were the half-finished sleeves of an uncompleted cardigan and several pieces of embroidery. There was a small television set which they hardly ever switched on, both the Colonel and his lady preferring to listen to the radio.

"Let me carry the tray. You go and put your feet up, poor darling, you deserve a rest."

Thankfully, she retreated into the drawing room, did put her feet up on the couch and pulled a crocheted rug over her knees. Michael followed with the coffee, poured out two cups – never mugs – and sat down. They both liked their coffee black and not too strong, brewed from grounds, of course, not instant, thank you very much.

"Tell me all about it, darling. How goes it on the rialto? Any sign of the little girl?"

"None at all, I'm afraid, but the big news is that Ernest is in the Iverdale Hospital and is said to be in a bad way. They say he's unconscious."

"What on earth can have happened to bring this about?"

"Word has it that his car had run off the road near the top of Long Harry. That's quite a stretch from here, as you well know."

"What would he be doing there of all places? It's well off his beaten track, isn't it?"

"A good question; suspicion in the Golden Unicorn had it that his being found there and the disappearance of the little Hirst girl are not unconnected."

"People can be very hard."

"Some would have it that he has had an unnatural interest in the girl. One person in the crush said that the Hirsts don't see it that way, but you know what gossip can do. He may have a deal of explaining to do when he comes round, if indeed he does survive. In a way I hope he doesn't, and that we could then go to his funeral in good order. Otherwise ..."

"Poor Ernest; what can have happened?"

"I gather that all this took place yesterday when the flood was at its height. Laura's disappearance and his being on Long Harry may be totally unconnected, of course."

"People enjoy thinking the worst – it's so much more exciting than the plain unvarnished truth. There hasn't been news like this in Holsterdale for years, not since the postman was murdered thirty years ago. That kept tails wagging for many a baking."

"I can't see what people are getting at. We've always thought of Ernest as a decent chap. His ideas at the PCC are always well thought out and cogently expressed. Mrs Hepworth, as the secretary, can't speak highly enough about him, and of course he's been a wonderful influence on Felicity Hepworth."

"Cogency is all very well but one cogent swallow doesn't make a summer."

"That proves nothing."

"I see him as being fundamentally damaged," said the Colonel, surprising his wife.

"What on earth do you mean, darling? Damaged? Surely not. He has always seemed such a well-balanced individual, don't you agree?"

"His infatuation with the girl, no matter how generously you interpret it is, to say the least, peculiar. His relationship with Felicity Hepworth and her parents is very different, close of course, and I know he's has spent many an evening with them over the years: but the way he has invaded the Hirst's household, I believe is a compensation for what must have been a very unhappy family life. He finds peace and contentment with them that he has never found anywhere else.

"I don't think he ever had what you and I would recognise as a happy childhood. So far as I can remember, he told me he was brought up by a succession of unsatisfactory maids, in India by Indian amahs, whilst his mother slugged dry gin rather more often than was healthy. Do you remember what he had to say about his mother? The picture he drew of her made Cruella de Ville seem a redeeming angel of mercy by comparison.

"It is a remarkable coincidence that he also went to Brotherwicks, the same prep school I went to – years before I was there of course. I had a jolly time at Brotherwicks."

"You didn't go at the age of eight though, and you went as a day boy, not as a boarder."

"True. Our experiences were bound to be radically different. He did tell me of the first day at Brotherwicks. His father was a professional soldier and had spent much of his tours of duty in India. Ernest had to be housed somewhere whilst his parents were abroad. In the vacations he was usually lodged with an unsympathetic widowed grandmother whilst his parents were living the life of Riley in the subcontinent."

"What did he tell you about his first days there?"

"His very first day was a savage eye opener. He was most graphic in his description. He recalled every detail as if it had happened yesterday. He was abandoned, as he thought, by his parents, and at the mercy of bullying on a scale I never had to deal with, both from older boys and even some from the staff."

"It was on the day Ernest asked me to act as an executor of his will. I knew he had money and to spare. Lucky in love and in fortune, and Ernest readily acknowledged he had been fortunate in both.

"Now I come to think of it, Ernest told me in some detail about his growing into manhood. The process was not straightforward in a boarding school and, especially, when parents were unwilling to deal with it in a sensible way. It simply was not done to talk about S.E.X, even in hushed tones. To be honest, I don't think parents knew how to talk about it intimately with their sons and daughters.

"Ernest told me a shocking tale when we were chatting in the parlour of The Golden Unicorn

"Again, it was almost as if he were talking about yesterday, not nigh on seventy years earlier. It was most disturbing and something I'd prefer not to share with you my dear. Suffice to say, it gave a certain insight into Ernest's character."

"Well if you'd rather not share, then I'd rather not hear! I think it's time for a cup of tea."

This didn't stop the thoughts passing through his mind, as he remembered the awkward conversation he had had with Ernest.

'Our dormitory at Brotherwick Fell was big enough to hold six beds. There was a locker behind each bed in which we kept most of our things. At the bottom of our beds was folded our extra blanket in case we were cold. These we brought from home so they were all different. Bear in mind that this was during the war and at night all the windows were covered with blackout screens. There was not much light that could leak out, but the staff kept a watchful eye by parading in the courtyard looking for any leakages after 'Lights Out'. They might have made better use of their time by keeping a watchful eye on what went on inside the dorms, but they couldn't see in because of the blackout screens.

'One night I awoke to find all the other boys clustered on a bed in the corner. They were all staring at a new phenomenon; a torch was focussed on Briggs's private parts.

"'Look what I've got," he had announced, and the others had all crowded round to see a single curly black hair! "Dad told me this would happen. He said that it's the start of a forest, and it tells you that you're changing into a man!"

'Then he asked us if anyone else had a short and curly one yet. No answer, though one or two of us sneaked a feel.

'Then he told us, "Pull down your pyjama bottoms and let's have a look. You might have missed something." We made a close inspection as the flashlight was passed around, but the cupboard was as bare as our bottoms.'

'Then he asked if we could make our willies go hard. We all agreed, some of us reluctantly, me included, that we could by fiddling around with it and demonstrated.

'"Not that way, you twats. Do it this way," And he breathily demonstrated what he called 'tossing off'.

'"If you do it long enough you'll get sensation," he grunted.

'At that very moment, as if on cue, and before we could try it out for ourselves, the door banged open and a senior monitor came in. This was serious.

'"Right, back to your own beds and bend down." Two more monitors appeared at the door and the first one whispered to them, "Right, okay for a team tanning?" All three produced a black gym shoe each, ready for action.

'"All right, trousers down, let's see your bare bums, all of you."

'Starting at the end nearest the door they marched, follow-my-leader fashion, round and gave each one of us an almighty vicious pasting with their gym shoes. After three circuits we had all taken six of the best thwacks.

'"Now up with your pants and into bed. It's long after lights out and silence."

'We were in no shape to rebel at this injustice. Our bottoms stung so much that I don't think any of us bothered with trying to get 'sensation' that night. The flogging for the time being had postponed all that experimentation and curiosity.

The Colonel was glad he'd not shared Ernest's unpleasant story with his wife. He knew this sort of thing to have been true, in many, if not all boarding schools at the time, but it had still made very uncomfortable hearing. He wished it had not so vividly come back to his mind.

CHAPTER 27

REG TALKS TO THE DREWS

It was now the evening of Thursday October 14th. Reg had reinforced his resources and was ready to complete the tale of Ernest and his modest beginnings.

He was first to enter the dining room, having spent the afternoon snoozing in his room. He had not eaten since his lunch with the Drews and was hungry.

Francis came to his table and remarked, "You had a lot to say for yourself at lunchtime. Did I hear you say you knew that chap what came here last night?"

"Do you listen to all your clients? A bit of a nosey parker, are you?"

"Not always, you weren't 'alf laying it on thick though. I couldn't 'elp hearing, but it were that interesting so I hung about to listen. Is there more to the story?"

"Quite a bit more. If you want to know how things develop, you'll have to wait until the Drews arrive. Where are they? You seem to know everyone's business. You must know what they've been up to this afternoon."

"Well I did 'appen to hear them say they were goin' for a walk if it cleared up."

"You do surprise me."

"You know 'e skedaddled; left at about midnight and never comed back."

"Yes, I do know he's gone. But God knows where to and why."

"Any roads on, the dining room's fillin' up so I've duties to perform." And with that he went to take orders from the other tables.

The Drews were last to come in and sat with Reg, eager for what more he had to add to the intriguing narrative. By this time, Reg had eaten his stewed prunes and custard. Their arrival delayed his going to the bar, so he ordered a coffee at the table and sat with them.

"The weather had dried up and we took the opportunity for a stroll – nothing ambitious but we went further than intended."

"The going was rather muddy so we had to change our filthy shoes before coming down. Sorry we're late."

"As we strolled, we talked a lot about your Scottish adventures and could hardly credit what you'd told us. We're actually excited and really hope you have more to tell us about … Rosy, did you say that was his name?"

"Yes, I did, but this afternoon his name came back to me. He was born Ernest Silver. The stage name he later adopted was Ambrose Piercy. Rather a mouthful, don't you think? So we knew him as Rosy."

"Did you have any dealings with him after the Riddell Company?"

"I did. He didn't stay with the Riddells all that long. He didn't appreciate what their expertise was doing for him, so he left and pursued the audition trail, occasionally finding work enough to keep body and soul together. It was at an audition some years later that we bumped into each other. Neither of us was having much luck so we hatched a plot to try our hand at comedy in the music hall circuit. Music halls were on their last legs but there was still a living to be made. We contrived a comedy duo which turned out to be a pale imitation of the Murgatroyd and Winterbottom act."

"Who on earth were Murgatroyd and Winterbottom?"

"They were quite a successful double act in the 1930s. They

were comedians in their own right – Tommy Handley and Ronald Frankau."

"Never heard of either of them."

"Oh dear, I forget the generation thing. Tommy Handley was a big radio star during the war; I.T.M.A. It's That Man Again."

"Did your act work, then?"

"We never topped the bill or came anything near it, but we did make a decent living until the music halls were closed by the dead hands of television. TV, even in black and white, rang their death knell. Comedy acts that had survived up to then were discarded, thrown on the scrap heap, us included."

"What a shame."

"Indeed, but that's the way of the world, darling."

"We did keep in touch briefly, but our tides naturally drifted apart."

"So that was the last you heard of him?"

"Not quite, Mr Drew. He and Margery found themselves in a touring production of *An Inspector Calls*. They married at the end of the tour and, as the saying goes, they lived happily ever after. Except they didn't."

"Don't tell me it all went wrong."

"No, it started pretty well; they had a daughter, Connie, who grew up to be a promising actress. She was asked to audition for a soap whilst still at the Guildhall."

"That's a well-respected theatre school, darling," Mr Drew helpfully pointed out.

"Quite right, Mr Drew. Sadly, Connie died in quite the most bizarre circumstances. I don't want to go into the details just now, but she died, full of promise. You can imagine how devastated Ernest and Margery were. Margery had to withdraw from the rehearsals of the TV drama she was in, and it took her a long time to return to her lively and active self. She would be approaching seventy, I think. Connie's funeral was attended by her fellow students and a largish cohort of theatre friends. I was not able to go but I did my best to console them for a while. That wasn't easy as we lived on opposite sides the metropolis.

"I've not much more to tell you, I'm sorry. I had hoped to catch up with Rosy when he found himself here last night, but he did a bunk, as you know, during the night. I'd love to know what was rattling around in his pretty little head."

"Amen to that. What's on the menu for pudding?"

"Rhubarb crumble, or prunes and custard; both acceptable but I can recommend the latter. See you when you're done!" And with that offhand recommendation, he repaired to the bar.

"Well, I never did? What a tragic end to the story."

CHAPTER 28

PROPOSAL, PROPERTY AND PROBLEMS

The marriage between Ernest and Margery came as a bit of a surprise to both of them, much more so to Ernest than to Margery who had 'ideas worth pursuing'.

Ernest kept himself to himself whilst in Scotland and he had deliberately not formed relationships with any of the other actors in the company. In fact, he saw no point in upsetting what seemed like well-established pairings. The owners of the company, and the actors they employed, were a strange and ill-assorted bunch; there was no great temptation to link up with any of them.

Margery's maiden name was Dawson. At that time neither she nor most of the others were members of Equity and so were not required to register a stage name. They must have toyed with aliases. The Riddells were the proprietors of the company and no doubt were known by their registered stage names.

Ernest didn't stay long with this company. When he left he had no intention of ever meeting any of them again; he wiped his feet, so to speak.

For years after leaving Scotland, Ernest had undergone a frustrating theatrical career of interviews, failed auditions, and small parts that barely kept the wolf from the door. One day, twenty or so years after he had abandoned Scotland (he was by this time about forty years old), he was auditioning for a role in *An Inspector Calls* and he bumped into Marjorie Dawson, now acting under the stage name Margery Dawe. Instant recognition and instantaneous friendship formed when they were both cast in the play in the important roles of father and mother – husband and wife. It was a touring engagement, so Ernest and Margery had a couple of months in close company and, in a mild way, they fell for each other. Ernest found out that her courting with Pete all those years ago had not lasted. No harm done.

The Priestley tour was about to end, a time when temporary friendships and associations between cast members are often put on the back burner. One evening, between matinee and evening performance, already in makeup and costume, Ernest came up with a startling proposition to Margery, quite out of character and out of the blue, almost as if he was quoting a line from a play. He declared (that's the only way to describe it, as if he were aiming at the back row of the stalls), "What do you think of the idea of getting married?"

Its spontaneity astonished even Ernest himself. He wondered what on earth his mouth was doing and why had it done it with such dramatic force.

"Married! Did you say married?" replied Margery, more than somewhat unsettled by the ferocity of this unexpected outburst.

Ernest croaked back in a throaty whisper, "That's the word." He was amazed at the word, but his mouth had opened and that precise word had popped out. He must really have said it.

"Were you proposing, then?"

"No! I mean yes, I suppose I was." He could hardly believe his ears. Was he really saying this or was it some strange alter ego?

"You silly thing. I've been aching for you to say those words, but I'd more or less given up hope of your ever getting round to it. Haven't you noticed that I've been itching to climb into your bed for weeks?"

"You've been what? Climb into my bed? We've had the odd

Proposal, Property And Problems

drinks in your room or mine, in Newcastle and Coventry. But you never invited me to stay in yours or hinted that you would like to linger longer in mine. We always ended sleeping separately in our own beds."

"We have shared bathrooms, sat on the same toilets, brushed our teeth in the same basins over the weeks we've been touring – but slept in the same beds? No. Never. I thought you must be queer or something. Now, just before the tour ends I had given up hoping."

"Well, I never. Oo, heck. Well, well, well."

"So, is that it, then? 'Oo, heck. Well, well, well.' Have I barked up the wrong tree? Yet, out of the blue you came up with the unexpected enquiry, asking that we get married."

"I didn't exactly put it that way. I said, what did you think of the idea of getting married?"

"You meant in the abstract? Oh, I see now. You weren't thinking that getting married applied to us in particular?"

"Well, no. I really wanted to know what you thought about the concept of marriage before asking. ... So what do you think? No silly question, I know what you think so ... I'm getting tongue-tied."

With a sudden outburst Ernest declaimed, "Will you marry me?"

Margery replied, remarkably calmly, "I didn't know you had those sorts of words in your extensive vocabulary. Were you quoting from a long-forgotten masterpiece that seemed to fit the occasion?"

"No, not that!"

"Then what?"

"Let me ask it again, this time more gently: will you marry me?" Then Ernest added as an afterthought, as if he'd been asking to play a round of golf, "I'm game, if you are."

"If this means you are proposing, and I may say it's a

peculiar way of doing so, get a move on. The curtain goes up in ten minutes."

"I'm game, if you are." Ernest repeated.

"If you truly are proposing, is that all you have to say – I'm game if you are?"

Ernest realised the game was up, and on bended knees before her he pleaded sincerely and directly "Margery dear, will you marry me? Please say yes."

"Of course I will, darling."

It was the first day of what turned out to be a long, prosperous, and happy marriage between two forty-year-olds. They married in a Registry Office in Clapham soon after the tour ended.

The marriage was a success. They lived together: avoiding asking too many awkward questions; putting up with inevitable separations; testing each other on lines; shopping and living together in what closely resembled harmony. They had very few quarrels and mostly a bundle of laughs.

Margery had a much more successful career on the stage than Ernest, who struggled to get parts, great or small. She was quite often on television; Ernest rarely. She was more experienced than he in quick thinking on the hoof, stage craft, speed line learning. In fact, she was a quick study – read the dialogue twice and it was in.

In the TV work, she became expert in hitting her marks. She had become proficient in movement and voice production. Her voice remained musical after years of unforced projection. She had a knack of instant characterisation. This had resulted in more success at auditions and she had made better use of the fit-up experience than the less-talented Ernest had.

Margery had appeared in a couple of award-winning films with her name actually listed in the credits (albeit low down). Whereas Ernest had had now and again nabbed walk-on roles incidental to the plot, Margery had been lucky to land character roles in strong and eye-catching storylines on TV, with runs that lasted for weeks or months – one for over a year. In that time, she had accumulated quite a fortune. Rather than spend it on fast cars, sailing boats and expensive holidays – all of which Ernest would have been tempted to indulge in – Margery had bought a semi-detached villa in a rundown, but one time elegant and tree-lined square in Hackney. She had paid for it in full out of savings without a mortgage. At the time, the sums of money involved were tiny, but well beyond Ernest's very limited means.

They had been married only a couple of years when the house next door was put on the market, and between them they bought that too. To be fair to him and his self-esteem, it was at Ernest's suggestion that they went ahead with this second property purchase. They jointly took the decision, but it was Margery's savings that paid for this new transaction.

Ernest had a practical streak and some skill in his makeup, thanks to the woodwork master at Brotherwicks. Having more 'resting time' than Margery, he devoted his time and skills to refurbishing and redecorating both houses. Once smartened up, the rooms were fit to be let as desirable theatrical lodgings. Managing this property had become Ernest's supporting role in their marriage. However, he was at the same time able to make occasional useful pocket money in adverts and voiceovers. He eventually refused touring opportunities to leave himself free to manage the lettings.

It was at this time of comparative prosperity that Ernest bought the Armstrong Siddeley. It was a wild extravagance, especially because the car spent most of the time in the garage – owning and running a car in London was a no-no.

There was, however, an impediment in the marriage at the start. Both wanted a family but no matter how hard he tried, in bed Ernest experienced a vivid and perturbing visitation of a ghost from a time long gone. It had haunted him throughout his life, had, in fact, prevented him from ever making any sort of close relationship with anyone, male or female. Now he had a firm and, he hoped, a lasting connection with Margery, but in bed this spectre prevented him ever reaching a climax.

Margery came to believe that her original doubts about Ernest's sexuality must have been true. One day she faced him with this devastating question, "Ernest, darling, don't you enjoy sex? It's supposed to be the be-all and end-all of life and love, isn't it?"

Ernest didn't immediately know how to answer the challenge, but he summoned up these words: "I don't know how to enjoy sex. I start out thinking sex is going well but each time I almost reach a climax, I see every detail of an event that happened nearly thirty years ago. My erection deflates and I just cannot carry on. It isn't your fault and I don't think it's mine either. But it's a road block that stops me in my tracks. I'm floored. I've never spoken to anyone about that afternoon. I hated it and I hate myself. I cannot help but turn away from you, just when it is going well. I turn over but find no rest; sleep eludes me afterwards."

"You poor dear. Oh, I'm so sorry. Could you tell me about it, or would that be too painful?"

"I don't know what to do. I have considered counselling but I've never had the courage to go through with it. I chicken out. I don't believe it would help anyway."

"Look. Why don't you tell me what happened. It's dark. Let's settle down. We'll hold hands and you can start whenever you want. okay?"

"This could be bedtime exorcism. Otherwise, if it doesn't work out I truly should give you the chance of something better with someone else."

"Don't talk rubbish, darling. Divorce is not an option. It is not on the agenda and it never will be, I promise. We're staying together through thick and thin."

"I don't deserve you. okay. I'll give it a try. We'll give it a

Proposal, Property And Problems

try. Settle down for a rocky road." He stared at the ceiling – he couldn't face her, not then.

"At the age of ten, I was at Brotherwicks – it's a boarding school. I went when I was eight to the prep school. War came and the senior and prep schools amalgamated as one, catering for about 150 boarders between the ages of eight and eighteen. The headmaster and governors of the joint school had found a stately home ready to give them board and lodgings, so to speak. That alone is a long and complicated story, so I'll spare you the details. I'll cut to the chase.

"On the day in question, the juniors had been playing rugby and had larked about afterwards in the showers, squirting cold water at each other from a hose pipe – all of us pink and naked and having innocent fun, screaming with excitement.

"After I had dressed for supper, I was passing the same shower room which was occupied by the team, like us stark naked but without the screaming and the innocence. As I walked past I stopped and looked in. The team captain, who was naked and without a modesty towel, advanced towards me and demanded to know what the hell I was staring at.

"I replied, 'Nothing.'

"He corrected me, 'Nothing, sir, if you please!' And he gave me a fierce clout over the head with the back of his hand as a reminder. 'Now, what were you staring at, boy?'

"'Nothing, sir. I was just passing on my way to supper, sir.'

"'What's your name, boy?'

"'Silver, sir.'

"'Be at my room after supper, before you go to prep. Do you know my room, the head boy's room?'

"'Yes, sir. I think so, sir.'

"'Be there at six-thirty. PT shorts and shirt, and bring a clean snot rag. A clean one, mind. Understand?'

"'Yes, sir.'"

Margery interrupted, "Nothing to haunt you or me so far."

"No. But I don't want to continue."

"You mustn't stop now. You've made a good start. *Courage, mon ami, le diable est mort*. What was he called, this head boy? Did he come from a decent family?"

"At the time, I didn't know his full name. We all called him 'Langhorn, sir', if we had to address him. We always used surnames, even among pals, or nicknames of course. It was sissy to call even your best friend by his first name."

"You should continue. A dark secret shared is a problem solved. Let's think positive."

"I hope you're right about problems solved. All right, then: take another deep breath."

He continued, "I turned up at his room promptly. He sternly commanded, 'Enter,' in answer to my timid knock. I entered, dressed as instructed in PT shorts and white Aertex shirt, with a clean handkerchief in the breast pocket.

"He was wearing a turquoise silk dressing gown and was lounging in an easy chair, his left arm on the chair arm, his right hand cupped over his crotch. His bruised legs were bare.

"There was a bed next to the wall, by its side an upright wooden chair. On the bed was a small pile of open *Lilliput* or *Men Only* magazines with pages open at rude pictures of naked women.

"I stood for a while, then he said, 'Did you shut the door properly?'

"I replied, 'I think so, sir.'

"'Make sure. Pull it to. Then you see that little hook at the top? Hook it over. We don't want any interruptions, anyone coming in when we're busy, do we?'

"I did as instructed. The hook was high up; it was hard to fit into the slot but, after a couple of tries, I managed it and we were securely locked in.

"Then he said, 'I think I'll lie down. Take my dressing gown and hang it on the middle hook by my raincoat, not the end one.'

"He stood up and turned his back to me so that I could ease the robe off his naked and very hairy shoulders. As I hung the gown on the middle hook he flopped onto the bed and lay on his back. He ordered, 'Right, now sit on the chair beside the bed and look at my face. What do you see?'

"'I don't know what you mean, sir.'

"'My face, idiot! Take a good look at my face and tell me what you see – every detail.'

"'Your face is very swollen, sir, and you've got a black eye; your face is badly bruised. There's some blood dribbling from your mouth and some on your cheek too.'

"'Anything else?'

"'Your lips are swollen and badly torn.'

"More. What more can you see?

"'Your left eye is bloodshot, completely blood red. I can't see any white in that eye, sir. Have you been in a car crash, sir?'

"'Not a car crash. That's rugger for you. You need balls to play rugger and sometimes you get hurt, like I did yesterday and again today. But wounded or not, you still turn out again and again to play. Rugger is a man's game. What else do you see?'

"'I don't know sir.'

"'Character. That's what you see, stupid. Character comes down the family tree. My grandfather had character, my father has character (that's why he's rich – you don't make a fortune without character) and I have character, masses of it. That's why I'm captain of rugby, I'm first bat in cricket and I've been appointed head prefect. Learn to recognise character when you see it. I'm proud of my record. It's not the only thing I'm proud of. You wait and see what I've got that makes me the envy of every boy in the school. Do you envy me? Don't answer that now. I'll leave you to answer that question later on. Did you bring your snot rag?'

"'Yes, sir. It's in my shirt pocket, sir.'

"'I hope it's a clean one. I'm not having your snot anywhere near me. Let's see it.'

"I pulled it neatly folded out of my pocket.

"'That's okay, now use it to wipe my mouth; mop up the blood carefully.'

"I did so. There wasn't much wet blood, most of it was dried on; I cleaned it up as best I could.

"'Bloody hell. Your gentle mopping is more savage than a kick in the balls in the scrum. Now you've finished, tuck your snot rag under my pillow where you can find it. You'll need it later on.'

"That done he said, 'Now look at my body. It's a fine specimen; don't you wish you had a body like mine?'

"'Yes, sir. You have a very fine body, sir.'

"'More details. Come on. You've got eyes – use them.'

"'You are very hairy, sir.'

"'What about muscles. Put your hands on my chest and feel my pecs. Stand up if you can't do it sitting down.' He flexed his muscles and I could feel them ripple under the hair.

"'Now feel my six pack. You have to put your hands lower down.' I did that, not with any great pleasure.

"Then he said, 'To continue this appraisal of my body we must go even further down. Do you know what they call what I'm wearing down there?'

"'No, sir. It looks a bit like skimpy underpants, I think, sir.'

"'That's a jock strap, idiot.'

"'I'm sorry, sir. I've never seen a jock strap before.'

"'It keeps your balls out of harm's way when you're in the scrum. Look after your balls. They are very important, did you know that?'

"'No, sir.'

"'No, well, I don't suppose your balls are. ... Let's have a look.'

"He pulled my gym shorts down and said, 'Mighty oaks from

little acorns grow. You wait! Pull your shorts up. Why did you pull them down?'

"'I didn't, sir. You did.'

"'Are you accusing me? Have a care with your loose accusations.'

"'I wasn't.'

"'Oh, never mind. We're wasting time. If we're going to continue your examination of my body, you're going to have a look and see what's underneath my jock strap.'

"'I don't want to, sir.'

"'So, what were you staring at this afternoon in the shower room? You wanted to see well enough then. Weren't you impressed?'

"'I don't know what you mean, sir.'

"'Well, now's your chance to have a good look. And there's more to follow that'll make your eyes water!'

"'I don't want to, now, sir,' and I started to cry.

"'Blubbing won't help, so stop that. I didn't ask you to my room to do what you want. It's what I want that matters and I always get what I want – no exceptions. Do you understand?'

"'You're head boy and I'm only ten.'

"'Good answer. Now get your fingers under the elastic, pull the jock strap down and you'll see what you really are aching to stare at.'

"He grabbed my left hand and shoved it under the elastic.

"'Now pull, you cringing bastard.'

"I pulled at the elastic but my fingernails got caught in his hairs. He shouted, 'Bloody hell, you don't have to tear my pubes out by the roots. All right, stop and we'll try another way.' He was determined that I undress him. What pleasure he got out of all this was and still is beyond me.

"It's too disgusting. I'm sorry but I just can't go on. The details are too horrendous to relate."

She replied that he had gone so far, omitting not even minor details, and that it was obvious the event remained etched into the back, not to say the front of his mind.

"You must go on." She added that this outpouring was maybe cleansing his mind forever – but a partial eclipse in itself wouldn't do. Convinced by her words, and in the hope that what she said would make a difference, he did continue.

"Langhorn turned away from me onto his side and told me to pull the elasticated back down first. This time it came away quite easily. That done he rolled again onto his back."

Margery again interrupted to say that she could guess what he made him do. And she was right. After it was over she asked, "How did he force you to do such a thing?"

"Torture can make even the strongest give in. He had my genitals in his fist and every time I hesitated, he squeezed. And he forced me to mop up afterwards.

"After it was over he dismissed me with a curt, 'You've had your fun. Keep that snot rag as a memento, while I have this fag. Now piss off. Bugger off, why don't you?'

"I ran from his room and down the corridor. A voice shouted, 'Silver, over here, lad.'

"It was the dreaded Mr Cawthore.

"'You know the rule – no running indoors. How many times do you have to be told? Where are you going in such a hurry?'

"'Sorry, sir. I'm late for prep, sir.'

"'And what's your excuse for being late for prep?' I didn't know what to say.

"'Answer me, boy.'

"'I was seeing the head prefect in his room, sir.'

"'What had you done wrong that he wanted to see you in his room?'

"'He had something to show me, sir.'

"'What did Langhorn want you to see?'

"I found an excuse and said, 'He told me I'd been insolent, sir.'

"'Langhorn is a fine young man. Look up to him. Follow

Proposal, Property And Problems

his example. Do as he does in every way and you won't go far wrong. You might even grow up to be a fine young gentleman like him: a fine upstanding specimen, an exceptional athlete, a sportsman and a scholar – though you're not making a good start.'

"Then he took my face in his hands, pulled the short hairs by my ears and forced me to stand on tiptoe.

"'Use your handkerchief to wipe your nose, you disgusting boy.'

"I couldn't use my hanky – it was wet through – so I wiped my nose with the back of my hand. Stupidly I licked my hand and it tasted salty. It definitely wasn't snot.

"I wondered what Cawthore would think if he knew what it really was. And what I'd been doing. And what I'd been invited to see and do. He'd have beaten me out of jealousy because I'd done what he desperately pined to do. That was only a guess, but he was the sort of man who ... never mind.

"'That's forty lines by tomorrow morning. Write "I want to grow up to be a fine upstanding man like Langhorn." Now be off with you, and walk!'

"I walked as fast as I could, went to the bogs and threw up."

Margery asked tenderly, "Is that the end?"

"Yes, it is," Ernest replied weakly.

"Give me a kiss then, and we'll try again tomorrow. We'll find out if telling me all this has unlocked your libido."

They kissed, turned over and for the first time in ages, Ernest fell asleep.

This unlikely therapy had worked. Not instantaneously, but Ernest was enabled, and after two months of determination and exertion they hit the bull's eye.

The moment when Margery said, "I think I'm pregnant," was greeted with what amounted to relief for the both of them. The nine months passed without dramatic interventions and Margery gave birth to a little girl. They called her Constance, after Constance Cummings; Margery had had a small but interesting part as a maid in a play with Cummings in the lead and they'd struck up a friendship.

Constance became the apple of both their eyes for many years; they shared her upbringing and she fulfilled all their dreams and promises.

Margery stayed at home to look after her until she was able to carrycot Connie to rehearsals. It was quite a lean time for them as Ernest had little success at auditions, and voiceover engagements were intermittent and unreliable.

Connie went to a local school which was not all that hot, to put it mildly, and they couldn't afford Italia Conti when the time came for that sort of thing. Connie was bright at school and took part in drama at all levels. She was excited to be cast as Mary, mother of Jesus, one year. All Mary had to do was to 'ponder in her heart', which needed no words at all. Anyone can ponder, but Connie wanted more than mere pondering. Her interpretation was sulky, which is not the right way to greet the Saviour of the World.

The year following, she was the Angel Gabriel – a much better part. The angel had important words to say.

Ernest was at home during all Connie's school days, so it was his job to listen to her reading, help her with spelling, show her tricks with numbers to make maths easier and help her with diction. When she started singing, first in the choir and later in solos, he helped her with voice production, clarity, breath control, rib reserve and all the necessary techniques involved in singing. He didn't realise at the time, but it was to arm him for the best acting role he was ever to undertake.

Her crowning moment while still at school was to sing, 'Let the Bright Seraphim' before the Lord Mayor of London and invited guests. She had a good and confident top C but wisely avoided Sutherland's top E.

After school, she was accepted at the Guildhall where she

instantly made her mark. She had developed into an attractive young woman. Her hair was a violence of curls, rather like her father's had been. Its colour, unlike his, was mousy so she went in for the blonde streaks which were very much in fashion in the late nineties. Her potential effect was spoiled when she put her hair up, as though she was intending to have a bath.

Connie's taste in clothes was outlandish: flimsy taffeta skirts teamed with violently patterned heavy pullovers.

When in her second year at the Guildhall, she was asked to audition for a pilot episode in what had the potential to develop into a series. If she succeeded and landed the part, she would have to leave college early. Both Ernest and Margery urged her to go for it. She prepared for it with advice from both parents and she went off to studios in Knightsbridge with their blessing.

She thought she did well at the audition. She could see there were powerful rivals so there was no certainty. You never know what is round the corner, especially in the theatre. One minute, no time to spit out, then months of drought. Connie knew all this from family experience, so it was with eyes open that she had decided on a career in the theatre. She stood outside the venue, waiting for another Guildhall student in her third year that she recognised.

Ernest was at home when a police car drew up outside the house.

"You are Ernest Silver, sir?"

"Yes, I am. What's happened?"

"And your daughter is Constance Silver. Is that correct?"

"Yes. Out with it, man."

"We're sorry to have to inform you that your daughter has died in an accident. She was standing on the pavement outside Star Studios in Knightsbridge and a man leapt to his death from the roof above and landed full on your daughter's head. She died instantly. There was no reviving her."

"Thank you. I must sit down. I feel quite faint."

"Head between your knees and try to breathe normally."

After a while he sat back and said, "Thank you for coming. This must be a sad duty for you."

"It is, sir. It is, indeed. Is there anything we can do for you?"

"No, thanks. I must ring Margery."

Connie's death was a devastating blow for both of them. Margery took on additional work, anything to keep herself busy and to brush aside the tears. With her fellow actors she was bright and excessively cheerful. It was a facade, hiding a broken heart.

CHAPTER 29

CHARLIE, CHASE AND FOLLOW

Maureen was over eager to find out what Charlie had to say and she was already at the Nattrasses when there was a knock at their door. Tom opened it to admit DC Susan Ingram. Introductions were made and the Nattrasses told the police what Charlie had said.

Ingram replied that she'd like to talk to Charlie.

"That's okay," said Mabel. "Talk to the lady, Charlie an' ell 'er what you told us."

"Hello, Charlie, my name's Susan and I want to ask you about Laura. Laura's your friend, isn't she?"

Charlie was sitting on his mother's knee and was crying. Weakly, he nodded his head but said nothing.

"Mrs Hirst, do you know how Laura and Charlie get on together?"

"They are not in the same class at school, but I think Laura 'as looked after 'im a time or two; in the playground and sometimes after school an' all"

"Do you know about this, Mrs Nattrass?"

"Oh, yes. I'm 'er godmother, you see. She comes 'ere quite a bit with 'im and they play drafts and that. They never say much about what they've bin doin'. So long as they're safe, that's all that matters."

"Charlie, do you look out for Laura at playtime sometimes?"

asked the DC. Charlie nodded his head, though he was still full of tears.

"Does Laura look after you?" she continued.

This time Charlie managed a weak, "Yes, she does."

"Why does she do that?"

"'Cos the big boys get at me."

The DC asked, "Mrs Hirst and Mrs Nattrass, both of you, has Laura ever told you about taking care of Charlie?"

"Not 'specially, but three or four of 'em in their class have been chosen to look out for kiddies as is unhappy and to take care of little ones if they're not gettin' on like. That's Laura and Fred and Jacob and another lass, I forget 'er name. They call 'em monitors or summat like that, so mebbe Laura 'as looked after Charlie now and again. She told me once that she took 'is 'and and they went for a walk at after school. That were some time ago, though."

"The other girl is called Emily," added Mrs Nattrass. "I've 'eard tell of all that an' all."

The DC pursued. "Does Laura take you for a walk sometimes. Charlie?"

"She does," muttered the still-tearful lad.

"Where did you go on these walks, Charlie?"

Mrs Hirst intervened, "I nivver said they went for walks lots of times. Just once did Laura tell me, that's all."

"Mrs Nattrass, did Charlie tell you about going for walks with Laura?"

"Oh aye, but I never thought nothin' about it. Laura comes to our 'ouse pretty often. They get on well together, Laura and our Charlie."

"Charlie, were you going for a walk with Laura after school the other day?"

"Yes."

"Any particular reason for going for a walk?"

"Yes, she said it weren't safe by the river."

"Why do you think she said that?"

"'Cos it were full," said Charlie."

"Did you talk to anybody when you went for your walk?"

"Yes."

"Who did you talk to?"

"Unk'lernest."

"Where was your Uncle Ernest when he talked to you, Charlie?"

"In 'is car."

"So that was when you saw Mr Silver?"

"Why didn't' you tell us afore, lad?" Harry asked.

"I din't think," replied Charlie limply.

"It doesn't matter. You've told us now. Thanks for that," said his mum.

"When Laura takes you for walks, where do you go?"

"I'm not tellin'."

"Come on now, Charlie, tell me where you go," coaxed his mother.

"I'm not tellin'."

"Come on, now, Charlie," said his dad. "When you go for walks with Laura, where do you go? It's a simple enough question."

"I'm not tellin'." Charlie was unusually stubborn.

"Why not?" shouted his dad.

"Please try to keep calm, everyone," said the DC. "Shouting won't help."

"I'm sorry. I shouldn't have shouted. You have a go Mabel, see if 'e will tell you."

Mabel tried, "Come on Charlie, tell yer mum where you go for walks with Laura."

"I'm not tellin'."

"Why not?"

"It's a secret."

"Who says it's a secret," asked the DC.

"Laura does ... and Unk'lernest."

Maureen impatiently demanded, "Are we gettin' any nearer to findin' Laura, with all this talk of walks and secrets and such like? Ask 'im if he saw 'er get in 'is car, for 'eaven's sake. That's what we cem 'ere to find out."

"I'm sorry, all of you." DC continued, "You said where you went for walks with Laura was a secret?"

"Yes. Laura said, an' Unk'lernest said."

"Is that true?"

"Unk'lernest says it's good to 'ave secrets."

"Let's get to the point," said Harry Hirst emphatically. "Did you see Laura get into Uncle Ernest's car when the river was flooding?"

"Yes, I did."

"Where abouts?" shouted Maureen Hirst. "Where was the car when she got into it?"

"I can't remember exackly."

Maureen tried to take the initiative, and gently asked, "If we go for a little walk could you show us, Charlie?"

"I don't want," Charlie cried.

"Right, then, let's get us coats on. Come on then, let's get on wi' it," demanded Maureen, who was determined to be first out of the door.

DC stopped her with a stern, "Leave that to the police." She continued, "a properly coordinated search is the best. Please do not take individual initiatives."

But Maureen was already at the door. DC Ingram commanded, "Come back here, Mrs Hirst. This interview is now closed. I will report back to my boss. I cannot authorise an initiative like that. My report will say that Charlie saw Laura get into Mr Silver's car. We can deduce that it must have been at the top of the green, above where the children had been playing football. I will also say there may be a secret hiding place that Charlie refuses to tell us about. I can assure you that if such a hiding place exists, it won't be a secret much longer. The police will find it.

"Thank you, Charlie, for speaking to me. I think you deserve a treat for that, don't you, Mr and Mrs Nattrass? And thank you all for your time and patience. In the meantime, I must ask you to stay here and try to be calm. If you wish to speak further, go to the incidence van on the green and someone will take time to talk to you."

With that, the questioning ended. Harry managed to persuade Maureen not to go it alone.

* * *

When the police had gone, the two families tried again to coax Charlie into telling where the hiding place was. The most he revealed was that it was under a big tree with shiny leaves. Maureen said it must be somewhere in the woods near the top of the green — it couldn't be that far away.

Charlie said, "Yes."

Upon this Maureen declared, "Right, that's not enough for me. I'm off to police van!"

And without another word she skedaddled.

But Maureen did not go to the police van on the green. She knew, or thought she knew, where the hiding place was. It was obvious to her: in the woods near the top of the green. She raced off to find it.

The woods were thickly covered in tall trees – sycamore, oak, but mostly ash. There was a thick undergrowth of rhododendrons, which in late spring were covered with a mantle of large, pale magenta flowers. Nothing grew under their branches. Most of them had been planted in the nineteenth century as decorative additions to the countryside and their dark green shiny leaves formed a dense cover under which no other wild plants could thrive, though a few creatures enjoyed the shelter they provided. Maureen thought that any one of these umbrellas of dark leaves could be Laura's secret hiding place, but which one? There were so many to choose from.

The woods were on a steep hillside. Rocks like knuckles were everywhere. Docks and brambles and bracken battled for dominance in the undergrowth, and the ground was slippery after the unusually heavy rains.

Maureen had made up her mind; she didn't trust the police to go looking for her daughter. Instead of going to the police van, she half-ran up the road past the likely spot where Ernest's car might have been when Laura got into. This must be where her lovely Laura would be. It was no place for a frantic mother to be racing, but Maureen's spirit was up; nothing and nobody was going to stop her from her headlong and desperate race.

The woods were dark and the tangled undergrowth grabbed at her hands, her hair, her clothes. Maureen stumbled many times as she coursed madly from one rhododendron to the next. She stopped herself sliding down the slope by clinging onto branches of gorse and bracken, which scraped her hands viciously. She found nothing in any copses that she peered into. She staggered from one clump to another. After fruitless searching for over an hour she tripped over a boulder and fell onto the wet undergrowth. Her ankle twisted and hurt like fury. She tried to get up in the hope at least of limping, but the pain was excruciating and she fell again, slipping down the steep slope. She grabbed at loose branches and managed to prevent herself slipping headlong into the roaring river, which was menacingly close. She could hear the roar of the river deep below her. She had foolishly landed herself in a daft place with nothing to show for it.

"Where is she?" she cried aloud in agony.

* * *

Tom and Mabel had neither encouraged nor calmed Charlie's troubled breast. Since Harry couldn't help in this fruitless exercise, he excused himself by saying he was going to follow Maureen to the police van on the green.

Harry briefly and breathlessly explained the situation to the sergeant on duty and said that he had followed his wife here.

"Where is she now?" he asked. The desk sergeant replied that Mrs Hirst hadn't been to the van at all that day.

"Bloody Hell! Where's the silly bitch gone now?" he shouted.

There was no time to waste; Harry chased off without explanation.

The silly cow must have gone looking for Laura's hiding place herself, he thought. *God knows where she'll be, but I have to find her, pump some sense into her crazy noddle and drag her home. I might have lost a daughter but I'm damned if I'm going to lose a wife as well.*

He sussed that Maureen had gone into the woods. It was obvious that the hiding place was in there somewhere. If not, he was flummoxed.

It was quite a steep climb on the road up to where he imagined Laura had got into Ernest's car. He looked for tyre marks but found none – the heavy rain had taken care of that. He stood for a moment trying to visualise what had happened up here only yesterday. In his mind's eye, he traced the footsteps, not only of his wife, but more especially of Laura and Charlie Nattrass.

But he must find Maureen; he wasn't going to lose her too. Much as Maureen had done, Harry powered into the woods, searching every dark rhododendron. Each time, there was neither trace of Maureen nor of Laura.

He dived back and forth for nigh on an hour. He paused for breath and to consider where to go and what to do next. His eye was taken by a small patch of red amongst the dark green gloom below. He focussed his eyes carefully and realised that the red belonged to the anorak Maureen had been wearing. Was it an optical illusion or was it truly her?

The steepness of the hillside made for a hazardous descent, so he had to place his feet carefully to stop himself skidding headlong into the roaring river at the foot of the steep slope. When near enough he bellowed, "I'm coming. Shout out to help me find you."

With all her might, and there was very little left in Maureen, she cried out. Her feeble voice was quite unable to guide him. But he did reach her after dangerous slithering and sliding to where she lay. He anchored his legs on a heavy tussock and attempted to lift her, but the slippery ground made any movement impossible and first-aid out of the question. His vain attempts almost precipitated them both into the ravine.

"Why the hell did you go looking for Laura all by yourself? You were stupid, you know that? And now I can't lift you and there's no way I can be dragging you up this slope. I daren't leave you to call for help."

No reply.

"I went to the police following you and they said you hadn't been to them. Then I left in a rush to chase after you. Hopefully they may already be on their way to look for Laura, and you and me too, after hearing Charlie's story."

Maureen was past caring; the pain, the cold and the sheer despair had left her numb. Her torn hands clasped and unclasped but she said nothing. Harry didn't think she had heard a word he had said.

This wet and bedraggled couple must have been lying there for an hour when they heard voices. Harry saw flashing lights above them and shouted out to let them know where they were. A quick assessment by the police of the Hirsts' predicament meant that ambulance and paramedics arrived swiftly, but it was still almost dark by the time the Hirsts were back in their home. Maureen's ankle was not broken, so there had been no trip to the hospital.

The police ticked off the Hirsts, saying that they had made matters worse by taking off like that. They also said it would have been a deal easier if they'd stayed at home and let the police take initiative. Also, chasing off like that, without saying where they were going, was downright stupid and a waste of police resources.

Harry acknowledged the truth of this and declared how sorry they both were.

Maureen added, "We was desperate, wasn't we, 'Arry?"

"Desperation isn't necessarily the best reason for taking precipitate and foolish actions like you both did. We still hope to find Laura, and we really are doing our best. We understand how desperate you are to find Laura, but what you did today was time wasting and did nothing to help us find the child."

"We will give the woods a thorough search in daylight tomorrow. Be sure of that."

This did nothing to alleviate the Hirsts' worries. "What are the chances of finding Laura?"

"There is still hope." The chances were dim after all that time, but the policeman wasn't prepared to say so just yet.

When the police and medics had gone, Harry and Maureen had a chance to talk things over.

"Thanks for comin' to get me, Arry."

"You should never have run off like that."

"I know, but I were that bothered. I threw caution to t' winds."

"I could have lost the both of you. They'll find Laura, I'm sure of it, but we have to keep ourselves safe and strong for when we get her back."

"I know, love, it were daft, but I were that desperate and couldn't abide with what that detective were askin' Charlie. She were gettin' nowhere. Charlie's a simple lad an' 'e didn't know what to say."

"Charlie was doing his best, love. You can't blame him."

"I don't, an' I know they 'ave to get things right in their 'eads, but it were gettin' them nowhere."

"Listen love, Tom isn't all that impressed with Ernest, is he? What do you think?"

"Just now, I wish Laura 'adn't got into 'is car, yesterday. I've nivver thought that afore and I've been right glad 'at 'e took 'er for rides now and again. She loved it an' I weren't the one to stop 'er."

"Yes, but now we're faced with the dead certainty that she *did* get into his car yesterday … or was it the day before? Anyhow when the flood was at its worst. And now he's been found, unconscious, miles from nowhere, and she wasn't with him."

"It doesn't bear thinkin' about. What could he have done wi' 'er?"

"God only knows. But he wouldn't have done her no harm, that's for sure. He'd look after her even on 'is death bed; we can be sure of that."

"Aye, that we can."

"Now you keep your feet up. I'll wet the hanky again with cold water for your ankle, and then I'll make the tea. We've got to keep ourselves together, no matter what."

CHAPTER 30

RECOVERY! RECOVERY! RECOVERY!

Friday, October 15th

At the Iverdale General, Doctor Shah was making his usual early morning rounds. Sister Graham reported to him that she had noticed some signs of recovery in Mr Ernest Silver. He had been in a coma since his arrival there Wednesday. Whereas before he was more or less motionless, she had seen some stirrings and movement. She had tried to talk to him – did he know his name and so forth – but there was nothing more than his eyes momentarily flickering. She had asked him if he could hear her and had received not a murmur of response.

Dr Shah, when he came to Ernest's bed, took his pulse manually and looked at the displays on the screens, then leaned over him and asked his name. Only a faint murmur of response, but it was a murmur.

"It's good to see, Sister. It's early days but I think we can say he's making good progress. Now and again sit by him. He may be uncomfortable. If you get really noticeable reactions, ask the nurse to sit him up a little. That can help restore circulation more effectively.

"We'll keep the drip feed, and of course the oxygen. When he gives clear signs of regaining full consciousness, try flat Coke from a spoon."

Progress, once started, went on apace. By lunchtime he was sitting up and seemed fully aware of his surroundings.

The policeman on watch duty informed DI Worth that Silver was conscious. It was too early to initiate an interview. That would wait upon medic's permission. It was far too early to consider taking him to the police station in Shepley for a formal interview. Meantime, the 24/7 duty watch had to continue, and nobody other than authorised medical staff could be permitted to visit or speak to Mr Silver. That Hirst woman especially must be kept away.

Recovery was slow but there was some improvement with every passing hour. Mick Hardraw, the night nurse on duty, spoke to him during the night, though not about anything special. It was not exactly a conversation; it was on the lines of, 'How are you feeling? ... Have you got a headache? ... Would you like your pillows puffed up a bit? ... Would you like a drink? ... Can you hold your mug yourself?" The monosyllabic responses at least indicated that Ernest understood the questions, and Hardraw was able to puff up the pillows, or not puff them up, as demanded by the patient.

The next morning, Hardraw had gone off duty after reporting the progress of his patient; a fresh nurse was ready for action. On the basis of his report she had Ernest properly sitting up. He was capable of holding a mug in both hands to drink the flat Coke. They tempted him with a little breakfast, but he indicated that he was not hungry.

By lunchtime the ward sister told him he was making very good progress for a man of his age. Out of curiosity and by way of conversation she asked him how old he was and when he said eighty-five she nearly fell off her chair in disbelief.

He was not yet recovered enough to face the sort of questions the police intended to ask him, but simple questions like these he answered with more complete sentences and more comprehensive answers as the morning went on. He was now most comfortable sitting up and seemed to take notice of his surroundings.

The whole of Saturday passed in a similar vein, and by lunchtime, his tummy told him he was hungry and he could eat: but not everything. The tough meat he hardly touched, but there was rice pudding for afters and he greedily ate the lot, strawberry jam and everything. He then drank weak tea with milk and a little sugar.

CHAPTER 31

TALKING AND TELLING TALES

Saturday morning was when the Colonel was usually dispatched to do the weekend's shopping, and today was no exception.

"May I sit with you, Norris?" Col. MacDonald had spotted the rector as he was entering the café and was in need of someone to talk to – any port in a storm – the Rev would do.

"By all means, Michael. The toasted teacakes here are the best in town, don't you agree?"

"Definitely," came the reply, as Norris took a hearty bite.

"Flood affect you at all, Michael?"

"Not at all. Our house is well is well above the flood plain so we rarely find the rain a bother. The church and the rectory are both well out of harm's way of course."

"Yes, indeed. Sad news about Ernest. Is he still in hospital?"

"So far as I'm aware."

"And no signs of the girl?"

"None. The Hirst's must be heartbroken."

"I went round to see them to offer what consolation and prayer I could, but they were out."

"An unusual man, Ernest. Well named though; Ernest I mean. One would have no problem with saying he was in earnest. I find him interesting and well-meaning. Would you agree, Norris?"

"He has worked wonders with our choir. But not, I think, a happy man."

"I believe he found happiness, or at least contentment with the Hirsts, but he seemed to have a special connection with their daughter. Nothing to worry about, that relationship?"

"Tosh, no. White as driven snow. That's my opinion. Aileen would tend to disagree – we have frequent arguments on that subject, as on many other bones with which we contend."

"He's told me horrific tales of his early school days. We went to the same school, though a generation separated us, of course. He was in the school when it went into the country during the war, with a scratch staff. Even so, we had much to chat about. I think after what might be called a sticky start, finally he settled down and more or less enjoyed his later days in the school."

"You must enlighten me about all of this, it sounds fascinating."

"I will, Norris. I will. Are you in a hurry to get away, it could take some time?" The colonel promised as he drained his cup of coffee.

The Colonel began by saying that he had had many conversations with Ernest over the recent years.

"As you know, Ernest has a fabulous memory. Our conversations would go like this:

'Ernest, you have told me fearsome stories about bullying by staff and senior boys. Surely your years at Brotherwicks can't all have been dreadful?'

'Quite the contrary. It had its downs and its ups, but isn't life very much like that?'"

Norris interjected, "You don't have to be a parson to know that."

"'And my years in Holsterdale have been on the up since I first arrived here.' Ernest said in all earnestness, and he really meant it."

A further heart-warmed interjection from the parson, "That's good to hear, and I believe he has found peace in his time."

The Colonel returned to the narrative.

"'Did you make friends at Brotherwicks, Ernest?'

'I did. A lad came one term after me. He had been ill with scarlet fever and his coming to school had to be put off until he had recuperated.'

'And the name, perhaps?'

'Mark Isadore Rosetree. He was almost exactly a year younger than me, but he was a brain so he was in the same form as me. His older brother Matthew, who eventually became head prefect, was three years older.

'Mark and I sat together, helped each other with prep, tested each other with spellings and did our best with reading French short stories to each other. In other words, we gave each other a lift. I loved to be with him and we were inseparable, except in sport. He didn't like games and did his best to get out of them. He'd rather read a book than turn out on the playing fields. He just couldn't get on with being cold and wet when he could be in the library, warm and dry.

'The school in its wartime premises was surrounded by a garden and fancy rhododendrons which, in flower, were a magnificent sight to behold. After flowering, all the boys were ordered to dead-head these huge bushes. We were told that failure to do so would result in them not budding next year. It was a bothersome but necessary chore. On one of the dead-heading days, Mark and I were counting the heads one by one in French. Matthew was supervising us with a team of other boys. He'd overheard us and told me my pronunciation was not all that hot.'

"What book are you reading in French?" he asked me.

"*Le Mystere de Slim Kerrigan*, sir." He might have been the elder brother of my best friend, but he was a prefect and rules are rules and titles are titles.

"Bring it to my room after supper and I can teach you a thing or two."

"I have to see Mr Cawthore after supper so I can't do that, sir."

It was a made-up excuse, but I had an experience in a prefect's room that I didn't want to repeat, even at the hands of my best friend's brother. He never repeated the invitation.'

("Here's another tale worth repeating, Michael.")

'One afternoon, Mark dug me out in the prep room and told me the Head wanted to see me urgently. Such a summons had to be hastily complied with.

'In his study, Dr Waterton, as always wearing his gown and with serious expression on his face, was pacing up and down. "Come in, my lad. Would you like to take a seat?"

'I sat on the edge of the nearest chair. Such invitations in his presence were rare.

"Your dear mother has just rung ..."

"Oh, really? She's never rung me before. What does she want?"

"Hold your tongue, boy. Be respectful to your mother."

'After a pause he continued, "I've asked Sister Friday to be here in support. Your mother has just rung with very distressing news."

"Dad's dead, isn't he?"

"Oh dear, oh dear, yes he is. I'm sorry to have to tell you but, yes, he has passed away ... killed in action ... on active service. He must have been ... a very brave man. We shall offer prayers for his soul in assembly tomorrow morning. ... A glass of water for the boy, Sister."

"Is mother coming to see me?"

"I'm afraid not. She has another engagement so she is unable to be here to comfort you. We are trying our best to take her place at this very sad time."

'I didn't say so, but I was glad.

"Would you like to sit here for a few minutes? Sister and I can leave you in peace for a short while to compose yourself."

"No, thank you, sir."

"Would you like me to send for a friend to come here to be with you at this sad time?"

"Can I go now, sir?"

"Of course you may."

'I left the room, ran to my dorm and wept into my pillow. My pillowslip was wet through when Mark found me there and did his best to console me. He lay on the bed and gently stroked my hair. It was lovely to have him snuggled up warm and close beside me. Mark instinctively knew what to do: say nothing and let the kindly warmth of his body do the talking.

'But I had to get a grip. After living only a couple of years in a boarding school, I had been taught how to behave like a man. I must hide my feelings. You can have feelings, but you must never let them show. I got up, pushed Mark to one side and went to the bathroom to wash my face. I wasn't going to let the rest of the mob see my distress. Bugger the lot of them (I had learned to swear).'"

Norris interrupted by asking Michael if he would like another coffee.

"Yes please, Norris. A cappuccino this time. And a glass of cold water. My mouth is dry with all this talking. Here's some change."

"No, that's fine. I'll pay."

Norris returned after a few minutes with two fresh coffees and a glass of water.

"The poor man didn't have it all his own way in boarding school. His mother left a great deal to be desired. How callous to inform her son remotely, by means of a telephone call to the Head, that his father had died.

"What I didn't know, Michael, until many years later was that Pops had not died in action at all. He was killed with three young passengers, all of them officers, when he crashed his car into the side of a bridge. Mother had told the Head to dress it up and make the lad think his dad was a hero – which clearly he wasn't. But to me Pops was everything then. And he still is my hero, even if he had been drunk. I found that out much later when I read the result of the inquest.'"

Norris again. "You repeat his tales awfully well, Michael. You must have spent a lot of time with Ernest."

"I did. He came to the house quite often, sometimes after a PCC meeting. We'd have a noggin of whisky sometimes, to calm ourselves down."

"Were my PCCs hard to take? I always thought they went pretty well: frank exchanges of views, though nothing ever changed as a result."

"They could be a bit hairy when those women got going."

"Oh, dear me. Can we change the subject – any more tales of the unexpected?"

"There is one more I would like to tell. What time is it?"

"Good gracious me. It's half past twelve. I should be home by now, but do continue. In for a penny. More coffee?"

"No, thank you. I should be high on caffeine if I had any more. Last tale before we go our separate ways then. Ernest told me …

'Towards the end of the war, Mark and I were at the bottom of the garden chatting when we heard the big school bell tolling four rings, then a short silence, then four more rings and so on, repeatedly. It wasn't an air raid warning. That would have been a continuous tolling until we were all safe indoors.

"We'd better go and see what the fuss is all about." We buttoned up and ran. As we approached the school buildings, we could see boys marching into the chapel, marshalled by prefects.

'Mark and I took our usual places near the back. The music master was playing a solemn melody on the organ.

"Someone else has had his chips, that's for bloody sure. Who the hell is it now?" By now I could swear like the rest of them, though there were some words I never used then and avoid using now.

'This was not the first time that the school had assembled to be told dire news from abroad.

'In the open countryside the school and its scholars had never been bothered by bombs. We'd heard news on our battery-operated valve radios and we'd been made to listen to Churchill's rousers. We'd seen the odd aeroplane fly overhead, but they were always 'ours', not 'theirs'. The war seemed remote, even uninteresting. Okay, on parade we wore Army Cadet Uniforms, we went on route marches and we'd gone to the range to shoot 22s at paper targets. Apart from sweet rationing and the terrible meals with watery cabbage and tasteless boiled parsnips, the war was somewhere else. It and we could have been on different planets.

'The music stopped and we sang a hymn with the line, "Though never more in one place all may gather, guide our endeavours, enfold us from harm."'

'It has a good tune and we sang it lustily, as if we meant it.

'Dr Waterton rose to his feet, walked solemnly to the lectern and addressed us thus:

"It is my solemn and sad duty to tell you of the heroic death of one of our noblest old boys. He was an example to us all, on the playing field and in his studies. He was a model of probity and good sense. This fine young man was a leader in his private life, here at Brotherwicks and perhaps more importantly in his service with the RAF."

"Who the hell is this model of saintly virtue?" I whispered to Mark.

"Buggered if I know," he whispered back.

"I refer of course," continued the Head, "to Pilot Officer the Hon. Hilbert Raymond Dornoway-Langhorn, only son of Lord Langhorn. We send our heartfelt condolences to Lord and Lady Langhorn at this time of sad loss – a loss we are proud to share. Let us now bow our heads and pray for this courageous young man who has left us in the prime of his honourable and exemplary life, for a life in the hereafter. He has died in service to this great country and is risen in glory to a better life with the Lord in whom we all trust. Hilbert was good enough to lend his time and his talents to this great school, which is much the poorer without him. As we kneel, let us offer up our private prayers and thank God for Hilbert's immense contribution to our individual lives. Let us pray."

"I'm off," I shouted to Mark as I noisily barged through the lads in the pew next to me and rushed out. I spewed my guts out in the doorway of the chapel, through which the whole school would later have to traipse holding their noses.

'I was given six hours detention and a week's gating for this offence during a solemn moment in the life of Brotherwicks. If only they knew.'

Michael said, "Only recently Ernest told me how he had bumped into Mark, some thirty years after they had kissed tearful goodbyes to each other when they left Brotherwicks for the last time.

"National Service had intervened without incident. They'd both spent some time in Germany; Mark had lived in Gottingen, a university town untouched by the war. Ernest was stationed outside Hamburg, which had been comprehensively flattened by the Allies. Both young men had taken the opportunity to learn the language and to run the risk of VD by living on the 'frat of the land'. Fraternization with the Huns was strictly verboten, but rules are there to be broken and who were they to stick to the rules?

"After the army, Mark, as promised, had gone to Oxford and Ernest had drifted into the theatre. They had never written or phoned each other. It was as if they had died to each other on parting. This, after they had meant so much to each other at school.

"They met again when Ernest was sitting over a coffee in the Exchange Theatre in Manchester. He was passing the time before going to see Margery in some new play or other. A man asked if he may share the coffee table …

'Of course you may.'

"After he had sat down the man suddenly tapped Ernest on the knee.

'You can't be Messy Silver, surely?'

"Nobody had called him that these past thirty years.

'I am Ernest Silver. Who are – No, you can't be … Yes, you are … Mark Rosetree. Well of all the happiest of coincidences. How lovely to see you, Mark, after all these …'

"They stood and two unembarrassed fifty-year-olds embraced each other as if the years between had never passed.

'What have you been up to all these years?' they asked each other simultaneously.

'Well, I'm Mark Rosenbaum, now. We decided to revert to our rightful name, Matthew and I. It's no longer necessary to hide the fact you are a Jew. How about you? What bushel have you been hiding under all this time?'

'Oh dear, it's a long story. In the theatre one way or another. I'm here to see my wife, Margery, in this play. Can't even remember the bloody title. I must buy a programme to find out. And you, after Oxford?'

'Good degree, teaching English, married, wife not well, three sons – eighteen, seventeen, and fifteen – living in Stroud. Hard going on a teacher's salary, even in a public school, but we manage. So your wife's an actress, then?'

'Yes, pretty good too. Goes under the name of Margery Dawe. And how about your brother Matthew? I always thought he'd do something out of the ordinary.'

'Gay. He came out shortly after he left the Navy – two years National Service. He makes a very good uncle to the boys, who adore him. Mother and Father weren't happy when he came out, but he survived, and after a struggle, so eventually did they. A follower of Peter Tatchell, by the way.'

"Just then the bell rang for the audience to take their seats in the auditorium.

'I'm in the stalls at stage level – complementary seat!'

'Lucky you. I'm in the attic." Mark shouted over his shoulder as he raced upstairs, 'See you in the bar afterwards.'

"Ernest called after him, 'Too true; I'm looking forward to a long chat!'

"But they didn't meet in the bar afterwards, there was no long chat and certainly no temptation to resume their erstwhile loving friendship, which had been severed at that emotional embrace on the last morning at Brotherwicks."

"Look at the time: one forty-five," exclaimed Norris

Both would be in hot water from their wives, and faced the unappetising prospect of cold soup and a crust of dried out bread. They hurried to their cars and drove home.

Norris and Michael, on their separate arrivals, were both greeted with the same questions, word for word, "What on earth have you been doing all this time? And did you get all the shopping you were sent for?"

Both, though separated by half a mile or so, thought it would be pointless to retell the stories they had exchanged. Would their wives be interested? Probably. Perhaps Peggy might have asked questions given the right cue, and Aileen would certainly have had something trenchant with which to top and tail the stories.

* * *

Meanwhile, in the Iverdale General the police were making a start. Mr Silver was sitting up in bed, propped up by numerous pillows and seemingly fully conscious. He had been taken from the intensive ward and now, at the police request, he had been moved to a private room where he remained under constant watch. His emergence from the coma had started slowly but had gained pace remarkably. He complained of a headache to eclipse all headaches. His speech was slow and slurred, but he was able to say to the nurse how he felt, that he knew who he was, to say he was uncomfortable and to ask where he was and why was he there.

Dr Shah was intensely interested in, not to say amazed at, the rapidity of Ernest's recovery: that was why he was there dressed for a round of golf later that afternoon. He had arrived on hearing that Mr Silver's rate of recovery had been unusually rapid. He wanted to see for himself, and to assess the man's situation vis a vis the police.

Shah spoke to the recovering patient, "Good afternoon Mr Silver, it's good to see you sitting up and taking notice. How are you feeling?"

"I have a ... stonking headache ... a few aches and ... pains here and ... there."

"Where in particular? Take your time. No hurry."

"My left ... leg hurts like I've been ... kicked by a mule."

"We can help with the pain, but I really want to know how far your recovery has come since the accident."

"What acci ... dent?"

"You had an accident and were brought here unconscious."

"What kind of accident? ... When?"

"Two days ago. You were found unconscious in your car on Thursday afternoon and you were brought here by ambulance."

"What ... day is it ... now?"

"Early Saturday afternoon."

There followed a long pause during which neither spoke.

"How long ... have I ... been here?"

"You were brought here on Thursday afternoon. That's about two days ago."

An even longer pause, in which the doctor exchanged questioning looks with Nurse Mold.

"What ... happened?"

"You're tired. I think that is enough for the time being. No more questions. I'll prescribe medication for your headache and pains in your legs."

Shah rose and said to the nurse, "See that he gets plenty of rest. If he wants to talk, try to engage him in gentle conversation. That should help to speed up his recovery."

As he left, he remarked that there was a surprising gain in awareness in his patient, far better than he had expected or even hoped for.

When he closed the door behind him Shah told the PC on duty to report to his superiors that the patient was recovering and was almost well enough to be interviewed, possibly the next day, but no earlier.

The PC rang in to tell DI Worth the good news.

Worth rubbed his hands with what amounted to glee, and told the PC that the 24/7 duty watch must continue, and that nobody other than authorised medical staff may visit or speak to him.

"And that Hirst woman must be kept away!"

He pointed out to PC Harris that no matter how pleased they were with his progress, it was still up to the medics to say when they could talk to the man.

"We can't barge in just because we want to. I think I'll send DC Fairweather to talk to him in hospital, as a potential witness. She'll treat him gently. No point in rushing like a bull at a gate. See what he has to say. No pressure on him at first. But he'll have to agree to put himself forward as a witness. We can't go in with guns blazing until he first volunteers to act as witness. I'll have a word with the hospital and see if they can get him to say he knows something.

"If it comes to arresting him, we'll take him to the police station in Shepley. We have enough evidence for Mr Silver to be arrested and charged, at the very least with child abduction. It wouldn't take long for us to get that far. He'll ask for bail and that means going before the magistrates. They don't sit 'til Monday so we'll get things going on Monday. If bail is granted, and that's highly likely, he'll be sent home.

"God help him when the word gets out that Silver's back at home. We'll have to keep a look out for trouble."

BOOK THREE

THE END OF
THE BEGINNING AND
THE BEGINNING OF THE END

CHAPTER 32

TELL IT ON A SUNDAY

It was Sunday morning, October 17th, in the Iverdale General. Breakfast had been served at the usual unearthly hour. Ablutions completed and teeth brushed, Ernest was sitting on the chair by the window when Dr Shah entered on his morning rounds. He was accompanied by Sister Wakefield.

"Mr Silver has had a good night, Doctor, and has eaten all his porridge and a light cooked breakfast," she said. "Temperature only slightly elevated. He's made a remarkable recovery."

"You have indeed, Mr Silver," Doctor Shah said. "How's the head ache this morning?"

"Thumping away, but bearable. The paracetamol seems to be doing the trick, thank you."

"I am glad to see you continuing to improve. I can tell you that you have recovered remarkably. There must be something strong in your overall constitution that you have done so well. Now I must tell you that the police are making a thorough investigation about the day you were found unconscious in your car.

"A schoolgirl has disappeared recently and it is feared that she may have been swept into the river and must be presumed drowned. The police believe you might be able to shed some light on the circumstances of her disappearance. I consider you are well enough for us to let the police interview you. The officer is here. Her name is DC Fairweather. However, I can only agree to let her talk to you if you feel up to it yourself. If you would like more time, I could ask them to delay questioning you for another twenty-four hours. I believe you are fit enough to cope now, but it is up to you."

"I think I can manage. I still have a terrible headache, though. I hope they won't be long. Who is the missing girl?"

"I think it is for DC Fairweather to tell you what they know. She will fill you in with the details. Shall I ask her to come in?"

"Please do."

DC Robin Fairweather entered and introduced herself.

"I'd like you to answer just a few questions. It won't take long."

"I hope not. I still feel a bit groggy."

"First, please confirm your name and home address."

He did so.

"It seems a hundred years since I last set foot in my house."

"Thank you, Mr Silver. You were found in your car in a steep gulley in the middle of the North Yorkshire moors. There is a famous hill known as Long Harry. Do you know it?"

"I've certainly heard of it and maybe I have driven that way once or twice."

"It was near the summit of Long Harry that your car was found with you in it. You appeared to have only minor injuries but you were unconscious and suffering from exposure and hypothermia."

"Was I really?"

"The car was largely undamaged, apart from a few scratches and dents in the bodywork. Can you explain why you were there so far from your home in Holsterdale?"

"I'm sorry, I really can't explain it."

"No idea at all?"

"Truly, none."

"I see. Nobody else might have driven you there."

"Nobody else is licensed to drive my car. No."

"So you must have driven it yourself?"

"Yes, I suppose I—"

"Yet you don't recollect how you got there? A car doesn't drive itself, does it?"

"Of course not. What a question."

"So you say you really don't know how you got there? Did you stop anywhere on the way?"

"I don't know. I'm sorry, my mind is so confused. I really don't know."

"All right, we'll leave that for the moment. Now, can you remember why you set out in your car in that filthy weather?"

"Oh, yes. I wanted to drive up to the Holst Falls to see the waterfall in flood. It can be very exciting."

"What time would that have been?"

"Well, it had stopped raining when I set out, but—"

"No need to be precise – roughly?"

"I should think about half-five, give or take."

"Thank you. Now for a more serious matter. We are investigating the disappearance of a young girl who vanished on that same afternoon. It was Wednesday, October 13th. Would you tell me all you can remember about what you did that afternoon?"

"As you say, it had been raining heavily. I spent most of the early afternoon reading. After a cup of tea, and when the rain eased off, I thought I'd drive up to have a look at the Holst Falls which, as I said just now, can be spectacular in flood conditions."

"Did you drive there straight away?"

"Yes, more or less."

"You said a moment ago this would be about half-five."

"I'm not sure. I think about fiveish."

"Did you stop anywhere on the way?"

"I can't remember. I'm a bit confused, that's all."

"Understandable. No hurry. Some children say they saw your car stop near the green where they were playing football."

"Do they?"

"Did you stop on the way to the waterfall?"

"Let me think – oh yes, I may have stopped to watch the kids with their ball; I was a bit worried that they were perhaps playing too near the river, which, as you well know, was in serious flood."

"Did you know any of these children?"

"Some of the younger ones, I go into their primary school – St Mary's, that is – to help with their reading programme. I also tell them stories."

"Do you know any of them by name?"

"Most of them, in Reception certainly, and I have kept in touch with some as they have grown older."

"Do you know Laura Hirst?"

"Yes, I certainly do; lovely intelligent girl. But don't tell me she is the girl you are looking for?"

"Yes, we are. She didn't come home for tea after school as she usually does, and she has not been seen since."

Ernest burst into a flood of tears. "Oh dear, oh dear, oh dear," he sobbed. "Poor Harry. Poor Maureen."

"It seems you know the family well, then. Do you?"

"I do … Yes, indeed I do. I have helped to look after Laura since she was a two-year-old."

"How well do you know them?"

"Please, do you mind? This is so distressing. I'm sorry, I can't help. … Oh dear. … Where's my handkerchief? I'm sorry, I'll be all right in a tick."

He took a moment to wipe his eyes, blow his nose, and then he made an effort to compose himself.

"I'm sorry, I lost it. Can I have a drink of water? My mouth has suddenly gone dry. Wet eyes and dry mouth – silly isn't it?"

There was a bottle of water on the bedside table. Fairweather poured some into a plastic mug and passed it to him. He drank it thirstily.

"I asked you how well you know Mr and Mrs Hirst and their daughter."

"Very well. Very well indeed. I frequently babysit – well, Laura is no longer a baby, but you know what I mean. I met them through church when I retired here a few years ago. Maureen cleans for me every week. Very helpful and thorough she is, too. We have become very good friends. They usually cook me a delicious meal when I go to look after Laura and we eat together."

"Did you see Laura amongst the kids playing football that afternoon?"

"I'm not sure. It was rather foggy as I recall. She would likely be there larking about with the boys – she is quite a tomboy."

"You're certain about that? That you didn't actually spot her with the lads."

"I said I wasn't sure. I don't recollect seeing her."

"One of the boys has told us he thought he saw her go to your car."

"Who said so? Which boy was that?"

"One of the boys."

"He must have been mistaken."

"In fact, he said he saw her by your car."

"Did he now? I wonder which little liar it was."

"You're sure she didn't go to your car and get in."

There was a long silence, then she repeated the question.

"I'm sorry, I have a terrible headache. Can we stop now?"

"One last question: did Laura Hirst get into your car that afternoon? Did she, or did she not?"

"I don't remember. I can't remember."

"Did she?"

"No!"

"Thank you, Mr Silver. That will be all for now. You have been very helpful and we appreciate it. I am glad the doctors are pleased with your progress. Some people hardly recover from a heavy blow to the head. We may need to ask you further questions, but I think that's all for now. Goodbye, Mr Silver."

DC Fairweather escorted him back to his room, handed him over to the PC on duty and departed. Ernest shrugged off his borrowed dressing gown, lay on the bed, turned on his side, buried his head in his pillow and wept.

CHAPTER 33

SHADOWS ON THE ROAD AHEAD

It was now Sunday on October 17th late afternoon. Evensong, poorly attended as usual, was over. *Thank the Lord*, thought the rector as he plodded his weary way home. The only saving grace was that it was at last fine and the setting sun cast long dark shadows on the road ahead. There were other, less romantic, shadows looming on the rector's horizon, one of which was the reception Aileen was bound to be preparing for him.

Aileen was developing a bad cold and didn't go to evensong. Had it been a proper evensong she might have risked going, well wrapped up of course: but evensong was one of Norris's concoctions of which she did not approve.

She was waiting, ready to pounce, with a cup of tea for him. "How did it go, darling?"

"Dreadful. I one-fingered my way through the hymns and we said the psalm and canticles. I might as well not have bothered. Hardly anyone was there to listen or even to take part."

"Why not? The weather has cleared up. No reason to stay away on the rain's account. You're later than usual. Where's the delay?"

"Ernest's had been detained by the police. Rumours are rife that he's—"

"Oh dear. Poor man. What can that be about?"

"Please, no more speculations. I'm fed up with it. Gladys and

Moira from the choir came to me afterwards and told me in no uncertain terms that children should not be in the choir, not anymore. I asked them why not and they simply said, 'what do you think?'"

"And what do you think?"

"That Ernest had an unhappy life until he came here and that at last he has found peace with himself."

"At peace with himself?"

"And with God. I take some credit for helping him on the road to salvation."

"That's a bit much, Norris."

"No, I truly do. At the very least I believe he has found true friendship and I honestly know he has made a creative difference here in this small town. He is welcomed with a smile almost everywhere, has a good word to say about everyone. Look how he has enjoyed the company of that odd couple Jacob Smith and Leslie Pickles, and Michael and Peggy MacDonald. He's often seen at the Hepworths and he gets on well at the Bowling Club. I'm not going to rake over the coals of the Hirsts with you. I know what you think and we disagree profoundly on that, but you have to agree that he's well met across the board. He is greeted nicely at the Co-op and he always chats with the men and women at the till, without pride or prejudice."

"Talking to tradesmen politely isn't exactly a token of joy, Norris. Being polite to them is one way of getting what you want out of them. Politeness from them comes from training. It is not a badge of friendship. It may be simply that his earlier life by contrast was not as good as this one. You've told me of his school days. Terrible, but life isn't necessarily everlastingly coloured by that. Most people simply forget what they did at school. I know I have done. What about his, shall we say, years ante-Holsterdale?"

"Tinged with sadness certainly. His daughter was killed by

a suicide, which devastated his wife. Then she died of breast cancer because detection came too late."

"More than just tinged with sadness, I think, darling. Why have we been so lucky? We're still together."

"Yes, we are, but three sons, two divorced and the third unmarried living with his boyfriend – none of them church goers. You call that luck?"

"Happily, they still come to see us, darling."

"When they think about it. Yes, they do, and I still love them dearly even at a distance."

"So what's going to happen to Ernest?"

"Darling, I'm afraid that's anyone's guess. I really don't want to think about it ... I wonder if a prayer might help?"

"It's worth a try, Norris. Can't do any harm. Might even do some good."

"Very well, then. Shall we kneel?

"Defend him, O Lord, with thy heavenly grace ..."

CHAPTER 34

EARLY ONE MORNING
– AND AFTERNOON

Transcript of interview with Ernest Silver relating to the disappearance of Laura Hirst.

Interview conducted by DS Watson and PC Harris
Monday 18th October. 09.16 hours.
DS Watson: Good morning, Mr Silver.
This is an interview in a boardroom at the Iverdale General Hospital with Mr Martin Ernest Silver, conducted by me, Det. Sergeant Watson, and PC Harris. Today's date is Monday, October 18th and the time is 09.16 hours. Please answer all questions as fully and truthfully as you can.
First, would you please confirm that your full name is Martin Ernest Silver. Is that correct?
Silver: Yes.
DS Watson: And your address is 31 South Street, Holsterdale, North Yorkshire. Is that also correct?
Silver: It is.
DS Watson: Before we continue, we would like to clarify that we are asking you questions on events that took place on the day of the flood, Wednesday, October 13th. You have agreed to be questioned as a witness. Is that correct – that you, as it were, came forward to continue as a witness?
Silver: That is true, yes.

DS Watson: Thank you, Mr Silver. We'd like to ask you some questions relating to the flooding of the River Holst. Do you recollect that day?

Silver: Yes.

DS Watson: You will also recollect that yesterday morning DC Fairweather spoke to you in hospital as a potential witness to the disappearance of Laura Hirst on the day of the storm, that is, on Wednesday, October 13th.

Silver: You don't need to continue repeating the day and date. But yes. I do indeed. I am very sad to hear that Laura is missing. Do you realise how precious she is to me?

DS Watson: A young lad in the village has told us he saw Laura approach your car, which was parked overlooking the green where children were kicking a ball about. You thought he must be mistaken. Is that correct?

Silver: Yes, I did say that.

DS Watson: He has also said he thinks she might have got into your car. You denied it. Have you anything further to say about that?

Silver: No, that's how it was. That is, she didn't get into my car.

DS Watson: But did she come over to your car?

Silver: Er ...

DS Watson: She did come over to your car, didn't she?

Silver: Er ...

DS Watson: But she didn't get in?

Silver: I'm not sure.

DS Watson: She did not get into your car, is that right?

Silver: Yes. ... I mean no. No, she didn't get in.

DS Watson: So you did see her on that afternoon, didn't you?

Silver: Yes, I must have. Yes, it's becoming clearer now. Yes, I did speak to her.

DS Watson: What did you say to her?

Silver: Maybe it was something like, 'Isn't it time for your tea?'

DS Watson: Was that all you said to her?

Silver: There was no time to say anything else. She ran off home.

DS Watson: This boy says she might have got into your car. He didn't say anything about her running home.

Silver: Really? I wonder why not.

DS Watson: The boy's name is Charlie Nattrass. Do you know him?

Silver: I have taught him. He is simple. Do you know that? Do you trust the word of a boy who can't read or write his name?

DS Watson: Out of the mouths of babes, Mr Silver. Do you recognise the quotation? It's from the bible, Mr Silver.

Silver: I do.

DS Watson: Did you offer to drive Laura Hirst home, to give her a lift perhaps?

Silver: What would be the point of that? She was not all that far from her home, she knows the town better than I do and she's a good strong lass. I'd have had no worries about her getting home safely, okay?

DS Watson: Let's leave that for a moment. What did you do then?

Silver: I drove up to the Holst Falls, as I said when I spoke to Fairweather.

DS Watson: And Laura Hirst was not with you in the car?

Silver: No. As I said, she had gone home for her tea. It was her teatime, after all.

DS Watson: Mr Silver, there are some things that just don't add up. Let me change the subject for a moment. Mr Silver, you were found in your car in a deep gulley near the top of Long Harry. Why were you there?

Silver: I'm sorry, I have a dreadful headache. Does it matter why I was there?

DS Watson: Perhaps not, but it does matter that we found a pair of Laura Hirst's knickers in your coat pocket.

Silver: Ah, I can easily explain that. As you may know, I regularly sit in with Laura at the Hirsts when they go to the gym or jogging or whatever. Laura, at one time, had a bit of a problem with what she called 'having an accident' so I often carried a spare pair of pants, just in case.

DS Watson: *Have you a similar reason for carrying one of her school shoes in your pocket?*

Silver: *Are you saying you found one of Laura Hirst's shoes in my pocket?*

DS Watson: *I am, yes. In the pocket of your overcoat.*

Silver: *That doesn't suggest that she was in my car, surely, does it?*

DS Watson: *What do you think?*

Silver: *May I have a moment to think?*

DS Watson: *Take your time.*

Silver: *Thank you.*

Silence.

Silver: *I have had time to think and I believe I may have got it wrong. Laura did get into my car.*

DS Watson: *At the top of the green?*

Silver: *Yes, at the top of the green.*

DS Watson: *So you were lying when you said she didn't get into your car, yes?*

Silver: *I had forgotten. Remember, I have been severely injured with a blow to the head, so the doctors tell me. Do you expect me to be clear about every detail of what happened four (or is it five?) days ago?*

DS Watson: *It was a simple enough question.*

Silver: *I know.*

DS Watston: *So the young Charlie Nattrass, simple Charlie, was right, was he, when he said he thought Laura Hirst might have got into your car?*

Silver: *Yes.*

DS Watson: *Before we go any further, Mr Ernest Silver, I am arresting you on supsicion of child abduction. You do not have to say anything, but it may harm your defence if you do not*

Early One Morning – And Afternoon

mention when questioned something which you later rely on in court. Anything you do say may be given in evidence.

Silver: I see. Oh dear. What do I do now?

DS Watson: I am terminating this interview. The time is now 10.01 hours. You will be taken to the Shepley Police Station where you will be formally charged and questioned under oath. That is all. Take him away and hand him into the custody of the duty sergeant.

Interview terminated.

* * *

Transcript of interview with Ernest Silver, arrested on suspicion of child abduction.

Interview conducted by DI Worth, DS Watson and PC Harris
  Monday 18th October. 11.07 hours.

 DI Worth: This interview is conducted by myself, DI Worth with Det. Sergeant Watson in attendance. PC Harris is making a recording of all that is said and done during the interview, and is operating the timer. The interview is with Mr Martin Ernest Silver of 31 South Street, Holsterdale, who is charged with abduction of a minor.

Today's date is Monday, October 18th and the time is 11.07 hours. It is noted that Mr Silver has declined the presence and services of a solicitor. Is that correct, Mr Silver?

Silver: Yes. I can't think how he could help.

DI Worth: So you're happy that we continue questioning you in the absence of your lawyer?

Silver: Not exactly happy but, yes, go ahead.

DI Worth: Very good then. To proceed, where were you intending to go in your car on that stormy day, from the top of the green?

Silver: To look at the Horst Falls.

DI Worth: Did you go to the Horst Falls with Laura Hirst in your car?

Silver: I didn't want to. The wind was very fierce and the heavy rain made driving very hard.

DI Worth: So you didn't go to see the Horst Falls? Then perhaps you drove to Long Harry instead, yes?

Silver: No.

DI Worth: No? You didn't drive to Long Harry? So where did you go with eight-year-old Laura Hirst in your car?

Silver: I drove up to the Horst Falls. I didn't want to. The weather was foul and driving nigh on impossible and my arms hurt with the effort.

DI Worth: Yet you did go. Why did you drive to the Horst Falls, Mr Silver, with Laura Hirst in your car?

Silver: She persuaded me.

DI Worth: Mr Silver, you're asking me to believe that an eight-year-old slip of a girl twisted you round her finger and made you drive on, against your better judgement?

Silver: Yes, that's how it was.

DI Worth: Mr Silver, you're an educated man, a well-respected man in the community, yet you truly want me to believe that this young girl was able to persuade you? What happened when you got there?

Silver: We stopped for a pee and she ran ahead. I couldn't catch her and ... I tried to stop her ... but ... she was ... faster than I ... I'm sorry ... I can't go on...

DI Worth: You have already been read your rights. Do you understand them?

Silver: I do.

DI Worth: I am formally charging you with abduction of a minor in the person of Miss Laura Hirst. There may be further charges pending further enquiries. You may apply for bail.

Silver: I wish to do that. How do I go about it?"

Early One Morning – And Afternoon

DI Worth: We'll put you before the magistrates this afternoon, first on their agenda. The sitting begins at 2.15pm. If you wish, you can apply to the magistrates for release on bail and it will be granted or denied based on the evidence put before them. Have a good story ready. You may have a lawyer present at the hearing. He or she can plead for you.

Silver: I understand. Thank you.

DI Worth: The interview is suspended at 11.54 hours. Hand Mr Silver back into the custody of the duty sergeant, Harris.

Interview terminated.

Ernest Silver was taken into the cells.

* * *

The magistrates sat in the courthouse in Shepley. On that afternoon, the first item on their agenda was to hear a claim for bail from Mr Ernest Silver of 31 South Street, Holsterdale. The charge of abduction of a minor was read out. Ernest was still wearing the track suit bottoms and fleece borrowed from the hospital. Speaking from the dock for himself, he formally applied to be released on bail.

The police were asked if they had any objections. Their reply was to say that they believed he was very unlikely to abscond, and they deemed that he would be not liable to repeat the offence whilst at home. They did not consider him a suicide risk.

Ernest said that he would sincerely promise to be on best behaviour while at home. He also added that he greatly regretted the distress he might have unwittingly caused to his friends, especially to Mr and Mrs Hirst, who he regarded as his best friends in Holsterdale.

He was asked to report to the police station in Shepley once a week, on Monday mornings, until the time of his trial. He would be informed of the date of the trial which would be, in the first instance, in front of magistrates but might be transferred to a higher court. He was advised by the bench that in his own interests he really should engage the services of a lawyer.

Ernest thanked the magistrates for this advice and said that he would consider it.

He was granted bail on his own assurances for the figure of ten thousand pounds. He was thereafter released and told he was allowed to return to his home.

He was then taken to the police station where the police returned to him his wallet and keys.

It was later that afternoon that he ordered a taxi and was driven home. He decided to sit low on the back seat of the taxi when they reached Holsterdale to avoid being seen.

There was thankfully no-one about when he let himself into his house. It was just short of half past five in the afternoon.

CHAPTER 35

THE EVENING AND THE MORNING WERE THE CURSED DAY

By early evening on Monday, 18th October, Silver's arrest and abduction charges were public knowledge. News gets around fast in a small town like Holsterdale.

Maureen and Harry had not stirred all day, and now they sat at the table, knowing they should eat but neither of them could stomach the idea of food. Laura would not be coming home.

They had known in their hearts that she must be eternally lost but had had held out hope right up to the knock on the door. The look on the face of the policewoman who had come to help break the news of Ernest's arrest was enough to tell them. No words needed to be uttered.

They were kind, and supportive, but Harry and Maureen had just wanted to be left alone with their grief and the knowledge that the friend they had trusted had taken away their precious daughter.

And now another knock on the door and in burst Tom Nattrass.

"'Ave you 'eard? 'E's 'ome! They've let 'im out on bail!"

Harry couldn't believe what he was hearing.

"'E can't be. They can't 'ave let 'im out!"

Maureen let out a banshee howl that cut Harry to the core.

Tears and howling screams poured out of her as she raced out of the house, not bothering with her coat as she rushed out into the night.

Harry shouted, "I'm after 'er. God alone knows what she'll do." Harry had never before seen or heard anything remotely like this ear-piercing shriek from her.

Windows and doors were flung open as she charged along Water Street and turned left into South Street. She was instantly followed by a curious mob. Here was an angry dragon with fire in its mouth.

When she reached 31, she grabbed a heavy stone from the rockery and hurled it with all the strength in her body, smashing the window of the sitting room where she knew the vile and duplicitous monster would be sitting.

She bawled through angry tears, "I 'ate you Ernest Silver. I 'ate you. You drownded my precious girl and I 'ate you. I 'ate you. I nivver want to see you again. Nivver. Do you 'ear me, Ernest Silver?"

Harry had caught up with her, and he was in time to catch her in his arms when she collapsed. All the strength in her had drained away after that outburst of violent anger and extreme distress. He half-carried her home through the noisy crowd, which had thronged to see the most historical event in their lives. Their cries echoed after them.

"I told you so!"
"Silver's a pervert, always was!"
"I never trusted 'im."
"Butter would melt."
"Smarmy bugger!"
"Paedo! Paedo! Paedo!"
"Murderer!"
"Grab 'im!"
"String' im up!"
Many better chosen epithets mingled with the boos and jeers.

The Evening And The Morning Were The Cursed Day

Ernest was in his favourite chair in the sitting room, still dressed in borrowed hospital gear when the rock hurtled through the shattered window. He was showered with shards of glass. The boulder landed on his feet, crushing the toes of his left foot. He heard the angry abuse and its sound crushed his spirit. Physically and mentally he was destroyed. There was nothing he could do, no explanation he could offer. He had never felt such cruelty, such enmity, such vile abuse. Half-fainting, he sank back.

About twenty freezing-cold minutes later, his backdoor bell rang. He tried to hobble to the door but the pain in his foot was excruciating and stopped him in his tracks.

A few minutes later, a voice shouted through his broken window, "Are you all right, Mr Silver?"

Ernest tried to answer but his voice didn't carry.

"I'll have to get in, sir. I need to speak to you."

Again the doorbell rang repeatedly and this time Ernest managed to drag himself on his knees to the kitchen door.

"I need to speak to you. Sit down, sir, please." It was PC Harris who had entered.

"Go ahead, Constable."

"We've seen the damage done to your property and we've arrested Mrs Maureen Hirst on a charge of criminal damage."

"Are you talking about my sitting room window?"

"Yes, sir, I am."

"I don't want Maureen prosecuted, Constable. Where is she now?"

"She's in custody, sir."

"She must be released, now. Do you hear, Constable?"

"But we have witnesses who saw her throw—"

"No, the window had been damaged by the recent gales and it just gave in."

"But we have witnesses, lots of them, who will readily testify that they saw—"

"I don't care how many witnesses you have ... and I refuse to listen ... to what they have to say. I don't want to know what they ... think they saw. I will NOT have Maureen Hirst prosecuted ... for damage ... caused by ... the wind. She and I are very good ... friends and it's not in her nature ... to do such a thing ... to me. She is my very dearest friend."

"Very well, sir, if you insist."

"I do insist, emphatically. See to it that lovely Maureen ... is released immediately."

"Sir, but what about the window? It'll need to be boarded up."

"I'll see to it in the morning. Now leave me, please." As the door closed behind PC Harris, Ernest sank back in the chair. He felt numb. How had he come to this? He closed his eyes and recalled the early days of his warm friendship with the Hirsts and the innocent love of their daughter.

Ernest fell into a deeper and deeper sleep, chilled in both mind and body. He saw his lovely Laura once again; vibrant and excited, urging him to drive closer and closer to the surging water.

* * *

Michael MacDonald had heard the commotion during the evening, and he'd heard of the charges Ernest was going to have to answer. The following morning, after he had breakfasted, he told Peggy he must call round to comfort his troubled friend.

The back door of No. 31 was not locked. It was unusual for security-conscious Ernest to leave a door unlocked. He went in. His friend was slumped on a kitchen chair. It was immediately clear that Ernest was dead. No pulse, nothing. And no wonder – the house might have been in the chill northern wastes with a cruel wind gusting through it, direct from the Urals.

Ernest was half-sitting, half-lying on the same chair he had sat on when PC Harris had called round last night.

The Evening And The Morning Were The Cursed Day

Ernest had not stirred.
Violated, he had died alone, icily cold.

CHAPTER 36

A TIME TO PEE AND A TIME TO CRY

Ernest struggled against the elements up the hill towards the old bridge – he dismissed the possibility of crossing into the picnic field today. Laura was excited to sit and thrill. She said, "Uncle Ernest, can I drive the car?"

"What on earth do you think I am? Dotty or potty? It's far too hard for me to drive. You silly girl, even to ask. Can't you see what hard work it is for me?"

"I could sit between your knees, like I did with Dad. Dad really had been steering but I sat on the seat between his legs and I reckoned to drive."

Harry had indeed sat her between his knees in the picnic field that time and let her pretend. But that was then, and in the field, and in the summer – and this was now, and on the road, and in a storm.

"No fear! Not in this weather!"

"Dad did that summer," she persisted.

"That was in a field, not on a public highway. A policeman would be very cross if he saw us do that, here, today. You really are the last word in idiocy."

"I'm not an idiot. How dare you call me that? *Well, me could sit on your knee and betend?*"

It was her use of baby language that made him waver.

"You're being persuasive again," he said, half-laughing.

A Time To Pee And A Time To Cry

"I know. Can I? Can I PLEASE?"

Stupidly and reluctantly he relented. He stopped the car for safety. "Come on then. Careful, now. Steady on." He made space between his legs where she could comfortably sit.

Laura climbed onto his legs, shuffled down comfortably between his knees and held on to the steering wheel. Ernest's hands wrapped round hers. He loved the feel of her firm, innocent and trusting hands under his; enfolding them like this was worth more than a bedtime cuddle. In spite of the increased effort he needed to cope with the elements. They struggled on in silent concentration. Battling with the elemental forces of nature caused him additional excitement and stress. He knew how foolish he had been, even how dangerous it was to drive like this with the rain bucketing down and a hurricane buffeting the car. He had to hold on tight with an unaccustomed firm grip to keep the car in the centre of the road which, yard by yard, was getting steeper. But nothing could undo his frantic delight in his daring. Surely there must be a guardian angel hovering above them, protecting Laura. So long as he was with her, they would both be safe; he knew it.

Mountaineers have written about an extra presence at their sides in moments of crisis, so for him this must have been his severest rock face, his crucial crisis. He understood what rock climbers' critical experiences were like. He was, and always had been, a confident driver. No harm could have possibly come from what had turned out to be a risky and dangerous adventure. He had never been excited like this before, but he knew that they both were safe in hands more powerful than his alone. Her head rested on his chest. His delight was redoubled by her confidence and trust. In a strange way he relaxed. Ernest had been fighting frantically to keep the car on the road. His headlights hardly lit the way, and the windscreen wipers had almost given up the ghost. Great concentration and physical strength were needed to be safe. He had plenty of the former, much less of the latter, so his arms were in agony and ached fiercely.

"Uncle Ernest, I need a wee."

His concentration was broken with a start.

"So do I. We'll stop in the next wide bit and we'll see what we can do about that." What a relief that he could at last have a rest, and a reason for resting, from this energy sapping torment. He drew into a gateway handily sheltered under a large tree – probably a beech, but this wasn't a time for arboreal speculation.

"Can you manage going to the toilet on the grass?"

"Course I can." Before getting out of the car, Laura kicked off her shoes and socks. "I can manage. But don't look." She pulled off her knickers.

"What did you do that for?" he exclaimed in alarm.

"Because last time I did it, I weed on my pants and shoes and 'ad to take them off anyway."

With that she opened the door, assisted not a little by a fierce gust which roughly yanked the door open and pulled her out. She chased out of sight and squatted.

"And you're not supposed to be watching," she shouted over the roar of the wind. Rain drenched her as she did what was necessary.

"I'm not watching, my sweet thing." Ernest himself disappeared behind the car and a convenient bush to do as nature intended and relieved himself. He thought about his mobile and opened the car door to retrieve it. *Better signal out of the car than in it*, he thought.

The mobile wasn't on the dashboard where he'd thrown it; in groping on the floor for it, he came upon Laura's knickers. He rammed them into his coat pocket.

"We'd better turn round and go back," he bellowed. "They'll be worried if you're not back in time for tea. Especially in this weather."

She shouted back, "But we're nearly there. I'm going on!" She was already halfway up the steep road and over onto the grass. Her tough little feet were barefoot.

Ernest hollered, "No, Laura, I'm sorry. We must go back." Either she didn't hear or she ignored him.

She shouted back, "I'm going on by myself."

This outlandish action shook Ernest to the core. He'd experienced her extravagant ideas and behaviour before, but nothing equalled this excessive wilfulness. Why would she take such thoughtless action? He had to chase after her. His running days had been over years ago, but he couldn't let her loose like this. Extreme measures summon extreme exertion, and with a strength he didn't know he possessed he grabbed her shoes before racing after her. He had to catch her before she reached the top of the hill with only the river beyond. Laura was already halfway up the slope. He had to stop her before—

He slipped and stumbled on the wet grass, gashing his knee when he tripped on a rocky knuckle. She was faster than he; she was out of sight when, breathing heavily, his heart a steam engine pumping furiously, he reached the top. Before him and about a couple of hundred yards upstream was the waterfall, magnificent and powerful. Below him, brown and hungry, flood water raced through a narrow and deep stone-lined gully downstream. The racing water almost submerged the ancient stone bridge. The flood's appearance was unexpectedly smooth with an oily flow. It was eerily quiet. He was astounded. He anxiously scanned this violent scene for Laura, but the rain battered his eyes and he didn't see her. Then she appeared below him as if from nowhere, running towards the water's edge with her coat wide open and her arms outstretched in imitation of Ali the albatross.

Surely not. It appeared to him that she was attempting to join in, to embrace the huge energy of the water, the fierceness of the wind and the downpour. No ordinary kid would do such a wild thing. Most children of her age would indeed be scared by the sheer ferocity of wind and water, but Laura was no ordinary child.

Ernest deeply adored Laura, but he now realised he had no idea what went on in her head at all, not now and, for that matter, not ever. At this moment he certainly knew that he truly did not know Laura at all. That he had never actually known her. This awful truth terrified him.

He hollered again but the wind carried his voice away; she either didn't hear or didn't want to. Was this strange young animal scooping up the magnificence of this monstrous scene and inhaling its intensity into her very soul? It was fanciful but what else could he think? She was possessed.

"Come back," he roared. "It isn't safe!"

She didn't budge; she was ecstatic.

Ernest slipped, slithered and tumbled down the steep slope in a desperate attempt to reach her and pull her back to safety. How his elderly legs had the resources to do this he had no idea, but a strange superhuman energy enfolded him. He sprawled headlong, careless of his own safety, thinking only of hers.

He could see upstream that a colossal tree in full leaf had been torn and uprooted from the earth and now careened downwards towards the waterfall. It loomed over the top of the cataract. Its submerged branches must have snagged against rocks: for a moment it hung motionless, a vast threatening gorgon. Then its massive trunk reared up into the air, poised for a moment, writhing into the leaden and storm-tossed sky.

Ernest's stomach turned to stone. Sprawled almost full length on the slippery turf he reached for Laura and grasped her ankle. He held on to it with grim determination. He would not let her go, come hell or high water. Holding on demanded more than he had strength to summon, yet summon it he did as the almighty events unfolded around him. He could not cry; he could not breathe; he could not shout; he could not even pray but he could and did hang on, all his strength devoted to clinging onto the most precious person in all the world.

He would not let go … yet it was more than even superhuman strength could muster. His heart, in contradiction, was both frozen and yet beating so rapidly he could feel its violent pulse caused by this awesome and elemental happening. His world was threatened and was disappearing as he grimly comprehended this dreadful situation.

The flood's pressure was too great, and with an elemental groan this huge tree plunged over the cataract with an enormous crash. Huge torn hunks of timber were flung carelessly into the air like matchsticks amidst a confusion of tattered leaves and fractured branches. Caught again by the current, the shattered remnants of the giant colossus sped towards the gully which consumed it, a gigantic mincing machine. A stray branch, a monstrous praying mantis, reared up out of the chaos and casually scooped Laura from Ernest's grasp. It flung her high into the dark sky, then down into the crushing tumult, where she was instantly consumed into that hideous brown water.

He prayed that her clothes might have caught on a branch and pulled her to safety; he prayed that she be flung clear onto the river bank.

The hideously damaged tree had casually murdered this most precious mortal and, not conscious of its fatal participation, it raced on until its vast trunk wedged against the old bridge. Instantly it formed an impenetrable dam. The pressure of the water and the momentum of the tree were more than the old bridge could withstand. Its ancient stones, weakened by this night's constant battering, could stand no longer and in a blink this historic landmark was shattered, its ancient stones scattered on the flood.

It was all over. Ernest was stunned with agonised disbelief. His darling had hideously been dragged from him into the maelstrom. Or could she be safe? Was she miraculously saved somewhere below? He knew in his broken heart that these questions had only one, inevitable answer: no.

The old bridge that had stood the test of centuries was shattered, its remnants forming gravestones over his beloved Laura's resting place. Its stones tumbled along, borne by a tidal wave that flooded down the valley.

CHAPTER 37

WHERE THERE'S A WILL, THERE'S A THRILL

It was the day after Michael had discovered Ernest. As soon as Michael got home, he rang Jacob to tell him the sad news. It was Leslie who answered the call. Jacob was in a field near the old bridge, mending a wall that had collapsed during the flood. Thankfully, Leslie was at home nursing a sore knee. Had he not been there, Michael, not having a mobile phone, would have had to wait until the evening to make contact. Les rang Jacob on his mobile and told him the news. Jacob said he would finish the immediate job and then return home early.

It had been about four o'clock when the two executors had a chance to talk about what to do next. It was therefore over the phone that this meeting with DSS had been arranged.

The colonel and Jacob Smith decided to meet at the offices of DSS. Both, with a laugh, agreed over the phone that the Department of Social Services was a strange place to find and read Ernest's will. Luckily, Ernest had told Michael that his will was deposited in the DSS vaults, and that DSS was the name of a firm of solicitors in Shepley.

The high-street premises that this ill-matched couple found themselves sitting in were briskly up-to-date, boasting colourful and expensive furnishings with a Scandinavian taste, miles out of reach of the economies afforded by IKEA.

The elegant lady manning the front desk asked them to sit. Mr Donne would be with them in a moment.

"Not what I'd expected, this fancy stuff," said Jacob.

"Indeed. Very, what shall I say? I don't know what to say but it is –shall we say, very..."

"Good morning, gentlemen. I am Wilfrid Donne. My receptionist tells me you have come to read Mr Silver's will. We have it to hand." The handshake was effusive, soft, and powdery to the touch. "Do come in to our interview suite."

Donne opened a large file crammed with papers, sitting on top of which was the will.

"How well did you know Mr Silver? You're not relatives, I take it?"

"No. Not related at all. As the saying goes, just good friends."

"Oh aye, we was pals, like."

"I see. Yes, well, I had had no dealings with Mr Silver before he called in only a few weeks ago asking us to help with his will. I took it on, and arranged an appointment with him two days later. On that occasion, before we started the actual writing of the document, we had a long productive conversation. A very long conversation indeed over innumerable cups of coffee. I was quite heady with caffeine by the time we finished that day."

"Spill t' beans, then."

"In your own time, Mr Donne. We're in no hurry," added the Colonel.

"Right. Here goes. I asked Mr Silver about his family. None, was his reply. He told me his only daughter had been killed in a tragic accident and that his wife had died some years later, cancer I think he said. I asked if he had cousins, and his answer was unusual. I think you'd like to hear what he had to say. Shall I go on?"

"Do. I'm curious. I've had many long conversations with him since we got to know each other six or seven years ago, but he never even hinted that he was or might be part of a wider family."

Donne riffled through the file and said, "Here it is. I made a detailed note of all he said. He had been watching that programme, 'Who Do You Think You Are', and it prompted him to delve into his own background. The result startled him and yet he said it made sense. As a child, he said, he was often dumped, his words not mine, during the school holidays with his hated Grandmother Silver. His researches started with her funeral and he found a collection of condolence letters and cards he'd never seen before. They had been in his father's effects. He trawled through them all and discovered that his great, great grandfather was one Hezekiah Silver, a Jewish businessman of some considerable substance. His great grandfather – let me see, Abraham Michael Silver – had built on his father's fortune and amassed great wealth. His grandfather, Peter John Silver had, in biblical terminology, wasted his substance on riotous living. Worse still, he had married outside the faith and been shunned by his family. This same Peter John had died young, only a few years after the marriage, in a climbing accident on the Matterhorn, leaving his widow Margaret Helen Silver with a baby son, who, of course, grew up to be Ernest's father Martin Hugh Silver. Mrs Margaret Hirst, Ernest's grandmother, was left with a baby son, a huge house and only a small income to heat it, let alone maintain it."

"Well, my words. So Ernest was Jew. He never hinted at the possibility and yet he must have known for some time. Ernest was straight-down-the-middle Anglican."

"Oh aye. 'E got on right well wi' t' parson. In t' choir an' that. Regular at church 'e were."

"I rather gathered that Ernest's grandmother was Church of England but she'd had more than enough of religion to last a lifetime. Ernest told me he never went to Sunday school when he stayed with her."

"May I change the subject?" demanded the Colonel. "How did Ernest seem? I mean, was he upset in any way, when he first came here? And when exactly did he come?"

"To answer your second question, he came here a mere three weeks ago, in mid-September."

"So that was the time when he asked me to be an executor. Was it about then that he approached you, Jacob?"

"Oh aye. Three week or four since, aye."

"And how did he seem?"

"It's difficult to say on first acquaintance, but I would say buoyant. Yes, he said he was late making a will, should have done so years ago but didn't think himself ready to die. Yes, I would say confident and lively; that's the word, lively. In fact, he boasted he'd lots of years left in him."

"Got that bit wrong!"

"He did indeed, Mr Smith. Just in time, as it turns out. But the theatre is all to do with timing."

"You imply he told something about theatre?"

"Oh yes, it all poured out when he was talking about his late wife, who had had something of a career on the boards."

"The old blighter! He kept that from us all these years, yet he spilled the beans to you, a comparative stranger – an actual stranger in fact."

"Returning to the first question you asked – how did he seem – I said buoyant. Actually, he seemed amazingly cheerful – happy. Indeed, I might even say joysome, if there is such a word. As far as the house was concerned, gentrification had set in big-time and so the property in the run-down square had become much sought after. There were actually two houses, and they fetched well over a million pounds. And he had no family to leave all this money to.

"But Mr Silver realised that his fortune would come like a win on the lottery to some of the people he had learned to like, respect and love whilst living in Holsterdale. He could lift a burden from their shoulders and his magic wand, again his words, would gently but completely waft their dreams into reality. Of course, they'd have to wait. He said he had no intention of dropping off the perch just yet awhile."

"'E got that wrong an' all."

"Indeed, regrettably so, Mr Smith," agreed Mr Donne. "One thing he emphasised was that nobody was to know that their good fortune was waiting in the wings and would eventually land in their laps. He jokingly added that he did not wish to tempt his friends into killing him off before due time, in a hurry to get an early hand on his dosh – he actually used the word dosh. It seemed strange coming out of his mouth. The contents of his will, he said, must be a darkest secret. 'The greater the secret, the more wonderful the outcome.'

"He, I thought strangely, said that secrets are important in life and in love, and just as important in death. He was visibly excited as he expressed this notion to me. He rubbed his hands together with glee as he said it.

"He then passed me a handwritten note with the intended bequests – names and amounts. The list was clear, the sums of money involved appeared to match his fortune, give or take the downs and ups of an outrageous stock market.

"There was one bequest I queried. He wanted to leave a substantial sum of money to an eight-year-old girl, Laura Hirst. He said he was certain beyond peradventure that she would make her mark in the world. He added that what she did would one day be a talking point on everyone's lips."

"'E were not wrong about that, were 'e?"

"Quite so, Mr Smith. He said he wished to cover the full costs of her education in school, in extra music lessons and all her fees and cost of living at university. I thought this unwise, and rather suggested he set up a trust for her and for other talented children in Holsterdale, whatever those talents might be. That way the money could be allocated, according to need, as a succession of grants when the children reached the age of eighteen.

"Silver thought that a brilliant idea. He in fact said he wished he'd thought of it first. He added that he knew a boy in the choir – he didn't mention a name - whose mother would welcome a monetary lift when her talented boy needed it. Mr Silver agreed to the fund idea – he said a hundred thousand pounds, which made me blink, and asked me to word it properly. He added that Rev. Norris Porter should be nominated as chairman of trustees to look after all this. It was a substantial sum of money and would need careful handling.

"After he had completed his list of bequests, Mr Silver added that there was one more that was perhaps the most important.

"He asked – 'Do you know the Hepworths of Holsterdale?'

"I replied, 'Who doesn't? A very influential family. They have a talented daughter, don't they?'

"'Indeed, they do. It is to her that I want to bequeath my double piano stool and all my piano music.'

"'I went to one of her concerts in aid of St Mary's organ fund. She played duets with an elderly man. That wasn't you, was it?'

"'Guilty as charged,' he answered jokily.

"'I should have recognised you. Do forgive me.'

"'Why should you? It was some months ago. To continue, she and I have played many duets on my piano. Felicity often came over to practise and I occasionally helped her to make piano arrangements of pieces of music intended for other instruments. After an hour or so working hard we would join hands to relax, playing duets together. If she arrived a little early to pick her up, Felicity's mother would sometimes come in to listen to us play.'

"'So, you want to leave her the duet stool and all your piano music?'

"Mr Silver spoke about the beautiful embroidery and said that Felicity loved the peacocks pictured in tapestry on the double seat. As it was merely a small personal bequest I agreed to include it, and all his music too.

"'You will need her full name and address.' he added.

"'Of course.'

"'Felicity Hepworth. She may have a middle name but that should suffice. The address – The Grange, Holsterdale.'

"'Is that all?'

"'Yes, I think so.'

"With that he ended. I think he seemed well satisfied that he had done the right thing.

"One further worry Mr Silver had: when all the bequests had been distributed, what should he do about the remainder? It might be a bit; it might be quite a lot. Who should fall heir to the residue of his estate? My suggestion was to leave it to some charity, to which he instantly replied that he would leave the entire residue to – let me see, what did he say? Yes, here it is – the residue to St. Joseph's Hospice in Hackney, London where his late and much beloved wife Margery had been looked after so sympathetically in her dying days.

"He left me to draft the will, using the draft document he had brought with him. He returned a week later to sign it, witnessed by two of our clerks. He told me that you both had agreed to be executors – he seemed contented, not to say delighted, with that and, if I may say so, so am I. Having carefully read and reread the will, he said how thrilled he was. Even after his death he would be bringing a ray of sunshine into so many lives."

"Thank you so much, Mr Donne," said the Colonel.

"I have one further question. Just suppose that a beneficiary (is that the right word?) refuses to accept the bequest, what do we have to do in that event?"

"Beneficiary is the right word. Is it likely that someone might refuse to accept what, after all, is a generous bequest?"

"I was just supposing, Mr Donne."

"I see. Most people are only too delighted to get a handsome windfall, wherever it comes from. However, were that to happen, the amount of that particular bequest would simply be added to the residue and would go to whomsoever Mr Silver had nominated to receive the residue: in this case, to the hospice I told you about earlier and as mentioned in the will. You don't think it's likely that someone would refuse a bequest, surely?"

"Not at all. Just dotting the 'I's, that's all. Thank you, Mr Donne."

"Here is a copy of the will for you both to peruse at your leisure.

"Oh, and by the way Mr Silver has included a pour-boire for you both – £5000 each. That is also written in the will."

"Nay, I don't know what a poor boy is but if it's spendin' money, it'll do. Ta very much."

"Don't thank me, Mr Smith. This is Mr Silver's, in my view, very generous wish, not mine."

"I think we both understand that it's our duty to make sure the terms of the will are upheld. How will the distribution be made?" The Colonel had moved on to practical matters.

"You may tell the individual beneficiaries as soon as you like. If you're in any doubt, have a word with me first. As to distribution, the best way is for DSS to deal with authorising and sending the cheques as appropriate. We'll need to find all relevant addresses of course, and it is likely that you would find that more straightforward then we."

"Thank you again, Mr Donne, and good day to you," said the Colonel as they departed.

"What's a poor boy, Colonel?" asked Smith tentatively as they strode to Smith's van.

"A pour-boire is payment for services rendered. It's French and literally means 'for a drink'."

"By Go'! Tha can sup a lot for five thou."

"Not the time for flippancy, Mr Smith."

"No, well, I didn't mean it, like. Me, I think it's a great honour to be asked. Did 'e do it? I mean about Laura drownin' an' that. I 'ope not, me. What does ta think?"

"Who's to know? The police will continue their searches and enquiries of course. They may have a better idea when they find the body if, indeed, Laura Hirst has drowned."

"What we've got in us 'ands, Ernest's will, is goin' to make some folks very 'appy."

"I hope so, Jacob."

"But as far as us friends is concerned, that's it. They can't persecute 'im now as 'e's dead."

"True, indeed, Mr Smith. The police won't prosecute a dead man, but persecution may continue even after death."

"I 'ope not. That I do."

"I too, Mr Smith. I do, indeed."

CHAPTER 38

WHERE THERE'S WILL, THERE'S A WON'T

Michael MacDonald and Jacob Smith each took their copies of the will home with them and showed them to their respective partners, Peggy and Leslie.

It took a while for these two households to absorb the details. The charities they took in their stride.

The MacDonalds thought the bequests to the Hirsts were lovely and generous, and expected that Harry and Maureen would enjoy the fruits of their labours. Ernest, at the time of writing the will, was of course still alive and kicking, and no doubt had high hopes that this windfall would help the family he loved so dearly to realise at least some of their dreams.

Peggy and Michael wondered at the bequest of Ernest's house and its contents to the Holsterdale Library. Peggy was a member of the library committee so the matter was of particular interest to her. What would the library do with the property? Its contents, especially his pretty comprehensive collection of books, would be welcomed, but where would they securely store the first editions?

"We have no facilities for looking after rare or precious books. The children's books we could give to the school instead of keeping them on our shelves, but the others, I'm not sure."

Michael supposed the library committee might sell the house, but who or what would benefit from the money raised?

Where There's Will, There's A Won't

He supposed that would be for the committee to decide once they'd laid their hands on the deeds, and before they took the step of selling. Maybe the sizeable house could be maintained for some other civic purposes. Peggy said she was glad the NSPCC was benefitting to some tune, but why was the hospice in Hackney so generously provided for? Michael couldn't answer that; Mr Donne had said something about a hospice, but the man had listed so many items and details and at such a speed that he had forgotten half of what he had said.

Then there was the section of the will that left a hundred thousand to set up a trust for the benefit of talented children. How on earth would that work? Who would decide who was talented and, more difficult, who was not? And who got what and how much? It would be tricky for poor old Norris to have to take all this on his plate, but the will said Ernest wanted the rector to chair the trust. Heavy burden ahead for the Porters. No doubt Aileen would put her oar in; that might help.

All this was speculation and food for thought to chew over at the dinner table.

* * *

Leslie's comment was his amazement at the size of Ernest's fortune. Where had it all come from? And why had Ernest never talked about his money?

"We never spoke of money. 'E telled us abaht 'makin' a contribution' to the cost of the trip to Blackpool an' such like, but 'e never admitted us 'at 'e'd paid for it or anything else up front like. An' why should 'e?"

"We should have put two an' two together and asked him. But we never did and he wasn't going to tell us without. He didn't boast about anything, ever, so he kept it to himself."

"What does ta think abaht 'im leavin' so much brass to t' 'Irsts?"

"Very generous, I'd say. 'E thought a lot about 'em and he'd be thinking his money would be very welcome. I bet he fair rubbed his hands when he wrote that bit."

"Laura 'asn't bin found yet. The Hirsts are bound to be right upset. I doubt they'll be in a right mood to 'ear the good news. Choose your words carefully, Jacob, when you go to see them."

"Aye, well, we'll see."

"Have you and the Colonel arranged where and when to break the good news?"

"Yes.. 'E rang this mornin' and we've decided. I'm goin' to the 'Irsts an' 'e's tellin the rector abaht the trust an' that. We've agreed to ask the solicitor to write to the library committee abaht the 'ouse bein' left to them an' then we'll go together to tell the library committee what they can expect – house and contents, like."

"Do you think they'll accept it?"

"I bloody well 'ope so. It's worth a lot o' brass."

* * *

Later that morning, Mr Jacob Smith went to 47 South Street to talk to Mr and Mrs Hirst.

Harry went to the door. "Come in, Jacob, do. What can we do for you?"

"Does tha wanna t a sup o' tea? I've just mashed it."

"Ta, Maureen. That'd be right nice."

"Sit yersell down, Jacob."

"Ta, Maureen, I will," Jacob said, as he sat at the table.

"What's to do now?" Maureen asked as she handed him a mug of tea.

"Ta, Maureen," Jacob took a sup of tea. "By Go," he cried. "By heck, Maureen, thi tea's 'ot. I near scalded mi sen."

"I telled thee I'd just mashed it. What does ta expect?"

"I'm sad about your Laura. No news yet then?"

"None. We've lost hope that there'll ever be. Just managing to keep ourselves together."

"Leave your tea to cool off a bit and tell us what you've come about."

"I'm bringing what I 'ope you'll tek as good news."

"They aven't fun' 'er after all this time?" Maureen shouted.

"'Fraid not. Maureen. I wish it was the news you want to 'ear more an anythin' else, but it in't."

"So what is it then?" Harry asked.

"Ernest Silver has—"

"Don't speak that name 'ere," Maureen screamed.

"But, Maureen he's—"

"I don't care what 'es done. If tha's come 'ere to speak 'is name, tha can go. Go on! Get out, Jacob Smith, get thi sen gone."

There was no point in staying. As Smith went, he said, "'Arry, come out wi' me. I need to speak to thee."

"Go on, 'Arry. Foller 'im and mek sure 'e dun't come back. I don't want 'im in this 'ouse no more."

Harry followed Jacob Smith and closed the door behind him.

"What have you come for, Jacob?"

"Thanks for comin' out 'Arry. Ernest 'as left you and Maureen a very big sum o' money in his will."

"She won't have it, Jacob. And I don't want it neither."

"But it's twenty thousand pounds, 'Arry."

"I don't care if it's two-hundred thousand, I don't want 'is fucking money. And you know what Maureen thinks."

"You can do a lot with twenty thou, 'Arry."

"It's tainted money, Jacob. Give it to someone else. We don't want it and we won't have it. Take his fucking brass and leave us be."

Harry hacked back into the house and banged the door shut behind him.

* * *

Jacob returned home, proud of what Harry had said and done. It was tainted money, and Jacob wished he could abandon his duties as executor and leave all the work to the Colonel.

When he told Leslie how the Hirsts had reacted to their 'good news', he added that he wished he could give up being an executor. Les told him he had duties to perform.

"Yes, well, I don't see why I should have to. Silver has done the dirty on the 'Irsts, so why 'av I a duty to mek sure 'is will works out? I can't force 'em to tek the bloody money. I don't want 'is will to work out. The 'Irsts don't want 'is brass, an' neither do I. 'E can keep 'is five thou. I don't want 'is brass neither."

"Yes, but what about the charities. They will lose out if they don't get 'is brass. They'll get it anyhow, but you can make sure they get it as soon as possible if you do your duties properly and promptly."

"Oh aye. Well, I 'ave to see they get 'is brass. They don't need to know where it's comed fra an' that it's tainted like.

* * *

Meanwhile the Colonel had visited Rev. Norris Porter and his wife about the trust. As luck would have it they were in and, even luckier, they had just brewed a coffee.

"Would you like a cup? Instant, I'm afraid."

"Thank you. That would be very welcome." A simple untruth but, in the circumstances, warranted. "A dash of milk and no sugar."

Aileen served the coffee as asked for.

"Now what can we do you for, Colonel?" said Norris. "Nothing to do with Mr Silver, surely. I must say his death and the circumstances of the same, in fact the whole tragedy, is very distressing. Has the funeral date been decided?"

"No, this is nothing to do with the funeral, but it has to do with Ernest."

"Spit it out, Michael," said Mrs Porter, "for heaven's sake. You have a face as long as a foot."

"First, I must tell you that Ernest, only a couple of weeks or so ago, asked me to act as executor of his will. Just in time, as the saying goes. I agreed and, in that capacity, I have had access to his will. You are not personally mentioned in his will; he hadn't led you to expect otherwise, I hope?"

"Not directly, no. We had discussed a Mediterranean cruise together next summer. We could never have afforded such a luxury, and he had very generously said he would undertake all our expenses. Apart from that we have no expectations. His death puts the kibosh on the cruise, of course."

"He hasn't left us the cost of a cruise in his will." Mrs P. timidly asked. "You're not here to tell us that?"

"Not that we have any expectations," interjected the Rev. "Ernest was, by Holsterdale standards, one of our wealthiest parishioners."

"No, there is no bequest – not to you personally – but indirectly, yes. The fact of the matter is that Ernest has willed a very considerable sum in trust and he specifically asked that you, Norris, be chairman of a named trust."

"And what is the considerable sum, Michael?" It was Aileen who wanted to know the gory details.

"One-hundred thousand pounds, Aileen."

"And the trust is for what purpose, Michael?"

"I was coming to that. It is to provide a bursary as needed for young talented children of the parish or rather, I should say, of the town. We can all guess who he was thinking about, though no names are mentioned in the wording of the will."

"You're referring to Laura Hirst, of course. Is there any news in that quarter?"

"None, I'm afraid, but I think we all know that she must be assumed dead after all this time. Whether Ernest had anything to do with her disappearance is anyone's guess. I hope not, as I'm sure you do too."

"And we shall never know from him, guilty or not," Aileen added unnecessarily.

"Indeed, Aileen. I know Ernest felt more than mere fondness for Laura, but I never felt she was ever in any danger from him, did you?"

"None whatsoever," said Norris immediately. Aileen's response was a rather more guarded, "Perhaps not."

Michael continued, "He assured me that Laura would become prime minister one day. She had such extraordinary energy, drive and imagination, and she frequently embellished his stories, much to his delight and admiration. Embellishment is stock in trade for PMs," he said.

"You're right, Norris. I had many long conversations with him. He told me a great deal, perhaps almost too much, about his school life, but it came as a surprise when the records revealed that Ernest had been a professional actor. McCullough, of course, had Ernest DBS checked before he could let him loose on the children. But even that had not shown that up. The DBS shows only that there are no police records indicating doubtful behaviour."

"I wonder why he wanted that theatrical part of his past to be hidden from our eyes. And isn't it remarkable that he successfully maintained the secret all this time, without leading either of us or anyone else to suspect that sort of background? I now think that his better-than-average reading of the Gospels might have led me to wonder why he was so exceptionally good at it. But I wasn't seeking answers to questions I wasn't asking."

"Remember, I half-suspected it. Do you remember what I said about that theatrical dinner party? It fits in perfectly. No, I'm not surprised at all. I wonder what sort of actor he was? Probably not so very good." That part of the conversation was satisfactory in Aileen's eyes

"Can we get back to the hundred thousand trust fund, please?" Aileen was far more curious than Norris about this vast sum of money, and where on earth it had come from.

"Quite right, Aileen. The will does not specify what kind of talent Ernest was thinking about. It could be music or dancing or sport or woodworking – you name it."

"And who is to decide on what talent is exceptional, who is to nominate candidates, and who to decide on the amounts of the awards?"

"That would be for you and your committee, Norris, to decide and define. Aileen would help, might even allow herself to be on the committee to make sure things went the way they should."

"And would this trust be so named as to be associated with and funded by Ernest Silver, or would the trust be attributed anonymously?"

"The will doesn't say either way, but even if it were anonymously attributed, people would quickly guess where such a large sum could come from. Ernest's dead – here comes a hundred thou."

"People would know, whether they were told or not. I can't take it on, Aileen. Whether I wanted to or not, it would commemorate Ernest in people's suspicious minds and would be associated with the disappearance and death of Laura Hirst, found drowned or not. Unless by some miracle she is still alive."

"But it could make such a difference to some of our parishioners. I mean, think of Clifford Johnston. He has a brilliant young treble voice. Think what Mrs Johnston could do with a grant to pay for excellent singing classes. She couldn't hope to pay for such without a grant. Not taking it on is denying Clifford the opportunity to develop. I wonder if even Mrs Johnston would accept a grant, knowing it to be associated with Ernest Silver and connected with Laura's death? Ernest and she were best friends in the choir."

"If you don't take it on, you're denying him what could be the chance of a lifetime. Take it on, Norris, and you'll have one grateful parishioner."

"No, Aileen, I've made up my mind. Michael, I cannot accept the responsibility for such a large sum of money. What happens to this money if neither I nor the parish can accept it?"

"If you refer it to the parish for their decision, it could never be anonymous. The cat would be out of the bag. I would have to refer your decision to do so to the solicitor. My guess is that it would simply revert to the residue, and that would mean, according to the terms of the will, that a hospice in London would get an extra hundred thousand pounds."

"That settles it them. Let the hospice have the money."

"No it doesn't. The trust is to be set up and it must be presented to the PCC at least. They may have a different view. Just because you won't accept chairmanship of the trust, somebody else might. You are not in a position to cancel the trust just because you have reservations about chairing it. You're making a big mistake, Norris." Aileen was not letting go a fortune so easily.

"And I've made a big mistake, Aileen," said Michael. "I should have asked you to leave the room and told Norris only about the bequest in private. At the time it didn't seem to matter that you were here when I told Norris about the bequest."

"I agree, Michael. Now listen, Aileen, nobody, but absolutely nobody must know what you now know about Ernest's bequest and that I have refused to take it on. Indeed, rejected it utterly. I want your solemn promise that you will never speak or even hint at the bequest, the trust and more particularly the sum of money. I speak of one hundred thousand pounds. I will never utter those fateful words again, and neither must you. Agreed?"

"No. You can't make me do that. Ernest has left money to set up a trust and you are in no position to let it go like that. No, I will talk about it whenever the opportunity arises. That trust can be so important to so many people who are not going to be exactly grateful if you deny this help."

"Back to the drawing board then, Norris! I will talk to the solicitor and see what can be arranged to deal with this. I think perhaps the town council will have to be the ones to take the final decision."

* * *

Colonel MacDonald and Jacob Smith met, told their respective and rejected tales to each other, signed off the bequests to the charities and authorised DSS to remit the cheques.

"The matter of the trust will have to be delayed until the PCC and the town council have had a look at it and perhaps found a willing chairman. If not, the hospice in Hackney may yet receive a huge windfall, much larger than expectations and, indeed, much larger than Ernest had intended. But Margery can serenely rest in peace after that."

Ernest had saddled this curious pair with impossibly awkward tasks, which they had carried out to the best of their abilities. They had worried over every minute they had spent executing his will. They both applauded the actions and reactions of the Hirsts and of Norris Porter.

Aileen Porter had put the cat among the pigeons, and they could heartily wish she had kept her mouth shut. But had she not done so, justice might not have been done and intended generosity denied.

Their duties were not over until the matter of the blessed trust was settled. There could be no sigh of relief that it was all over until it was, indeed, all over. But the ball was still in their hands.

CHAPTER 39

IT'S NOT OVER YET

It was matins, on Sunday, October 24th, two days before the funeral. In the notices, Canon Porter reminded the unusually small congregation that Mr Silver's funeral was to take place next Tuesday, at 11.30 AM. He expressed the hope that there would be a good attendance to pay respect to the valuable work Ernest had done over recent years with the choir and also as a valued member of the PCC.

There were no children in the choir, and precious few other members. After the service, Norris spoke to those in the choir who had remained, still in their cassocks and surplices. He was aware of the trying circumstances, but repeated the hope that there would be a good turn out from the choir to celebrate the fruitful years Ernest had spent, both in time and in energy, in building up the choir. Could he have a show of hands of those intending to be there? Only two hands were raised.

"And how about you, Nathaniel? You'll be playing the organ surely?"

"Can't promise. I had planned to go over to see mother, as I usually do on a Tuesday – buy her shopping and so on. I'll see if I can fit it in."

"Thank you all for being here this morning. Frankly I am disappointed at your collective decisions to be absent, but I am speaking to the absentees, not to those of you here just now. Mr Silver has transformed the choir and the congregational singing. I had hoped you might overlook recent events and be at his funeral. I'd like to think you will change your minds and be here on Tuesday, eleven-thirty, a full turn-out is the least we can do to celebrate his invaluable contribution and commitment to our worship in this place. That is all, ladies and gentlemen, thank you for remaining behind."

After they had disrobed, two sopranos, Gladys Hunter and Moira Shepherd, came to him in the vestry.

"Hello, Moira, Gladys, what can I do for you just now?"

Gladys took the initiative. "We told the kiddies not to come into the choir this mornin'."

"It was improper of you to do that. If anyone should take such a draconian decision, it would be Mr Tweddle."

"Yes, well," Gladys continued, "young Clifford Johnston is that upset at 'is friend Laura bein' missin'."

Moira interrupted, "She must be dead after all this time."

"Regrettably so, indeed, Mrs Shepherd."

"And they don't want no reminders of that evil man. He must have groomed young Laura 'Irst, 'ad 'is way wi' 'er and then drownded 'er to destroy the evidence."

"Don't say such a thing, Mrs Shepherd. There is no evidence for such statements."

"No, well that's what they're all sayin'."

"That's right, Gladys. An' what other kiddies 'as 'e been after int' choir and, for that matter, at St Mary's School?"

"And as for Nat Tweddle, 'e won't be at funeral, no matter what 'e said about 'elpin' 'is mother out."

"But they got on so well, Ernest and him. They worked together so effectively, an invaluable team."

"Are you blind or summat? Nat 'ated 'is guts."

"Mr Tweddle never gave any indication!"

"No, well, 'e wouldn't, would 'e?"

"'E's that meek an' mild. 'E could see how you got on with that man. ... Nat's not one for upsetting apple carts."

"But Nat 'as more music in 'is little finger than 'im. Nat coped, no that's not right. What's the word I'm seekin', Moira?"

"Tolerated, Gladys. Any roads on, Nat put up with 'im and' took the line of least resistance."

"Bless me. There's been an iron curtain between me and my flock. Now the shutters are opening up. I'm seeing Silver in an entirely new and less sympathetic light."

"Thank you, Mr Porter."

"I take it you won't be sitting in the choir stall on Tuesday?"

"That's right. An' it's likely you'll be playin' for the 'ymns on the piano."

"Oh dear! What a dismal anti-climax. But I'm most grateful that you have spoken so openly to me. I just wish you had brought this to my attention earlier. I think I see a way how I might have been able to prevent this terrible catastrophe, which has not only visited us in our erstwhile sheltered community in Holsterdale, but also I might have made Ernest's life more comfortable – more true to itself, if not exactly happier."

With a heavy heart, Norris walked thoughtfully to the rectory. He was in for an 'I-told-you-so' episode when he got there, and he was in no hurry to speed that particular plough.

He was proud of his willingness to believe face value presentations. What was more, he was genuinely fond of Ernest, who was inclined to be vain. He was on easy hail-fellow-well-met terms with everyone he came across, be it in church, in the choir, on the bowling green, at the cricket club as a chatty but knowledgeable spectator, on the PCC, and memorably within the school, in the shops, and in the street. And he had struck up amicable relationships with Jacob Smith, that strange builder of dry-stone walls and notorious crossdresser. It was as though Ernest was on easy terms with all walks of life. Indeed, Norris was envious of Ernest's social facility, equally welcome at the Hepworths' mansion and in Smith's cottage.

The now-public knowledge that Ernest had been a

professional actor suddenly made sense of his social ease. Norris thought that, as an actor, Ernest must have taken on many roles, from murderer to detective, from hero to villain, from pantomime dame to genuine crossdresser – of course Ernest would see nothing odd in Smith's proclivities, and would feel perfectly at ease being seen as Smith's friend without fear of snide gossip.

You name it and Ernest must have lived it and have actually experienced it.

Aileen had described Ernest as having swallowed the Hirsts whole. Norris didn't see it that way, and had defended Ernest's reputation in the face of her frequent onslaughts. And now he was in for a further attack. She had asked 'What did he expect?' when Ernest's arrest was made public. She perfectly well understood Mrs Hirst's violent reaction. Everyone knew about the stone throwing event. Maureen Hirst's star was in the ascendance, and many public voices said they would have thrown the stone first if they had thought about it.

***

Aileen was developing a bad cold and had stayed at home, dosing herself with paracetamols and hot milk, with honey and rum enhancements.

"Is that you, darling?" she called out when she heard the kitchen door open. Her attacks always opened on a gentle note.

"It is I," Norris replied as he hung his wet coat over the fire guard to dry.

"What was the atmosphere like today?"

Norris knew that the best form of defence was to keep talking, give Aileen no time or opportunity to speak. He started as he intended to finish and gave a long-winded but watered-down version of what he had learned in his vestry after the service. Intermingled with all this were his thoughts and interpretations.

After half an hour had passed, exhaustion set in. Quick as a buffalo at a waterhole, Aileen splashed in, "What did I tell you?" It was a variation of I-told-you-so. Before he had time to counter-attack she asked, "And the funeral on Tuesday? You're not expecting a big turn out to pay their lasting loathing of the man?"

"I'm afraid that is likely. Tweddle offered a lukewarm excuse that he might be too busy looking after his ailing mother. He is too lily-livered to tell me outright that he wouldn't be there. But he won't be there, I'm certain of that. Mrs Shepherd told me Tweddle despised Ernest. And I shall have to play the tunes on the piano."

"You always told me they got on really well, Ernest and Tweddle."

"I did, but it seems I was wrong."

"Not for the first time, Norris, and it won't be the last." Then she added as a coda, "There's none so blind as he who will not see."

It was time for retreat and Norris took refuge in his study. Safely inside, he sat at his desk and sketched notes for the dreaded funeral sermon. That done he turned to his hymn book. It was opportune to give that under-used and out of tune Bechstein an airing. He looked up 'The Day Thou Gavest, Lord, Is Ended'. By the time he had played it through three or four times using the melodic lines on a single stave, he was reasonably fluent. The congregation, such as it might be, would sing at whatever pace he could manage.

He had an idea that Elgar's Sospiri might be in his now out-of-date cassette collection. After much searching he found it and uttered a silent prayer of thanks for deliverance. The day of miracles was over. He fitted it into the cassette player, but it must be years since he had last used it. Quite right: it didn't move a muscle. He resolved to get new batteries at the Co-op on Monday morning.

Oh golly, it was four and his evensong was due to start at half past. Too late for a sandwich, he rushed down the road to open the church. There was no queue impatient to get in. Normally Tweddle would spend most of the afternoon playing the organ, but not today.

Norris went in, switched on the lights.

Half-past four came and the church was empty. He thought that the words of the Nunc Dimitis seemed highly appropriate. He found a dusty copy and, thinking of Ernest, he read aloud,

"Now lettest now thy servant depart in peace, according to Thy word."

It was a short canticle, but after he had completed it, including the doxology, he had recited all that needed to be said and he was glad there was nobody there to listen. Norris dreaded the funeral on Tuesday.

CHAPTER 40

THE FUNERAL

"How did it go?" Aileen had not gone to the funeral, pleading illness and she had offered a sore red nose as evidence.

"It went."

"Who was there?"

"Jacob Smith and Leslie, joined at the hip as usual, and Michael and Peggy MacDonald. Both couples sat about halfway back, and just in front of them were Mr and Mr Hepworth and their daughter, Felicity. They asked me as they came into church to announce an invitation for a cup of tea after the cremation, to all those who would like to come back to the Grange; very kind of them, I thought."

"I'm glad you didn't come back for me! I assume you went along?"

"Yes I did, and I assumed, as you say, that you would rather be excused. Also in the congregation were two elderly gentlemen, both almost completely bald and pink as if they'd both stepped out of a hot shower. I asked them afterwards why they were there, and they chorused that they had known Rosy from way back. The name Rosy didn't make sense to me but I never had chance to ask them about it."

"No incidents, then? No demonstrations?"

"The hymn started hesitantly, but when Felicity saw that I was struggling she, encouraged by her mother, came to my aid

The Funeral

and played beautifully, although I think her parents and I were the only ones singing.

"The Elgar Sospiri is a very moving piece, I chose it particularly for the solemnness of this occasion, but the tape broke shortly after it had just got going. This rather spoilt the effect and left us in silence. However, just before the commendation prayers, Felicity asked if she could play a short piece by Schubert.

"She announced to the small congregation before she started playing that it was an arrangement for piano that she and Ernest had worked on together, of a string quartet called 'Death and the Maiden'. It was very moving.

"When the service was nearly over, I was glad to see Maureen and Harry Hirst enter. They stood at the back. I thought they must have remembered all the good times with Ernest and I thanked God for it. However, as we passed them, in one final indignity for Ernest, Maureen spat on the coffin and then collapsed in her husband's arms. No forgiveness in that household; just great hurt that will take a long time to heal.

"The road to hell is paved, Aileen. What a waste of good intentions. Ernest's final journey he took in a desecrated box, but I am thankful to say he was not actually alone. The MacDonalds made their apologies, but Jacob and Leslie, the two pink gentlemen and the Hepworth's came with us to the Crematorium. Felicity shed silent tears through the brief ceremony, clearly deeply distressed at the loss of her mentor and friend.

"Afterwards, as I came out, the two pink gentlemen were being driven away to the station by Mr Hepworth so, as I mentioned, I was never able to ask them about 'Rosy'. But Jacob and Leslie came up to the Grange for tea, and I gave Felicity and her mother a lift.

"Mr Hepworth joined us almost as soon as the tea had been poured. I have to say, after the alarms and excursions of the funeral, it was very pleasant to have a quiet conversation, while Felicity played the piano in the next room. Like many of us, I think music was proving to be her best comfort.

"'These scones are delicious!' Leslie typically, was the first to break the ice. 'But I like them best with butter, I don't usually go in for whipped cream and raspberry jam!'

"'Me an 'all!' agreed Jacob, who seemed uncomfortable in the smart drawing room at The Grange.

"'You must leave room for some of this fruit cake,' said Mrs Hepworth. 'It's a specialty!'

"I decided I would forgo the pleasure. 'A busy rector's work is never done, and I'm afraid I still have other things to attend to.'

"'Then you must take some with you, and a piece for poor Aileen too; I'm so sorry she was indisposed this afternoon.'

Aileen smiled at this as she popped a second piece of said cake onto her plate.

"Before I left I thanked them for coming to the service, and said how offensive I found rumours that are rife in the town. You know I was very fond of Ernest and am saddened by the way this overshadows his memory.

"I asked them to thank Felicity for her rescue in time of need during the service. She played that piece by Schubert exquisitely, and it was entirely appropriate to the occasion. I shook hands all round and as Mr Hepworth showed me to the door he took the opportunity to thank me for coping so well with the funeral, as well as with the mixed emotions in the congregation. He also stated quite emphatically that he and his wife give no credence to the rumours in the town.

"We are convinced that Laura's death, as it surely must be, was no more than a tragic accident," he stated.

"I have to say, Aileen, that I totally agree with him."

Aileen wiped the last crumb of Mrs Hepworth's fruit cake from her lips. "Well you know my thoughts on the matter, and nothing will change my mind!"

The Funeral

With that she had the last word.

EPILOGUE
REUNION IN MAYFAIR

[annotation: ☆ New Chapter]

It was early evening on Tuesday, December 8th at King's Cross station taxi rank.

"Where to, sir?"

"Grey's Hotel, Marley Street."

"Thank you, sir. Grey's it is."

Peter had chosen Grey's Hotel in Mayfair because it was discreetly tucked away. It was the perfect address for a golden reunion.

"A party, is it, sir?"

"Very much so, thank you."

"Enjoy yourself then, sir."

"I'll do my best."

Seven minutes later the cabby announced, "Grey's Hotel, sir, on the dot."

Having thanked and paid the cabby, Peter entered the portals and went to the reception desk.

"Good evening, sir. Can I help you? Residence or restaurant?"

"I have a private dining room reservation for this evening; the name's Freelay."

"Oh, yes, Mr Freelay. I'll ask a page to take you there."

At that moment a rickety, aged person prised himself out of a nearby chair, grabbed at his Zimmer frame and lurched very slowly towards Peter, who was still at the reception desk.

"Peter, how nice to see you. Long time no see!"

The reunion had been arranged with the aged one entirely on the telephone, so they had not met until this very moment.

"Now let me see, you must be Oswin Makepiece."

"The very same. Tapdancing, as you see, is no longer my forte."

The page led them to an elegant dining room to one side of

the restaurant. They followed at snail's pace behind the suitably elegant young man.

"Here you are, gentlemen. I'm told two more will be coming. I'll make sure they find their way here."

A female waiter was already in attendance. "An aperitif, perhaps?"

"What do you think, Oz? I think champagne cocktails are in order, don't you agree?"

"Steady on, old chap! Budget considerations."

"On me; the sky's the limit. Sixty years in the theatre is no mean achievement, and it must be celebrated in diamond style."

"If you insist."

"I do insist. Right, young lady, champagne cocktails if you please."

"Who else is coming? You mentioned Brigitta on the phone. I suppose she will be here."

"Certainly. A bright young poppet, she was. Lovely china blue eyes, as I remember."

As if on cue, no playwright worth his salt would risk it, the door opened and in sprung a spritely old lady wearing dark glasses, no walking stick, elegant black outfit, set off with an array of jewels (probably paste) that clattered as she galloped in. The gorgeous effect of this well-thought-out ensemble was rather spoilt by white trainers on her well splayed feet.

"You must be Peter, the only begetter of this wonderful occasion."

She launched herself at him for a kiss.

"Bless my cotton socks and scarlet suspenders, you've worn well, Peter. Are you in possession of the elixir of life? What is your secret? I must make a note."

"Ponds Cold Cream, actually!"

"Where do you get it? I've been searching and, believe me, searching. Tell me now, immediately, I must make a note."

As she made no effort to do so, Peter didn't feel it necessary to let on that it was Tesco's own brand.

"You've survived the ravages pretty well yourself, Briggie. What's with the dark glasses?"

"Blind as a bat! Can't see beyond the end of my nose. Have a white stick but I keep it in my capacious handbag, out of public view. Now let me see – silly inappropriate phrase in my 'blind as a bat' situation, but it will pop out – is there someone else here? Oh, thank you, young man."

She unerringly reached for the cocktail from the salver offered to her. The 'young man' was in fact the female waiter: an easy mistake for a blind bat. Some bats are not as blind as they say they are when it comes to grasping a drink. They can find a cocktail in the dark if challenged, and Brigitta was the living proof.

"Oh my God, yes, there is some little person lurking over there." She pounced towards him. "You can't be – you must be – indeed, you are! No, don't get up." She dived in to spray another kiss.

The closer contact told her that the wizened creature was indeed Oswin Makepiece.

"Was that your real name? Twirlpin – or are you Makepiece? Somebody famous had the name but my mind is no longer sharp enough to remember who it was. A nineteenth century actor probably."

Then without a pause she continued, "Sorry to hear about your lover, Twirlpin – now that is a name for a tap dancer. AIDS was it? No don't tell me, preserve me from the gory details. Too distressing and really not the subject for a dinner party. So, what are we having? Started well with the champagne cocktail. No, don't tell me, I like surprises."

Yet again, with brilliant theatrical timing, the door opened and in strode an elegant old man, upright back, smartly tailored, powder-blue suit and silver waistcoat topped by a rather too, too flouncy grey satin bowtie. He was wearing, yes, that is the right word, wearing a silver topped walking cane, more for show than for support. Peter, with undisguised impatience in his tone, asked, "Who is this vision-entrancing I see before me?"

"Rawsthorne, don't you recognise me, you old shaver?"

"But you said you weren't able to—"

"Changed my mind, *vieu haricot* – man's privilege, don't you know."

"Waiter!"

"Sir."

"A surprise extra guest; please set the table accordingly."

Brigitta, sensing that she was going to be upstaged by this elegant octogenarian, asked, "So who else is to adorn our festive board? Let me guess, it can't be Faith Dunaway-Culbertson. She must be older than God by now."

"Yes," Peter supplied the answer. "She was as much as ten years older than us."

Rawsthorne snatched the conversational initiative. "She was, I agree, ten years older than we." (correcting the grammar en route.) "Positively elderly by our standards. We were teenagers before the term had been invented. Methinks she would have been just over a hundred today, had she lived. She died, you might be pleased to know, some years ago. Many years before that fatal moment, she had married a Von and spent the rest of her life in Germany. As I understood it, she never mastered the lingo, but when we knew her then she was hopeless at quick study."

Brigitta caught the conversational ball. "All in all, losing a hyphen and gaining a Von was a bargain for the poor woman. She'd never have made it on the stage – small beer and no fizz. One wonders why such lame creatures drift into theatre."

"Can't do anything else, probably."

Brigitta asked, "So who IS the late arrival, and why is he not here by now? You did say dinner at half-past seven did you not, Peter? If I can be on time, anyone can. In any case, I'm ravenous. What are we having at this festive repast?"

"Menu chosen by me with advice from the chef; I think you'll be impressed. It relates to those remote years we spent in Scotland."

"Not chicken in a basket! You couldn't possibly ask for that here; not at Grey's, for heaven's sake."

"Not that. Wait and see."

"So who is the laggardly layabout?"

"See if you recognise him when he enters." Oswin was already asleep and Brigitte's practised entrance speech had almost exhausted him. She had one last fling at talking before sitting at the table.

"So, Philip, were you related to the composer Alan Rawsthorne?"

"That's my story and I'm sticking to it," he replied indignantly.

"If true, the musical genes had not drifted your way; you were hopeless at the piano."

Peter had never been an actor, so was happy to remain silent and let the enthusiastic flood flow around him uninterrupted.

"Ernest Silver was a first-rate pianist and did a brilliant takeover from you, Philip, darling. Were you jealous?"

"Not really. Relieved, actually. I was envious of his blond curls and saw him at first meeting as a potential rival for Jimmy's amorous advances. Turned out he, that is Ernest, was not interested. He never turned to you for creature comforts, Briggie, did he?"

"Not at all. No, never. I have to say I was disappointed really, but I got over it."

Rawsthorne wasn't keen to hear more, so he continued hurriedly, "But he did get on well with the kids we took on as village folk in the pantomimes. They liked him and he made rehearsals fun. These canapés are delicious by the way! Janet, who had always done the kids' bit before, let the curly-haired, golden boy Ernest get on with it. Otherwise Ernest was not a bit interested, not in Jimmy or anyone else, whichever way the balls swing, so to speak. A bit of a loner; an asexual, if such a forlorn creature actually exists.

"He never wrote to me after he left – sort of disappeared, flushed down the lavatory of life, as it were. Did he keep in touch with any of you or anyone else, by the way?"

No reply. Oz was asleep, Brigitta was into her third cocktail and looking for a fourth, Peter preferred to reserve his comments for later and Rawsthorne, talking to himself said, "I don't know why I ask really, I'm not the slightest bit interested. How is he, by the way? He's not the missing guest at the feast, is he?

"Dead, I'm sorry to say." Peter would have continued but at that moment, in came the laggard.

In walked Reg, pink as from a Turkish bath and breathless as from a jog. Actually, he had run into the hotel as one might run upstairs before making a breathless entrance, to give the impression of haste. More truthfully, he was late.

"So sorry, everyone. I hope I haven't delayed proceedings. Tube stations and escalators will be the death of me. Taxi ranks! Don't talk taxi ranks to me. Anyhow, I'm here now. Hello, Peter old chap, sorry if I've held things up."

"No damage done, we're still alive. Now then, Reg, have a champagne cocktail. I'm afraid Philip has consumed all the canapés."

"So who's here, Peter? Let's see if I recognise anyone. You've mentioned Rawsthorne but you said he wasn't able to come. That must be you, Philip, with the crumbs down your frontage." And he advanced to shake the silken clad gentleman's hand warmly.

"And you must be Reginald Page. God, you've aged! How de do! *Ca va?*" cried Rawsthorne, as he brushed the offending crumbs onto the carpet.

The Funeral

"Bien, merci," he replied. "That's enough of that nonsense, Philip, thank you. Now, let's see?"

"Surely you recognise me, Reginald, darling," Brigitta pleaded.

"No, frankly, I don't. Sorry to disappoint. But who from my distant past would call me 'Reginald darling' in that curious way? Let me take a closer look."

He advanced unerringly on the only person wearing what appeared to be widow's weeds.

"Are you coming for a closer look or are you hoping for a great big sloppy kiss?"

"Both if I strike lucky." On closer inspection he drew to a shuddering halt. "This is not the fair and lovely Briggie, is it? It can't be. Let me sniff."

A deep inhalation removed all doubt and raised his spirits. "Chanel No. 5! Tell-tale signs of Brigitta Flaverson, the only one of our number who could afford the best perfumes on our paltry wages."

"Mrs Brigitta Interlock, now, darling. I married a zip fastener manufacturer and I now shop exclusively at Fortnum's." (The 'paste diamonds' must be the real thing after all.)

"Stand up and give me a kiss for old times' sake." She rose with what, given her age, had to pass for alacrity; more truthfully, she slowly rose to her feet. The knees were not as they had been in earlier times. As their lips finally parted, he said wistfully, "Gosh, Briggie, you used to be so beautiful. Where have all the flowers gone?"

"Gone to graveyards everywhere," she chorused in reply.

"How did you find this elderly, if still ravishing creature, Peter?"

"A couple of weeks in the wanted columns of *The Stage*, and she turned up."

"Oh yes, it's years since I trod the proverbial boards, but I like to keep up to date by taking out an annual subscription. Of course, I rarely read anything that relates to me, so Peter's ad descended on me like a breath of spring. Marc, that's my hubby, read the ad to me and told me to go ahead. 'You might see someone you actually want to see! It could be fun,' he said, and before I had time to make up my mind he had rung here and booked my usual room."

"He's not coming too, is he?" Peter was working out space round the table.

"Gracious me, no, darling. He can't abide luvvies. I've never dared lean on him or ask him to book a table at the BAFTAs. All that gushing makes him vomit – that's what he says anyhow."

"I don't have that sort of problem with my partner, Clive. He acts whenever the chance arises!"

"Do the chances arise often?" It was Reg who broke off his wooing to ask.

"Rarely. Frankly, he has no talent. I think Clive's addicted to auditions which rarely bear fruit. It was he who spotted Peter's ad and pointed it out to me. Not only does he like luvvies, he tries his hardest to become one himself."

"You should have brought him along with you. It sounds like he would have enjoyed our company."

"I did suggest it, but he couldn't come. Another blessed audition, this time for a murder set in one of the last remaining coalmines and frankly, he wouldn't fit in here – he prefers younger models. Let's face it, we are all on the steps of the Styx, parcelled up and almost ready for despatch. I tell you, I sigh with relief when he returns empty handed, not having found a beautiful mate. I fear that one day he will discard me for a comely youth. When that day comes to pass, I shall be desolate and, I confess, not a little envious."

"Sorry to interrupt this weepie tale. Shall we take our places at the table? Reg, can you help the Makepiece?"

Reg obliged and heaved the sleepy Oswin out of the depths of the settee and onto the nearest seat at the table. Peter sat at one end and Reg opposite. Between them, and facing Oswin, was Brigitta, nearest to Reg, and side by side with her was Philip Rawsthorne.

Two waiters entered, one with a large tray of elegantly arranged glass dishes which the other set, with an elegant flourish, in front of the now-seated diners.

"The first course, as you see, is prawn cocktail, and to accompany it a dry Chablis," Peter said.

"Inspired choice, Peter. Very popular in the fifties. Perfect for a diamond jubilee."

"Inspired, maybe," said Brigitta, "but I cannot allow shellfish to pass my lips! Take mine away, waiter."

"Would madam prefer some other dish?"

"No thank you, kind sir. Just pour me a large glass of the white. That will suffice."

"The Chablis? Certainly, madam."

"And, waiter, take mine away too," demanded the decorative Rawsthorne. "I have preserved my youthful figure by avoiding creamy mayonnaise. A lightly dressed tomato salad in its place and pacey-pacey, man."

"I'll do my best, sir. And in the meantime, may I pour you a glass? Chablis also for you, sir?"

"Obviously! And be quick about it. And, Peter, please wipe Twirlpin's face. The sight of his unattractive phizzog besmeared with mayonnaise, and with creamy prawns sticking out of his nostrils is unappealing and, quite frankly, disgusting."

"This is Oswin Makepiece; at least get his name right, for God's sake. For your information Morris died years ago."

"AIDs was it? I expect so. Careless."

"It was, and Oswin nursed him tenderly throughout. Such loving devotion can hardly be imagined. The effort took it out of the poor sod; he's been in care since just after Morris's funeral."

"Whichever he is, the sight of him sickens me. For goodness sake, clean him up."

Oswin had overbalanced and toppled head first into the

prawn dish. He was indeed seriously marred and mired. Peter did his best to scrape off the offending creamy confection from poor old Oswin's face, and wipe the mayonnaise from his worn and woolly H&M cardigan. He put a spoon in the old man's hand in the hope that some of the starter would actually enter his mouth."

The telephone rang just as Peter had sat down, and he was called over to speak. He listened and said, "Right, send them in." Returning to his seat, he was just starting to eat when a gentle knock was heard at the door. In came two handy looking men in buff-coloured coats with a wheelchair.

"Come along, Ozzie, time to go home." They gently lifted him into the wheelie and, with a polite, "Thank you, gentlemen," they departed with as little ceremony as they had shown on entering, the one pushing the wheelchair, the other carrying Oz's Zimmer frame over his shoulder.

"And then there were four," Reg offered with a smile.

Peter asked, "Who will be the next green bottle?"

Then Rawsthorne piped up, "It will be me if that tomato salad is not forthcoming instantly."

After a delay caused by the Oz cleaning up operations following the messy departure, the main course arrived.

"Coronation chicken, created in 1953."

"Bless you, Peter, how appropriate: a golden dish for a golden celebration, and the wine? Let me guess. Perhaps a rose d'Alsace?"

"Spot on, Reg. I must tell you that the menu didn't go down well with the chef. He said that two creamy courses are not recommended! It was only when I explained the specific reasoning that he capitulated."

"The main course has arrived, and I am still awaiting my tomato salad," was the petulant moan from the lips of the Rawsthorne. "And it's another creamy affair, woe is me, with pastry accompaniments – a double jeopardy for my o'er

The Funeral

stretched corsets to contend with. You might have warned me, Peter, it really is too, too bad."

"You said you weren't coming, so what was the point?"

"Ah, here comes my tomato salad. Set it down here, my man – oh, you're not a man. I like men about me that are – oh, never mind. A glass of that ghastly pink stuff, pacey, pacey."

"The chef apologises for the delay, sir."

"Shut your flaming mouth, let the fair damsel pour the pink and get out of my sight."

"Philip, darling, that's no way to treat an 'umble servant." Brigitte's voice was slurred as she reached for the bottle of Chablis.

"May I pour for you, madam?"

"Certainly, you may young lady. Be generous, if you please."

"And that is no way to treat your body, sloshing all that wine down your gullet," added the mouthful-of-tomatoes Rawsthorne, as he squirted tomato seeds down his waistcoat like rubies set in a silver sea.

At that very moment the door burst open and a vision in mint green velvet floated in making an extravagant entrance.

"Come along, Phillie, darling. You said you'd be tired of these tedious people by nine, and it's already quarter past."

"But Clivie wivey, I've hardly started this delicious food and I have had but a scant occasion to enjoy relaxing with these charming friends."

"No matter, love of my life, here is your cloak. Left the apartment without it, naughty boy! Slap your handy! And I've got a perfectly delicious surprise for you in the car. He's eighteen and darkly handsome. Latino at a guess, speaks very little English, but he has perfect teeth.

Rawsthorne rose with undue haste, blew kisses and shouted over his shoulder as he departed, "Toodle pip! You see how I am trammelled with heavy responsibilities and have onerous duties to perform."

He disappeared, shrouded in purple velvet, hurried along by the mint green intruder.

"And then there were three," Peter said ruefully.

"But, Pete, where's Briggie? She's disappeared." All they could see was a representation of chaos, such as no props department could hope to reproduce: wine glasses had toppled and were broken, the wine bottles were tipped over and their contents flooded the table; there was tomato salad, coronation chicken and broken bread rolls all in charming disarray. But no sign of Brigitta.

"I'm under the table! It's dark and cosy down here. Did you hide under tables when you were kiddies? I did and still do when the going gets rough."

In drunkenly sliding from her chair, Briggie had dragged the table cloth and half the contents of the table onto the floor around her.

"Come out of there this instant, Brigitta! Reg, help me get her out, please." She was singing, "*Twinkle, twinkle petit star, que vous etes je ne sais pas. Au dessus.*"

The rescue interrupted the chanteuse and was messy but successful. Briggie was seated on a dining chair, Reg preventing her from falling off it.

"Brigitta, listen to me: no singing. None! Do you hear?"

"Of course I hear, you're shouting. Even God, bless his cotton socks, could hear in heaven if there is such a place. It's naughty of you to shout, Peter. You should know that, so stop it."

"Brigitta, I'm taking you to your room. Now where is the key?"

"I feel sick."

"You can't be sick here. Now where is your key? Tell me quickly."

"In my capacious handbag and don't fuss me, Peter, I'm not used to it."

"Reg, find the fucking key and take her to her room, please.

If she's going to vomit, it's better that she throws up in her room, not here."

"Deed as good as done, mate." And after a successful rummage, the key was unearthed and the Brig was safely removed to her home port.

When Reg returned, Peter had told the waiter that the celebration was to be abandoned.

He had said to her, "Apologise to the head waiter. Tell him the food has been perfect but that some of the guests have spoiled the whole evening. I am very, very sorry. Would it be possible to serve coffee and brandy in the lounge, just for two? I don't suppose you have seen quite such a scene before in these walls."

"Some guests have their moments, sir, but mostly no, I haven't"

"And coffee in the lounge?"

"Certainly, sir. I'll see to it immediately. A cafetière for two?"

"Yes, please."

"Bad show this evening, Peter, but there was nothing I could do."

"Of course not. No worries"

"Are you paying for all of this evening's do?"

"I am and, in a curious way, I still think it's going to have been worth it. I'll settle up when we go and apologise for the messy outcome. I think I should be generous with tipping the waiters, especially the female one. She never put a foot wrong, in contrast to some of us who rather put our foot in it."

"Too true. May I help with the bill, or at least the tips?"

"Thanks, but no fear; I had put aside a thousand for it and I think I will have change, so thanks for the offer but keep your hand in your pocket. It's my treat and I think I'm going to be a winner."

"Okay, then. Now tell me, how did you get in touch?"

"I've more or less hovered over Morris and Oz, helped then through the awful AIDS business with Oz's lover. His nurse was a brick and Morris was a loving patient. It was dreadful to see Morris fading. At the time there was little understanding of what to do about the worldwide scourge. Consequently, I knew where to find Oz, though I haven't seen him recently since he moved into the care home. I contacted him there and spoke to him about my idea of a reunion well beforehand. He was keen, but I could tell from his tremulous voice that he was on his last legs. Actually, I was surprised that he had the determination to come, but he made it. Poor man, perhaps only a few days left in the supervision of people who care professionally, but not lovingly. Maybe that's too much to expect."

"And Rawsthorne? Where on earth did you find him?"

"You couldn't miss him! I got in touch through his amour, Clive, who was actually the one you couldn't miss; he always turned up at every audition, always dressed to kill, but unfortunately always killing his chances of landing himself a decent part. He never went for the right sort of roles. In a twisted way, he saw himself as butch. Deluded, of course, and so Rawsthorne turned up tonight after saying he couldn't make it."

"And me?"

""Well of course our meeting at Ernest's funeral was a pleasant surprise on such a sad occasion, but of course there's no time to talk at these do's"

"My hotel, as you call it, was actually a pleasant road house. I'd only been there a few days when late one night Ernest barged in, obviously in some distress. I recognised him instantly but he was barely civil to me, even though we'd worked together once or twice over the years. Then he bunked off during the night without paying the bill! I heard about his death through the local press and then, Francis, who was a lean and lanky lad working there and a gossip with an ear for bad news, told me about the funeral. So I went, not expecting you or anyone else that I knew to be there."

"I phoned him only a few days before he died, to tell him

The Funeral

about the reunion I was proposing. I asked if he knew where you were and he said he hadn't seen you for years. Said he would mention the reunion if he bumped into you. Did he say anything to you about me or the reunion?"

"Not a word. Did you get Ernest's telephone number through Equity?"

"Didn't need to."

"Why not?"

"I knew it already. I've known it for years, ever since he moved from Hackney when Marjorie died."

"How come? For God's sake, Peter, spill the beans."

"Do you remember that Marjorie and I were more than an item in Scotland? Well, it never really stopped. After the fit up experience, we both went for proper training. She went to LAMDA for acting and I went to Central for stage management.

"Our affair cooled off while we were in London but it never truly went cold. She had quite a bit of luck in getting good roles on stage, and on TV, whilst I went onto the continent to stage-manage operas and festivals and so on.

"I heard that she was getting married, at the age of forty for God's sake, to sexless Ernest. I had a bit of leave, returned to London and sneaked into the wedding. Well, not exactly into, but I was outside in the crowds when they came out into the street.

"Time passed; they had a kid, lovely girl called Constance. She grew up to look like a very good bet for the stage. She had presence and oodles of talent and she worked hard.

"Marjorie and I started to meet up. Often when she was supposed to be rehearsing she was actually with me and, to put it frankly, we became just as close as you can get. She refused to divorce Ernest, though he would have had ample grounds if he'd known what we were getting up to. I don't think he even suspected.

"One day I was in Oxford Street, buying cards I think, and in waltzed Marje with thirteen-year-old Connie on her arm. We greeted each other as long-time-no-see friends but it must have been obvious to Connie that we were making it up. We went for a coffee.

"After that chance encounter with them together, Marje brought Concon pretty often, usually to my flat. The first time there was a giveaway – Marje knew where the coffee was kept, handled the kettle familiarly and so on. Marje made Concon promise never to let on to her daddy about me. I think the girl enjoyed the secrecy and exciting conspiracy. She never did let on. I remained a hidden secret from poor old Ernest, who was in the dark, forever thankfully, enjoying domestic bliss with his small but at least loving family.

"Once Concon – she would be seventeen I think – was to be singing a solo in the school concert and I sneaked in on the back row to listen. Concon arranged it: Ernest and Marje were going to be near the front so we wouldn't meet. But they were late, the lights had gone down and their seats had been taken. There were just two empty seats only two rows in front of mine. I'm sure Ernest didn't see me but Marje did, spotted me and signalled to be careful.

"As soon as Concon did her bit, I snuck out undetected. Her singing and her projection were unbelievably marvellous, by the way. But Concon died. Did you hear about what happened? It was in all the papers.

"It was while she was in her third year at LAMDA. She was invited to audition for a television play that, if successful, might be developed into a series or even a soap. Ernest and Marjory were so excited, but tried to contain themselves. They waved her off with high hopes and good wishes. They waved her off with high hopes and good wishes and sadly that was the last time they saw her alive. She had done the audition and was waiting outside when scaffolding collapsed above her. She was

The Funeral

killed instantly. Marje was inconsolable as was Ernest. And of course, so was I, but there was nothing I could say."

"Then, some hardworking years later she died too. It was cancer and she ended up in a hospice in Hackney. She was only there a few days and it was all over."

"Can I ask you a question, Peter? You don't have to answer if you don't want to."

"Fire away. I think I can guess what the question might be, but go ahead and ask it anyway."

"Okay then. Was Concon yours or Ernest's?

"I'm not sure. She had my colouring. Mine? Yes, possibly."

"Poor Ernest. He had all the luck."

Peter ordered more brandy, and after a few moments silence he said, "First Concon, then Marjorie, and now this awful business. I'm glad we went to the funeral; we could have seen no greater evidence of differing beliefs. The Hirsts, engulfed in their own tragedy, and then the Hepworths and their charming daughter clearly grieving for a man they admired."

"I suppose Ernest was intended to be at this party. If he had lived to come, what would you have said to him?"

Peter replied after some thought, "I don't really know. I couldn't have confessed about my long-standing affair with Marjorie. However, I could have told him how I knew about their daughter's death.

The conversation at the Grange said volumes about his love, if that is the right word for the little girl. But maybe such relationships can go too far with sad consequences and unimagined hurt all round."

Reg agreed and said, "From what I understand, many people from Holsterdale would feel that 'sad long evening, and I have to make my way back to the Grand Palace where I am staying overnight."

Reg struggled from his chair, the combination of rheumatism and brandy hampering his aching knees; he shook Peter's hand with further offerings of thanks and departed, leaving him to order another brandy.

The evening of reminiscing and reminders of his own past mistakes drew more uncomfortable memories to the forefront of Peter's mind. Silently he raised his glass in a final salute to his old friend.

"Ernest; may he finally rest in peace."

Extract from the Holsterdale pioneer in January.

It is reported that the body of a young girl has been found downstream in the river Holst. It is thought it is the remains of the missing child Laura Hirst. Her body has been taken to the morgue awaiting identification.

Headline in the Holsterdale pioneer in February.

The inquest on the body of Laura Hirst has been concluded. The coroner's verdict is that the girl must have drowned in the river when in flood. There was no evidence to support anything but that it must have been a tragic accident.

The church was filled to capacity for the funeral of Laura Hirst, and the congregation joined in the familiar refrain of "All Things Bright and Beautiful", a fitting tribute to such a vibrant little girl.

The Rector thought back to the very different service he had led for Ernest. He wondered how many were remembering him now with forgiveness; Norris suspected that the thought on many minds would be, 'There's no smoke without fire' no matter what the evidence to the contrary.

He went on to speak movingly about the tragic event and after the service Harry Hirst thanked everyone for being there in a short moving speech.

Finally both Laura and her friend could Rest in Peace.

ACKNOWLEDGEMENTS

My deteriorating eyesight has meant that I have had to rely on several people to help me complete this book. I would like to thank them all for their many differing offers of help.

Barbara Davy, who has designed and painted the image for the book cover.

Ellen Shorrock for using her many and great IT skills to complete the appearance of the book: title, spine and blurb!

Penelope Tipping, my daughter who helped me with the finishing touches of the book.

Eliza Wilson, my granddaughter, who has typed amendments onto the PC at my dictation.

Nikki Ford for professionally editing and correcting my many and varied typing errors!

Nichola Swan, literary trustee of her late husband's work, who has made helpful suggestions toward my narrative progress through the book in the early stages of my its creation.

And of course all those people who have read my book and kindly written reviews.

Last but by no means least, I would like to thank Julia, my younger daughter, who has suffered the slings and arrows of my creative whims for the last eight years!